THE BROKEN BOUGH

THE BROKEN BOUGH

Nicola Thorne

This first world edition published in Great Britain 2001 by
SEVERN HOUSE PUBLISHERS LTD of
9–15 High Street, Sutton, Surrey SM1 1DF.
This first world edition published in the USA 2001 by
SEVERN HOUSE PUBLISHERS INC of
595 Madison Avenue, New York, N.Y. 10022.

British Library Cataloguing in Publication Data

Thorne, Nicola
    The broken bough
    1. Domestic fiction
    I.   Title
    823.9'14 [F]

    ISBN 0-7278-5681-2

Contents

PART I

Verity

One

C athy, fragile, delicate, had never appeared strong yet she had overcome many seemingly insurmountable obstacles in her life. Maude forced herself to try and remember this as she faced her sister who, her large luminous eyes welling with tears, was clutching baby Peg to her breast.

Life was so unfair, Maude thought, as she struggled to find words to console her sister. Here was she, the elder sibling, well off, well married, yet not blessed with Cathy's good looks and, more importantly, barren.

"Stanley and I would so love to have had children," Maude said twisting long, capable white fingers restlessly in her lap, "yet it did not happen."

"Maybe in time . . ." Cathy ventured putting the tip of her little finger in Peg's mouth as the baby began to cry. Cathy looked flushed and unhappy, wisps of dark hair clinging to her damp forehead.

Maude shook her head.

"The doctors say there is no reason it cannot happen, but we have been married eleven years. You had Verity before you'd been married a year." Maude bowed her head. "Somehow I don't believe it is the will of God." She leaned forward earnestly to address her sister. "Verity will have a very good home with us. Stanley and I will lavish every care on her. She will go to the best school, have the best of everything and besides," she looked around at Cathy's sitting-room cluttered with shabby furniture, *bric-à-brac* and children's toys, "you really have not room for her here in this small house. It is unfair to expect a girl to grow up in these conditions."

Cathy's flush grew deeper and she shifted Peg from one arm to the other.

"We had to move quickly after Billy died. This is only temporary. Besides, Verity is happy here. She has me and her sisters. She is loved."

"She will be loved by us, and you and the girls can see her whenever you want. Besides, the money we are offering you will make a great deal of difference to your circumstances." She pointed at Peg curled up in her mother's arms nearly asleep. "It will give Peg a better chance," she glanced around, "you can make some improvements." She gently took hold of her sister's free hand.

"Verity will have all the love we can give her. Every opportunity."

"It is not really my decision," Cathy said with a sigh. "I cannot make the girl do anything against her will."

That night Verity's sobs seemed to shake the house. Next to her, six-year-old Addie did her best to comfort her. Once or twice her mother stole in and the sobs ceased abruptly. Cathy stood listening at the doorway and then crept away again to the loneliness of her own bedroom and the large bed, half of it empty since her husband had been killed shortly after Peg had been born.

Cathy climbed into bed and after pulling the bedclothes up to her chin lay for a long time gazing into the darkness. She imagined she could still hear the sound of Verity's muffled sobs.

Was it cruel to send away her eldest daughter, or was it a kindness? Did it seem harsh now, but would not the benefits of a good education be seen in later years?

After all she was not going to strangers but to her mother's eldest sister – married to an engineer, fortunately placed and comfortably off with a large house on the outskirts of Bournemouth.

Cathy had never been very close to Maude; the sisters were very dissimilar personalities, even as children. Cathy was fey, petite, pretty, with brown curls, soft brown eyes and a winsome smile, clearly vulnerable, instinctively reliant on others. Maude was tall, awkward, plain, with straight brown hair, a broad nose and a wide mouth which seldom smiled. People noted how unfortunate it was that two sisters were so different: Cathy, good looking like her handsome father, Maude, resembling, both in looks and character, their mother.

Their parents had been farmers but Cathy had married a butcher, whereas Maude had married a structural engineer, thus anchoring herself firmly into the middle classes, well off and secure. After that the gulf between the sisters had grown ever wider, largely owing to Maude's social pretensions and the fact that she seemed to look down on Cathy.

Cathy, reliving the past, closed her eyes but knew that sleep was far away. As she had expected, Verity was aghast at the thought of being sent to live with her relatives to whom, though dutiful visits had been paid and received, she had never been close. Uncle Stanley was a tall, handsome, kindly man whose hobby was lepidoptropy, the collection and classification of butterflies. He gave learned talks to societies all over the country. Aunt Maude's tall, upright figure, her chalk white face with its large proboscis and its firm-set mouth, her hair set in two coifs on either side of her head, left her small nieces with feelings of awe, even fear, rather than affection.

In their Bournemouth house nothing was ever out of place with well-polished furniture and vases full of flowers. There was a cook and a maid, Doris, who wore a white starched apron over a trim blue dress and a little white cap with a blue bow.

After Maude left Cathy had told Verity about her aunt's exciting proposal trying to make it sound enticing: how she would have her own room, plenty of new clothes, a new school and, perhaps, a puppy. But even this latter promise failed to stem the tears.

Verity emphatically did not want to go and live with Aunt Maude and Uncle Stanley. Uncharacteristically in front of her mother and sister she broke down, finally fleeing the room for the security of her bedroom until she was joined at last by Addie who, because she did not want to lose her sister, also failed to comfort her.

It was hard to make light of the occasion. Uncle Stanley came personally to collect Verity and to take Mother, Addie and the baby back for tea to help her settle down.

There had been no more tears once the die was cast, Mother's mind clearly made up, the necessity for the move, its advantages clearly explained. There was not enough money to feed an adult, two growing girls and a baby. There was not enough money for the rent. There was no way Mother could go out to work with a young baby to look after. Thrown on the generosity of relatives it seemed only sensible to allow Verity to go and live with Aunt Maude and Uncle Stanley. And if things changed, why Verity could always go back.

Buoyed up by that promise and sitting now in her best green dress, her hair tied back and fastened with a bow, her expression grave, Verity gazed out of the window for the entire journey, never looking once at Mother and Uncle Stanley sitting opposite her, the baby on Mother's knees, or Addie by her side.

Verity was a grave composed young lady, only eight years of age but she seemed old for her years, as she always had to be as Mother's helpmeet. No two sisters could be more unalike than Mother and Aunt Maude who, in many ways, Verity knew she took after. Whereas she was rather stern and unbending like Aunt Maude, Addie was soft and cuddly, warm like Mother. Verity smiled little, seldom laughed. She was very good at her schoolwork and knew that at a more academic school such as the one she was now to attend, she could do better.

So after the tears had dried and in the privacy of her bedroom, once Addie was asleep, she had decided to do what Mother wanted her to do without fuss and go and live with her relatives. After all it was only an hour's ride away.

So she had said goodbye to her friends at school, emptied her drawers and wardrobe, packed her bags and there was no more fuss, no more bother, just a grim acceptance on her part which made it seem that, of the three, Mother and her younger sister were the most sad.

"Here we are," Uncle Stanley said brightly as the coach came round the corner and stopped outside the large red-brick house with a short drive that stood back from a leafy road on the outskirts of Bournemouth.

Almost before it had stopped he opened the door and jumped down, turning back to help Cathy and the baby, then Addie and, last of all, Verity.

"Welcome to your new home, Verity," he said gazing at her with an expression of sweet and sympathetic understanding which his niece found touching and gratifying.

"Thank you, Uncle Stanley," she said taking his hand and jumping down. Then as she turned she saw Aunt Maude walking slowly towards her, closely followed by Doris who rushed ahead to help the coachman with Verity's bags.

Aunt Maude came up to her niece, arms outstretched and enveloped her in a stiff embrace. It was the greatest show of affection Verity had ever had from her undemonstrative aunt and she was moved. She returned her embrace with an awkward kiss on the side of her cheek whereupon her aunt, equally awkwardly, put an arm round her waist and led her towards the house. Mother, Addie, Uncle Stanley followed and, bringing up the rear, Doris staggered along, almost bent double beneath the weight of a large suitcase and a clutch of smaller parcels and bags under her arms.

There was a smell of baking as they entered the house.

"Cook has baked a lovely cake specially for you, Verity."

"I can smell it," Verity said, sniffing the air.

"I hope you will be happy here, my dear." Aunt Maude looked anxiously down at her.

"I'm sure I shall."

Mother appeared most affected and hardly touched a crumb of the freshly baked cake, the scones and home-made strawberry jam, the egg and tomato sandwiches. However, she

7

drank copious amounts of tea, nervously lifting the cup to her lips and smiling forlornly across at her daughter as if, at last, she realised what was actually happening.

The conversation was desultory. The tension extreme. It was a very big step after all. Maude and Stanley were acquiring a daughter, ready made, and Cathy was losing one, part of her flesh. Of them all Verity appeared the most relaxed, as if resigned to her fate. She had been up to inspect her room which overlooked the back garden. It was quite a large bedroom compared to the one she had just left – she must no longer think of it as "home" – with a single bed covered by a pretty cretonne counterpane, a rosewood dressing table with silver-backed brush, comb and hand mirror, a small porcelain tray and a cut-glass bowl with a lid.

In the corner by the window was a desk upon which there was a vase of flowers. There was a wardrobe, a chest of drawers, a small cabinet and an easy chair. The polished floor was covered with rugs, and there was a fireplace in which had been laid a fire ready to light.

Doris had brought up her case and bags and they sat on the bed ready to be unpacked.

Mother had inspected the room silently, Peg still in her arms, and Addie had pranced around, unable to stand still and had looked rather enviously at her sister.

Uncle Stanley took Verity into his study to show her his latest collection of specimens and once again had assured her how happy he and Aunt Maude were to have her and what great care they would take of her.

Finally it was time to go. The coach waited outside and Cathy, rather a forlorn figure with the baby in her arms and Addie clutching one hand, walked slowly towards it while Maude and Stanley Carter, with Verity between them, stood on the steps all waving goodbye.

Home was an empty place without her mainstay. Cathy should have realised how much she would miss Verity who had done so many useful jobs. She had been a second mother to the baby and practically an elder sister to Addie. Verity's care for her younger siblings had enabled Cathy to take in more work as a seamstress. She was an expert dressmaker and, as well as making clothes, mended and darned and did alterations. Now she found that without Verity she was able to do less. The children required more of her time and the income from Maude and Stanley barely made up for it. She was about as well, or as badly, off as she had been before. But now it was too late, much too late to change her mind and ask for Verity back again.

Jack Hallam took off his hat and stepped almost diffidently into the living-room, looking round before laying a bunch of flowers on the table.

"Growd 'em myself," Jack said.

"It's very kind of you." Cathy brushed a lock of hair from her face and stooped to smell the flowers. "They have a lovely scent, Jack."

"Prize-winning blooms," Jack said a little smugly. "Nothing but the best for you, Cathy."

Cathy, who had been making a dress on the table, put the cover on her sewing machine and carefully folded the material and tucked it into a bag.

"I see I disturbed you, Cathy."

"That's all right, Jack," Cathy said with a smile. "Can I make you a cup of tea?"

"That would be very nice." Jack looked over at Addie sitting docilely in a corner of the settee reading a book and then peeped into the pram where Peg slumbered, the afternoon sun streaming in through the window.

"Verity at school?" he asked.

"Verity's not here, Jack. She went to live with my sister and brother-in-law."

"Oh!" Jack looked surprised. "For good?"

"For the time being." Cathy gazed at him defensively. "I'll go and make the tea."

When she came back, Jack had made himself comfortable

9

and was chatting amiably to Addie, who had put aside her book and was listening to him intently. Jack's visits had started after Billy's death, infrequent at first, latterly more regular. He arrived unannounced with some offering – fruit or vegetables or flowers which he had grown himself.

Addie was a pale, fey child with wispy brown hair and the faraway expression of a dreamer.

"I told Addie we could go over to the big house and have a look at the garden, that is, if you like." Jack looked diffidently at Cathy.

"When, now?" Cathy glanced out of the window.

"No time like the present, now that the sun is out. I've got the pony and trap outside."

"Why not?" Suddenly the day seemed better for seeing Jack Hallam and after tea Cathy sent Addie upstairs to change while she put the baby into a warm matinee jacket and matching hat which her mother had made.

The Tempest Newton family owned most of the land in the area including the house where Cathy now lived, the butcher's shop and dwelling they had occupied before and the cottage on the Tempest Newton estate which was the home of Jack Hallam, head gardener at Tempest Newton House.

Billy Barnes and Jack Hallam had been friends and drinking partners, a curious combination because Billy had been a jolly, outgoing sort of chap and Jack was rather shy and withdrawn, a man known for his green fingers: everything he planted grew. They both, however, did like a drop – Jack, as a single man, perhaps more so than Billy – and could on occasions be seen supporting each other out of the pub, a short way down the road, before separating and calling a cheery goodnight as each unsteadily wended his way to his respective home.

Cathy hardly knew Jack until Billy's death. He had been one of the pall-bearers at Billy's funeral and was a tall, robustly handsome man with a pronounced Adam's apple which was accentuated by a high stiff collar. He had thick, long side-whiskers and tanned weather-beaten skin because of all the time he spent out of doors. His most attractive feature was a pair of bright blue eyes which, set against his brown skin, made him look quite dashing. Cathy knew he had a bit of a reputation with women, but he was always most courteous and correct towards her.

Her husband Billy had been killed in an accident involving a runaway horse and cart as he attempted to stop it careering down the main street and harming someone. He had dashed out of his butcher's shop when he heard a commotion outside and, without stopping to think, had recklessly flung himself at the horse, catching hold it its bridle. The terrified beast, gathering speed, had dragged him a hundred yards or so and when Billy finally let go he fell under its hind legs, was subsequently crushed by the wheels of the cart and killed instantly.

In a way it was a very foolhardy act. No one had been in the cart but there was no doubt that if the horse had continued to career down the street someone might have been injured, even killed. Billy was regarded as something of a local hero and his widow was given fifty pounds raised by the local community as a gesture to Billy's bravery. Shortly after that, however, she received notice to quit the premises they'd occupied over the butcher's shop to make way for someone else.

This was the first time Jack had asked them out and, as they strolled round the gardens for which Jack was responsible, Cathy pushing the pram and Jack holding Addie by the hand and occasionally smiling at her, Cathy realised that a new note had been struck in their relationship and it suddenly seemed somehow right. She returned Jack's smile with a warm one of her own. When he smiled his blue eyes seemed to sparkle.

"Tell me, what made you give up Verity?" Jack asked as they stopped to admire the beautiful display of rhododendrons on either side of the long drive leading up to Tempest Newton House, still only a blot in the distance.

"Oh, I didn't give her up," Cathy said quickly. "My sister is childless and she is able to provide for Verity in a way that I am not able to at the moment."

"If there is anything you need . . ." Jack began, his hand nervously fingering his Adam's apple as if in an effort to squash it back out of sight.

"Oh no, nothing, thank you. My sister is generous in her support and my dressmaking helps out."

"Still, you were very fond of Verity." Jack glanced down at Addie who clung to his hand, not missing a word. "It must have been a wrench."

"It is for the best," Cathy said firmly. "The best for her and for the moment, at least, the best thing for us."

Jack took her arm and guided her along a path that led to the walled garden where he grew his vegetables with fruit trees, pears, apples and plums lining the walls. At one end was a greenhouse full of camellias at various stages of flowering: some fully out, others still in tight buds. Next to it was another with a huge vine running full length and covering the ceiling which in season produced sweet muscat grapes.

Jack led Cathy and her children along the rows of vegetables, explaining what was planted in each plot: cabbages and sprouts, peas and beans, marrows and potatoes. Another greenhouse was full of tomato plants. He became quite animated and lyrical when he talked about his work and it was certainly a change from butchering with that vague, unpleasant smell of dried blood and offal somehow permeating the premises where they'd lived.

"You've enough to feed the family, and more," Cathy said admiringly.

"And I take plenty to market." Jack opened the door at the far end of the garden and led the family on to a lawn from which they now had a good view of the side of the house. This was an Elizabethan mansion with many additions. It was gabled and turreted and looked like a small fortress with its tiny mullioned windows gleaming in the sunshine.

It was a heavenly spring day with the waxy buds on the Magnolia trees gradually unfolding, cowslips on the lawn and a carpet of bluebells starting in the copse at the side of the house in front of which a large fountain sent forth a jet of water high into the air.

They walked for a moment, Addie letting go of Jack's hand and running ahead causing Cathy to call out anxiously:

"Be careful now."

"She's all right," Jack said smiling and, glancing behind him, pointed to a bench and invited Cathy to sit down. The atmosphere now between them was very relaxed, almost intimate. "The family are very fond of children."

"Are they here now?" Cathy looked over towards the house.

"No. They are in London for the season. Their eldest daughter is coming out this year, being presented to the King and Queen."

"It's hard to imagine such a life," Cathy said with a sigh.

"Things are difficult for you, aren't they, Cathy?" Jack said gently and Cathy was aware that his hand hovered lightly over hers. "I am told Billy left you badly off, that you have difficulty paying the rent."

"Who told you that?" Cathy's eyes flashed angrily.

"It's common knowledge in these parts. You mustn't be ashamed of it."

"I suppose the agent told you?"

Cathy paid rent to the Tempest Newton estate and the agent had been a friend of Billy and, presumably, Jack.

"It stands to reason. When Billy died you lost your livelihood. Doubtless your parents helped a little?"

"A little," Cathy said lowering her eyes.

A very little. They had not approved of her marriage to Billy and they were not the first to rush forward to help her when he died. Her mother's attitude was that those who made their beds should be left to lie on them.

"Cathy," Jack moved closer to her and his hand finally dropped, lightly covering hers, "I . . ." he stopped and a flush stole up his neck and across his cheeks making his blue eyes seem brighter than ever.

"I would like to take care of you, Cathy. You know . . . I would like to marry you."

Sarah Swayle, mouth pursed, looked grimly at her daughter. In the background Joseph Swayle sat in his rocking chair smoking his thick briar pipe. Cathy's mother was sixty, and her white hair and careworn expression made her look older. She always wore black, her silk dress fastened right up to her neck, sleeves down to her wrists, ankles covered, sensible black shoes. There was very little that was soft or gentle about her; she seemed all hard corners and jagged edges.

She had been a farmer's daughter and then a hard-working farmer's wife all her life and there was yet no end to it in sight. Her husband, Joseph, ten years her senior, was crippled with arthritis and Sarah felt she still shouldered an undue burden of the work on the farm. Lacking sons they had to make do with paid help when they could afford it.

It had always been a cause of mortification to Sarah that, of all the children born to her, only two girls had survived. She lost two sons in infancy and miscarried another girl at a late stage, and she felt that somehow she had failed her husband, who was one of seven brothers.

In her youth she had been pretty and flirtatious, but it was almost impossible to imagine that now.

Joseph was the eldest and had inherited the Swayles' farm. When they were younger he had the help of two of his brothers, but they had married and moved out of the district to take on farms of their own.

And then wasn't it a misfortune that, of her two daughters, one was incapable of producing children and the other only had girls? Wasn't that double bad luck?

Cathy had been engaged to a prosperous farmer nearby, of whom her parents approved, when she fell for one of the slaughtermen from the nearby abattoir whom her parents didn't consider half good enough for her: dashing Billy Barnes.

Her parents were appalled at her jilting one well off,

industrious man for one so ordinary with so few prospects for advancement. They had even imagined that her fiancé might take over their farm and enable them to lead a life of ease as Joseph Swayle began to suffer from arthritis at an early age.

Billy, however, as well as being good looking and very much in love with Cathy, was also ambitious. He moved from slaughtering to managing a butcher's shop and, apart from his regular booze-ups on a Saturday night, had proved a good husband and devoted father. Despite his good nature he had never won over his mother-in-law and proved incapable of standing up to her.

Looking at her, Cathy could almost read her mother's mind. Jack would not be good enough for her, as Billy had not been.

"I despair of you, Cathy," her mother said as if to confirm her expectations. "What is it about Jack Hallam that has such appeal? He is neither rich nor particularly well placed . . . and he also drinks."

"What do you mean 'drinks', Mother?" Cathy demanded.

"Well, Billy drank . . ." her mother began darkly.

"Only on Saturday. I saw no harm in that. He was never cruel, or beat me or neglected me. You've always been unkind about Billy and I resent it, Mother, especially now that he's dead. Is this why you didn't help me when Billy died, so that I had to sell my eldest daughter to my sister?"

"*Sell*!" Sarah was clearly outraged and her eyebrows shot up to the top of her head. "*Sell*? Is that how you interpret your sister's kindness?"

"It was a condition of her letting me have some money. No offer of help came from *you*, Mother."

"And where was that help to come from?" Sarah's shoulders shook with rage. "Your father crippled with arthritis, as it is we can barely scratch enough together to make a living. Had you married Tom Fairbrother who was a good man *and* a wealthy one . . ."

Sarah suddenly crumpled into a chair and for a moment

15

Cathy thought she was going to cry. However she controlled herself and looked defiantly at her daughter.

"How is it that Maude can find a gentleman to marry, a professional man with a good income and you have to make do first with a slaughterman and then a jobbing gardener? Have you no pride, no wish to better yourself? You are blessed with good looks, Cathy. You could do much better."

"You want me to sell myself in the street?" Cathy cried shrilly, and it was she who finally burst into tears.

Joseph Swayle, grimacing with pain, leaned forward to try and touch his daughter's shoulder. He was a mild man, totally dominated by his wife, dispirited by the harsh course his life had taken, years of ill-health. It had started so well, and in her youth Sarah had been a beauty with rosy cheeks and a dimpled chin.

He too had yearned for sons, but it didn't stop him loving both his daughters, specially Cathy, the pretty, vulnerable one. It had always been obvious that Maude knew how to look after herself and would marry well. But Cathy's looks and gentle nature had seemed to make her prey to weakness, to irresolution, someone who swayed with the wind, never quite knowing her own mind or what was best for her. Being attractive she liked attractive young men and, for all his good qualities, Tom Fairbrother had none of the charm and certainly not the looks of Billy.

"That's no way to speak to your mother," Joseph said gently. "She is only thinking of your good."

"You know Jack Hallam, Father, you like him, don't you?" Cathy turned to him appealingly. "Addie likes him. He says he has come to care for her and little Peg. And he is not a jobbing gardener but head gardener to Mr Tempest Newton."

"I like Jack well enough," Joseph nodded, but he seemed half-hearted. "But I have heard that he does drink too much, which is why he never holds a job for very long."

"He has been with Mr Tempest Newton for five years," Cathy said defensively.

"And been twice threatened with losing his job. However,"

Joseph wriggled uncomfortably in his chair, "maybe if he marries you he will settle down."

"I don't know how you can speak like that," Sarah exclaimed, "encouraging the girl."

"Mother, she is her own mistress," Joseph said placatingly. "If I know Cathy, I think her mind is already made up."

"And if that is how you wish to make your bed you will have to lie on it." Her mother waved a finger threateningly at her daughter and swept out of the room.

Cathy sobbed silently for a while and then she raised her tear-stained face and looked at her father.

"What must I do, Father?"

"What your heart tells you," Joseph said sadly. "But I think we already know the answer."

Two

Verity sat watching her mother nursing the new baby, her
eyes only for him, the first boy. Little Edgar, a few days
old, had broken the long line of girls who had been born to the
Swayle and Barnes families. Besides Cathy, Jack stood looking proudly down at his son.

"Would you like to hold him?" Cathy asked holding the
baby out to her daughter, but Verity shook her head.

"Go on, he's your brother," her mother said encouragingly,
but Verity shook her head again and sat tight. In truth she felt
that, though he was to all appearances bonny, there was
something repulsive about the baby in her mother's arms.
It didn't seem right. His very existence bothered her and she
didn't like it at all. She and her sisters had been Mother's
children exclusively; now there was someone else taking all the
limelight.

Next to her, Addie, finger in her mouth, had one eye on Peg
who was playing with wooden bricks in a corner.

Instead it was Jack who took the baby from his wife and
strolled with him over to the door which led into the garden,
and soon they were out of sight. Verity continued to gaze at
her mother. Sometimes she felt she had become a stranger.
Instead of seeing her and her sisters often, as had been
promised, Verity saw them very little. The trap never
seemed to be available to take her over to the cottage on
the Tempest Newton estate where her mother lived with her
new husband.

None of them had gone to the wedding a year ago, not even
Aunt Maude or Uncle Stanley. It appeared that no one had

been invited, and Mother and Jack got married at the register office without letting anyone know.

So as not to cause a fuss, Mother had said, but Verity had known that this meant that neither Granny and Grandpa nor Uncle Stanley and Aunt Maude approved of Jack.

She didn't much like him herself. She who had been Daddy's girl couldn't understand how Mother could have chosen someone so different to her first husband. Father had been all bounce and jollity and affection – "hugs for my darlings" he'd cry – whereas Jack was cold, almost aloof despite his bright blue eyes which seemed to shine only when they looked tenderly at Mother. Mother said he was shy, but she was always making excuses for Jack.

She had said it was because he wasn't used to children. Now that he had one of his own perhaps he'd change. But still Verity knew she would never like him or the little stranger he'd held in his arms. Mother smiled a sad smile at Verity, her head on one side, her arms extended.

"Come over here, my precious." The tone of her voice was gentle, caressing. Verity's heart turned over with a love for and longing for Mother. She longed to be Mother's favourite again, the firstborn who had enjoyed her sole attention for two years before Addie was born. There had been jealousy with Addie too, but not so much as when Peg arrived and Verity had been almost put on one side while everyone sat round adoring the pretty new baby.

Verity moved across and sat next to Mother, aware of her comforting arm round her waist.

"I wish we were alone together again, Mum."

Cathy planted a kiss on the top of her head but avoided answering the question. Instead she said:

"Is all well with Uncle Stanley and Aunt Maude?"

Verity nodded.

"They never seem to have time to come and see me. Nor do you . . ." There was a reproachful note in Mother's voice.

"Uncle Stanley's been giving a lot of lectures. He's also helping to build a huge bridge near Durham. He's away a lot."

19

"That's only an excuse," Mother said lowering her voice and looking towards the window. "They don't like my husband."

Verity said nothing.

"Do they?" Cathy insisted.

"I don't know, Mum." Verity gazed at the floor.

"How can they not like him if they don't know him? It's because your grandparents are prejudiced against him. Jack is a good man. He has given me a home, security, a son. A son at last." Mother had an expression of such tenderness on her face that a spasm of jealousy gripped Verity once more. It was so strong that it seemed to shoot like a sharp pain across her chest.

"Are you happy with Aunt Maude and Uncle Stanley?" Cathy held her daughter away from her and looked at her intently.

Verity nodded.

"Truly happy? Because I thought that, if you liked, I would ask Jack if we could have you back here again. Would you like that? Be one big happy family as we were when Father was alive?"

"Oh Mum!" Verity responded by squeezing her mother tightly round the waist. "If only we could."

Gone suddenly was the dislike of Jack, the little stranger in the euphoria of the thought of being one big happy family again.

Maude Carter looked round Verity's bedroom where everything had been left as if waiting for her return. Then she went to the window and gazed on to the lawn where Stanley sat in a deckchair reading the paper. Suddenly the paper fell on to his knees and his head drooped, his chin resting on his chest. They had all seemed so happy together, Verity had settled down and was doing well at school.

Now the whole thing was up in the air while she took an extended holiday with her mother and stepfather. In reality the object was to see if she liked living with them again. There was every possibility that she would not return.

20

Despite her feeling of desolation, Maude mechanically puffed up a few cushions and moved things that didn't need to be moved and then put them back again in their place. Empty futile gestures, symptomatic of her loss.

She went into her bedroom and gazed at herself in the mirror before changing into an afternoon dress, then powdering her face, adjusting her hair. She examined herself again critically in the long mirror inside the wardrobe, turning around in her dress, noting her slim hips, her firm bust. They said some people improved with age and she thought this was the case with her. She had never been beautiful but she looked after herself and always bought good clothes.

Still, she could not help wishing that she had been more like Cathy, not only in looks but in temperament because, despite her air of fragility, even feebleness, Cathy always got what she wanted.

Despite her misfortunes, she seemed like the lucky one. Not Maude.

Maude put a dab of perfume behind each ear, selected a fresh handkerchief and wandered slowly down the stairs, taking pleasure as she did in the spacious graciousness of the house: the broad staircase with its rich ebony banister, the large hall with its highly polished tiles, the flowers on the circular rosewood table. The rooms opening off the hall, the drawing-room, dining-room, parlour and study, were carpeted with Axminster and furnished with antiques bought largely over the years she and Stanley had been married. The green baize door at the end of the hall opened on to domestic quarters: the kitchen, pantry and scullery.

She crossed the hall and walked slowly through the drawing-room, stopping to make an adjustment to a bowl of flowers which stood on a marquetry table, the bright blossoms reflected in the gleaming surface of the wood.

In every way, practically speaking, she was better off than Cathy who lived in a small cottage through courtesy of the Tempest Newtons for whom her husband worked. In every way she was better off than Cathy except for the new baby, what a darling he was. In her mind's eye she saw the baby's angelic smile, his chubby cheeks.

Yes, she envied Cathy and she always had. Jealousy of her younger sister had really dominated her life.

Through the open French windows she could see that Stanley still slumbered on the lawn, his paper now fallen on to the grass.

She stood for a while watching him. Everywhere was silent except for the occasional snatch of birdsong. The garden was beautifully kept, by her efforts and those of the gardener who came twice a week. Stanley liked to look after the orchard at the bottom of the garden or, occasionally, potter in the greenhouse. But he had not Maude's way with plants or her interest. He preferred to spend his spare time searching for localities in which to find his precious species of butter-flies, thinking nothing of walking five to six miles at a time as he examined every insect he saw along the way.

They had had an exceptionally happy marriage but for one thing, and for a time Verity had helped to make them forget their childlessness as they indulged her as if she'd been their own daughter.

Had it been a mistake? As if aware of her approach Stanley suddenly grunted and jerked himself upright, struggling to get his paper from the ground, searching for his spectacles which had also fallen down.

"It's all right, dear, let me do it." Maude knelt on the ground and carefully put the pages of the paper into proper order and handed him his spectacles.

"Thank you, dear," he said smiling. "Did you have a rest?"

"I was too fidgety." Maude sat back on her heels. "I was thinking about Verity. I miss her so, don't you?"

Stanley nodded.

"We had to let her go."

"It's only for a holiday."

"Somehow I feel it's so ungrateful. We did *everything* for her."

"I think it stands to reason that she wants to be with her

mother and sisters. Maybe we should have taken her to see them more often." They both knew in their hearts that this had been deliberate, in the mistaken supposition that the less Verity saw of her mother and sisters the more likely she was to forget them.

"I still think it's ungrateful. She had everything she could wish for here."

Stanley put out his hand.

"We did our best. We still have each other . . ."

"Would you like tea, dear?" Maude said abruptly, and got up.

Verity looked up from the table as the kitchen door suddenly opened and Jack stood framed in the doorway with a basket of vegetables in his hand.

"Your mother not here?" Jack asked looking around.

"She went with the baby, Addie and Peg to see Grandma. She told you at breakfast." Verity looked for a moment at her stepfather and then lowered her eyes to the book before her on the table.

"Busy with your studies, are you, Verity?" Jack said in a friendly tone peeking over her shoulder. Then he lit a cigarette as if to relax.

"Yes, Jack."

"I wish you'd call me 'Father' ". Jack placed a hand on her shoulder, a gesture Verity didn't like so she wriggled away. "The others do." He appeared not to notice her rebuff, or not to take it as such.

"But you're not my father," Verity said coldly. "My father's dead."

"You're a very uppity miss." Jack's manner and tone of voice suddenly changed and Verity suspected he'd been drinking. There had been something slightly unsteady about his gait as he came in, and she'd learned how to interpret Jack's manner and behaviour in the short time she'd been living with him. Jack slumped in the chair opposite her, a sulky expression on his face.

23

"I don't know why you didn't stay with your uncle and aunt or wherever it was you got all your airs and graces from."

Verity got up and, sweeping the books off the table, put them under her arm and made determinedly for the door. In a trice, however, Jack was there before her, blocking her way.

"Let me pass," Verity said angrily.

"No, I shall not before you call me 'Father' ". Jack sounded decidedly tipsy now.

"I shall *not* call you 'Father', now or ever. Now please get out of my way."

With a silly leer on his face Jack leaned forward as if he wanted to kiss her and as he did Verity swung the books towards him hitting him in the chest and, as he doubled over clutching himself in pain, she ran along the hallway and up the stairs to the small room she occupied at the top. Once there, she turned, breathless, to lock the door and then realised that there was no key. Simultaneously she heard Jack running up the stairs after her.

Thoroughly afraid now and regretting her high-handed behaviour she leaned against the door, her heart thumping painfully, as she heard his footsteps stop outside the door. She could hear his heavy breathing on the other side.

Verity closed her eyes and prayed for him to go away.

Suddenly the door was violently pushed open and she found herself knocked over and spreadeagled on the floor while Jack, his veins bulging in his neck, his face puce with rage, towered over her.

"If I'd a whip I'd take it to you," he snarled. "You are a haughty, imperious, objectionable little baggage. Ever since you came here you have interrupted our family life. There is only one way to deal with you, teach you a lesson . . . and this is it." Roughly hauling her to her feet he threw her across the bed as of she were a sack. Then he hoisted up the skirt of her dress, grasped the top of her stocking and threw himself on top of her, at the same time struggling to unfasten the belt that held up his trousers.

Verity felt she was suffocating. Her breath came in gasps

because of his weight on her chest. She clawed at the hand that was fumbling with her knickers as he tried to prise apart her legs and force himself between them.

His mouth then bore down hard upon hers and she could taste the bitter alcohol on his tongue as he thrust it into her mouth.

Verity closed her eyes, wishing that at the moment she might die, when Jack suddenly lay still, lifted his head and appeared to listen to some noise he'd heard outside. He then jumped off the bed, his trousers half-way down his legs and, hanging on to them, he went to the window and looked out. He hurriedly drew up his trousers, stuffing his shirt into the top and tightened his belt.

"Get up," he commanded roughly, "wipe your mouth, tidy yourself up and don't you *dare* say a bloody word about this to your mother or, by God, I'll have you and, believe me, it will be an experience you'll never forget."

With that he opened the door and shut it carefully behind him. Verity lay on the bed exactly as he'd left her, clothes awry, knickers pulled down over her hips, utterly dazed and shocked at what had happened to her. The lingering taste of his mouth on hers, the smell of him, made her feel nauseous and she thought she was going to be sick.

She could hear the sound of voices outside and knew that her mother had returned just in time to save her from a fate that surely was worse than death.

She had been within inches of rape by her stepfather.

The hated Jack had turned out to be everything she thought he would be, except that she had never thought of him as a rapist. She was an innocent young girl and she had not really known what "rape" meant except that it was a defilement, taking someone by force. In Latin classes the rape of the Sabine women had been somehow glossed over, never clearly explained except that it was some sort of violence perpetrated against them by the Roman soldiers.

Now she thought she knew exactly what rape meant or could mean, or would have meant had it happened to her.

Jack's trousers round his knees, his exposure of himself, had told her everything.

She heard voices inside the house and knew that at any minute someone would come up to find her. The thought of her young sister or, worse, her mother seeing her like this galvanised her into action.

She got up quickly from the bed, tidied her clothes, hurried to the dressing-table and ran a brush through her hair; patted her flushed face, then opened the window to try and let the cool fresh air of a chilly English summer's day blow in.

She quickly smoothed the counterpane and was taking the books up from the floor when there was a knock on her door.

"Are you there, Verity?" Addie called. "Can I come in?"

"Of course," Verity called back, her voice shaking. She still felt unsteady, and her heart raced alarmingly. She sat down on the bed again and attempted to compose herself with a fixed smile of welcome to her sister.

"Did you have a nice day? How was Grandma?"

"Grandma had a headache, which is why we came back early. We were going to stay for tea." Addie stopped and looked curiously at her sister. "Are you all right, Verity?"

"I have a headache too," Verity said with a nervous laugh, brushing her forehead with the back of her hand. "I had a little lie down and was almost asleep when I heard you come."

"Mum has brought the cake that Grandma made for our tea."

"Is Jack down there?" Verity asked.

Addie shook her head.

"Then I will come down. Give me a few minutes, there's a love."

It took Verity more than a few minutes before she felt she was ready to confront her mother and sisters, perhaps her stepfather too. She was so stunned and shocked by what had happened that she felt her whole life had changed fundamentally in seconds.

She had not liked Jack and it was now apparent he hated

her. They could not possibly live under the same roof together, not for a day longer.

She hated, feared and loathed the man who was married to her mother. Was this the way he treated her? Is this why there were so many grunts and what seemed like little cries of pain from their bedroom at night; sounds that were amplified in the small cottage? At times Verity would pull the blankets over her head because she didn't like to think what was happening to Mother. Now she knew what was happening to Mother. It was how adults behaved towards each other. On a larger and more terrifying scale it had nearly happened to her.

When Verity got downstairs the table was laid for tea. There were cups and saucers on it, plates and the cake Grandma had meant for them to eat at Swayles' farm. Mother, however, seemed in a good mood. She sat feeding the baby in the discreet way that she had, with her bodice undone but nothing unsightly, no exposure of bare flesh.

"Did you see Jack?" Mother asked, but Verity shook her head.

"Go and get him then, there's a dear," Mother said. "Tell him his tea is ready."

"Could Addie go?" Verity said wearily brushing her hand across her forehead once more. "I have a terrible headache."

"Oh dear!" Mother looked concerned. "Perhaps you'd better lie down, dear."

"I think I will, Mum, if you don't mind. In fact I may go to bed and spend the rest of the day there."

"You work too hard," Mother said, shaking her head, but she had a tender smile on her face, her eyes on the baby at her breast, as if she was really in another world, thinking about him and not about Verity at all.

Mother wouldn't miss her, Verity thought as she gazed at the ceiling. She was still terrified that Jack would somehow find a way into her room again and try and complete what he had set out to do. When she heard a step outside her door her heart

27

beat faster. But it was only Addie with some supper and the news that Jack had sent word that he would not be back before nightfall.

Finally Verity dozed and then she was suddenly wide awake as she heard someone stumbling on the stairs and cursing, and her mother's outraged tone as she hissed loudly outside the door: "Jack Hallam, you've been to the pub again!"

Then the door of Mother and Jack's bedroom shut and she heard a thumping noise and muffled screams, and now she could imagine exactly what was happening to Mother.

After a while there was a tap on her door and Addie slid in, her little face pale and fearful in the light of the candle that still burned by Verity's bed.

"Can you hear that noise?" she asked. "Is Mum all right?"

"I hope so," Verity said holding her little sister very tight. If she left, what would happen to her? Except that Jack had always seemed fond of Addie whereas between him and Verity there had lurked a sense of enmity.

"Father frightens me sometimes," Addie said.

"He frightens me too." Verity turned and looked at her sister. "I wish you wouldn't call him 'Father'. He isn't, you know."

"I know, but Mum asked me to. She said he would like it and she wished you would too."

"Well I shan't. Never. And Addie, look, you must promise me never to be alone with Jack. If Mother, or even little Peg, are not in the room then go somewhere else."

"But Father – Jack is all right with me," Addie said, hastily correcting herself. "It is only sometimes that he frightens me."

"Quite so. When he's been to the pub he *is* frightening and that is why I don't want you ever to be alone with him. Promise me?"

"Promise," Addie said clinging to her sister. "But you will be here to protect me."

"I may not be."

"But you said . . ." Addie began to whimper, "you said you wanted to stay to be one big happy family as before."

"You can't put the clock back," Verity said grimly. "Things change. People change. Nothing ever stays the same."

Mother appeared distressed by Verity's statement that she wished to return to Uncle Stanley and Aunt Maude. "But I thought you were happy here? We have had a very happy summer."

"I feel I must go back to them, Mum. Aunt Maude is lonely without me. She was very sad when I left last time I went to see her. Uncle Stanley is away so often. They have been very good to me. I don't feel it's fair." .

"But that's not what you said." Mother was sitting next to the baby's cradle which she shook gently. Little Edgar looked blissfully contented. But then he began to cry and Mother felt his bottom and said that his nappy needed changing and sent Addie to fetch a clean one.

When Addie returned, Verity sat watching Mother change Edgar and, as he lay there for a moment, naked, she looked with some wonder at his little appendage and marvelled that the same thing had been so big and ugly on Jack. She realised that she had learned in a most unpleasant way a great deal about the facts of life in a few short days.

Mother finished changing Edgar, put his dirty nappy in a bucket and gently rocked him to sleep again. Mother looked very tired and pale, as well she might because the noise in her bedroom had not stopped until the small hours of the morning. Verity longed to be able to speak to Mother but knew that she could not, neither about what happened to Mother almost nightly nor what had nearly happened to her.

She knew that she would not be able to tell anyone about that: not Mother, not Aunt Maude nor Granny Swayle, not Addie nor any of her closer friends at school. It had been a horrible, ugly, demeaning experience that would remain a close secret in her heart for ever; an ugly secret like a suppurating, almost fatal wound.

Jack had not appeared that day for breakfast. Mother said he had left early to take some vegetables to market and would not be back until late.

Verity knew then that this would be her last day alone with her gentle, kind adorable mother whom she loved so much but was powerless to help.

That very practical woman, Granny Swayle, would be sure to say in one of her favourite phrases that as Mother had made her bed she must lie on it.

Verity knew she must be very sure that this did not happen to her.

Three

F or the next few years Jack continued to work for Mr Tempest Newton but he was restless and dissatisfied. He was a man who liked change; he was stimulated by it, and he seemed to have been stuck for a long time in one place and with a growing family crammed into a smallish house.

In 1909 Verity turned fourteen. She was a tall, grave-looking girl who seemed to stand apart from the rest of her family as though she wasn't part of them any more. She had returned to her aunt and uncle, settled down and, as expected, did well at school. This remoteness from her family distressed her. She felt it was unnatural. She loved her brother and sisters and adored her mother, but school life was so busy, there were so many activities and Uncle Stanley encouraged her to spend long hours at her home-work in order to excel. She wanted to excel to show her gratitude to the Carters for what they had done for her.

In the spring Jack had an interview with Lord Ryland, who was even more wealthy than Mr Tempest Newton and lived in a castle near Sherborne, some thirty miles away. Cathy came along for the interview and made a good impression, as did Jack. He and his wife and family seemed the sort of people Lord Ryland wanted on his estate, and of Jack's ability there was no doubt. As well as being presentable, he was good at his job. He exhibited at all the local fairs flowers and vegetables which were better, bigger, finer and brighter, sweeter smelling than those of many of his rivals.

As well as a house and more money, Jack's status would

increase. He would have five gardeners under him whereas at Tempest Newton he had only one.

After the first meeting with Lord Ryland, which appeared to go favourably, they were taken by Lord Ryland's agent on a tour of the gardens and to see the lodge at the gate which was allotted to the head gardener who was retiring.

This was a substantial dwelling within sight of the castle. It had a sitting-room, a dining-room, kitchen and scullery, and four good-sized bedrooms. It had a cottage-style walled garden, conservatory and an outhouse. All the buildings, including the house, were of the same warm Ham stone as the sixteenth-century castle. It seemed like a time warp, so that one could almost expect a knight in armour to come charging down the hill. Cathy thought they would be so comfortable and happy here she could hardly restrain herself at the prospect of living in such a place and they returned apprehensively to the castle wondering how Lord Ryland felt about them. Would they have been shown the lodge if . . . But the suspense didn't last long. Lord Ryland had already made up his mind, as they had made up theirs. Jack was offered the job; it was accepted and they returned happy but weary to Bournemouth to break the news to the children and the rest of the family.

The move took place in the summer. Verity, on her summer holidays, came along to help with the younger ones because Cathy was pregnant again.

The day had begun extremely early, soon after dawn, when the van pulled by two large cart-horses arrived to remove the furniture. After a final inspection of the old house Jack, Cathy and the children had piled into the coach hired to take them to Sherborne and had followed the van. It was a slow journey and they were tired when they arrived.

The removal men had already started to move the furniture inside under instructions from Cathy, who had seen the new house again the previous week, and had worked out just where to put everything. Scarcely was the furniture in when a maid arrived from the castle to summon Cathy and Jack to see Lord and Lady Ryland.

"Four bedrooms!" Addie said excitedly. "Now you need never go back to Aunt Maude and Uncle Stanley," Addie went on looking at her eldest sister. In the cottage on the Tempest Newton estate the younger girls had had to share a bedroom and Verity's had been very tiny, almost a cupboard.

Verity smiled at her excited younger sister.

"But I *want* to go back to Aunt Maude and Uncle Stanley. It is my home."

Addie had never become accustomed to the loss of Verity. She pined for her all the time and, because of her distress, Verity's visits had become more frequent, though she always tried to time them to a period when her stepfather would be absent.

Now with more space, and being that much further from Bournemouth, perhaps she would come and stay. She would have to. She didn't relish that prospect at all, never having lost her fear of her stepfather's motives towards her.

"Oh here's Mum!" Addie shouted excitedly looking out of the window. Then in a slightly more subdued tone: "Oh dear, she looks so tired."

Cathy was tired and her daughters watched her walk slowly along the drive as if she carried the weight of the world on her shoulders.

"Poor Mum," Verity said sadly. "I'm sure she does not want this baby."

"How can you stop having babies?" Addie looked puzzled. "I mean how . . ." She gazed at Verity who looked away, not wishing to be reminded about the day her stepfather's assault brutally instructed her into the facts of life. Until then she'd been as ignorant as her sister, and sometimes she wished she had remained so.

Just then Cathy looked up, saw her daughters and, attempting a brave smile, quickened her step.

Verity waved from the upstairs window and ran downstairs, closely followed by Addie, Peg and Edgar holding hands. The two younger ones were inseparable.

Just as Cathy got to the door her children rushed out to greet her.

"Oh!" Cathy sank on to the bench on the lawn, thankful that it was a fine day as the house was in such a state of disorder.

"How were they Mum? How was it?"

"They were very nice," Cathy nodded her head approvingly, "particularly Lord Ryland. Lady Ryland, I think, was a bit stuck up. We were not asked to sit until she had left the room. Then Lord Ryland was very charming. Lady Ryland asked me questions about when my baby was due and whether it would prevent my husband from doing his work! I said that my husband had never had much to do with the children anyway and I didn't expect he would start now! Jack seemed a bit annoyed about that but Lord Ryland laughed and said men were well out of the way as far as those matters were concerned. I gather they have three." Cathy paused and waved her hand in front of her face. "Oh dear, I long for a cup of tea."

"Did they not offer you tea, Mum?"

"Oh, no. I expect Jack will have one in the kitchen when Lord Ryland has finished showing him around. He takes a great interest in the running of the estate and, unlike Mr Tempest Newton, doesn't leave it all to his agent." She paused, looking thoughtful. "Whether that is a good thing or not I can't say."

"Addie, go and make us all a cup of tea," Verity commanded, looking at her mother with concern. "Are you sure you're all right, Mum?"

Cathy rubbed her stomach.

"A little pain," she said wincing slightly. "Not much. You will find the kettle, teapot and tea things already in a chest in the kitchen," she told Addie. "I made sure that they were put there." As Addie obediently trotted off, Cathy put out her hand and took Verity's.

"I do wish you could stay for a few days. Addie is very good but I don't know what I'll do without you."

She looked towards the two younger children who were playing on the lawn. "Peg and Ed need such a lot of attention, especially Ed. He's into everything."

"I'm sure the people here will be very kind, Mum." Verity wriggled uncomfortably.

"But it's all so new," Cathy wailed. "They don't know me and I don't know them. Not only you but I'm further away from my own Mum and Dad." Cathy's eyes filled with tears. "Oh, Verity, I *do* wish I'd never let you go to Maude and Stanley. It's made you hard."

"Mum!" Verity looked shocked. "How could you say such a thing?"

"It's true. It has changed you."

"But Mum, I've got older. I was eight when I went to them, now I'm fourteen. I was bound to change. Besides they have been very good to me."

"I think you've grown away from us. We're too humble for you. Not good enough . . ."

"Mum!" Verity stamped the ground angrily. "I will not hear any more of this. It is most unfair and quite untrue. I do not think I am better than you. I love you but you were the one who gave me away and my home is with— Mum . . . are you all right?"

Cathy suddenly bent double, her hand clutching her stomach. With her other hand she groped wildly for Verity's.

"Verity, I am starting. Oh, I have nothing ready. Get Addie to run and fetch Jack and the midwife. Oh, Verity, help me go inside."

Panic stricken, Verity put her arm round her mother's waist and assisted her slowly towards the door just as Addie emerged with a tea tray, nearly colliding with them.

"Hurry and fetch Jack and the midwife. Mum is starting

her labour pains. Oh, and take Peg and Ed with you. There is no one to look after them here. Oh, what a day for this to happen."

Inside, everything was chaotic with bags, boxes and suitcases spilled in the hall, though there was some semblance of order upstairs where the furniture was in place. The beds, however, were not made and as Cathy staggered upstairs and into her bedroom, helped by her daughter, she collapsed on the unmade double bed and lay there gasping, her stomach already heaving.

"Oh, my . . . the pains are bad. Oh, my . . . I can feel the baby bearing down. It will not be long, Verity. Oh, darling . . ." she held out for her daughter's hand and squeezed it tightly, "don't leave me now. Quick, get some sheets from the box in the hall and then pray that the midwife arrives in time."

As opposed to her mother's near hysteria Verity suddenly felt calm, responsible and in control. She knew this was a serious, almost desperate situation and her role was a vital one. She flew downstairs and found the box containing the sheets, identified her mother's suitcase with her clothes and carried them upstairs.

Her mother wore a blue silk dress with high fastenings which she was trying clumsily to undo. As she stood up Verity put down the things on the floor, threw the sheet half over the bed and, having helped her mother to remove her dress, lowered her on to the bed while she finished undressing her.

"You'll have to help . . . the baby," Cathy gasped, opening her legs and looking down, and when Verity followed her gaze she saw to her astonishment a little head covered with matted fluff emerge from the gaping hole in her mother's body and then the rest of the baby wriggled out and lay momentarily inert on the bed before uttering a feeble cry.

"Oh my God!" Cathy cried, "you'll have to cut the cord. Oh, my baby."

36

"It's a girl," Verity said, and suddenly and with some pride smiled triumphantly at her mother. "Mum, I have another baby sister."

Aunt Maude was shocked that a girl of fourteen had assisted in the birth of a baby.

"Young girls ought not to see such things," she said, her mouth pursed in disapproval.

"Why not, Aunt?" Looking rather smug, Verity reached over and selected a macaroon freshly baked by cook in honour of her homecoming.

"Because it's not seemly, that's why."

"I don't see why not. I thought it was very natural, very interesting. Mum was very brave. She told me just what to do and I helped to cut the cord."

Aunt Maude, scandalised, raised her eyes to heaven. Verity even fancied she blushed.

"Just like my sister not to make preparations, to leave everything to chance." Flustered, Aunt Maude poured herself a fresh cup of tea. "Much as I love Cathy, she is deeply irresponsible."

"I don't see how Mum could possibly have helped it," Verity said crossly. "The baby was early. She didn't expect her. It was the exertion of the journey, the heat of the day. The doctor came and said there were all sorts of reasons."

Verity gave a smile of self-satisfaction. "He said I did wonderfully well and that I should be a nurse."

"What nonsense!" her aunt retorted. "Your uncle would be very annoyed if you entertained such a notion."

"But why?"

"It's not a dignified calling for a young lady."

"Then what do you want me to do?"

Aunt Maude looked surprised. "We don't want you to *do* anything, child. There is no need. Once you have completed your education we thought we might travel abroad for a year. Uncle Stanley suggested that you and I might go together and then he would join us. You will then be well educated and well travelled, an ideal bride for some fortunate young man."

Verity felt herself freeze. She put down her cup carefully on its saucer and stared at the floor, imagining the life of conformity and respectability her aunt and uncle had planned for her. Education, travel, an introduction to a "nice young man", a house in Boscombe or maybe nearby, babies . . .

Verity thought of the baby wriggling out of her mother and she knew that it would be far too soon for that sort of thing to happen to her, if ever.

Uncomfortable with her thoughts, Verity found it hard to sleep that night. There had been no more talk of trips round the world or marriage, for soon Uncle Stanley had arrived home and after an early tea had taken Verity with him to the common, butterfly nets in hand to look for varieties Uncle Stanley knew to inhabit that part of the grassland.

Uncle Stanley had been overjoyed to see her home because, whereas Maude didn't care for his hobby, Verity was his constant companion on his excursions.

Verity loved Uncle Stanley. More of a contrast with Jack was hard to imagine. He was so gentle and gentlemanly, kind, understanding, full of encouragement. He was softer than Aunt Maude and it was to him she turned in times of trouble, though it was true that such was the even tenor of her life, there were few of these.

For the next two years Verity saw little of her family despite her promise to her mother to visit as often as she could. Now that they had moved to Sherborne there was the distance to consider, but above all there was a reluctance on the part of the young girl to see too much of her stepfather. At the same time she was anxious for the welfare of the younger ones, particularly her sister Addie, who was much prettier than she was.

However, whenever she did see Addie there was no cause to

suspect that anything was amiss. There was no change in her naturally joyous and open character and Verity suspected that, for whatever reason, she alone had been the temporary object of her stepfather's lust.

Her mother never complained, though she frequently looked weary and was always alarmingly thin. Edgar and the new baby, Stella, flourished and, though the elder children went to the local school, they did well.

At sixteen years of age Verity was tall, graceful with long brown hair. She could not be considered beautiful, her features were too sombre, her expression always grave and composed. She seldom smiled spontaneously, but when she did it briefly illuminated her rather plain features, and her soft brown eyes seemed to sparkle with an incipient sense of fun. Compared to Addie or the winsome little Peg, Verity was unfortunate as far as looks were concerned, but in everything else, and as a result of the years she'd lived with Uncle Stanley and Aunt Maude, she had a distinct advantage over her sisters.

Verity was a serious, bookish girl and she could not have had better adoptive parents than Stanley and Maude Carter. Stanley, in particular, encouraged her to learn, never calling her a blue-stocking as others were sometimes cruelly inclined to do.

As a result of her superior education in a private girls' school Verity was better read, better educated and, thanks to Uncle Stanley, was interested in science, biology and allied subjects which were largely considered the prerogative of boys. From the point of view of intellect Verity and Uncle Stanley were perfect companions, and it was perhaps not surprising that Maude grew jealous of the relationship and from time to time showed her pique.

On the whole, however, these occasions were rare. Husband and wife had disparate lifestyles. Aunt Maude had her own circle of friends, ladies of a certain age who entertained one another to tea, played bridge and attended flower-arranging classes and concerts in the town. As they regarded Verity as their daughter, Maude and Stanley were united in their affection for her, and the result was a happy and harmonious household, one in which Verity, despite her initial misgivings, considered herself very fortunate to live.

Uncle Stanley had a very fine library consisting, as well as numerous books on butterflies, of volumes on entomology and botany. While he sat mounting his precious specimens, either purchased or collected, Verity used to keep him company sometimes by assisting him with his work or quietly reading close by.

Verity, who had just returned from a visit to Sherborne, looked up from her book to see Uncle Stanley gazing across at her. He pushed his chair back, removed his spectacles and addressed this young woman whom he loved as if she had been of his own flesh.

"And how did you find your family? Mother well?"

Verity seemed relieved to put aside her book.

"Mother always looks very tired to me. Addie does what she can but the two smaller ones are a handful. I wish I was nearer. I do worry frequently about Mother." Verity leaned forward as if about to confide in Uncle Stanley and then appeared to change her mind. Sometimes she longed to tell him about Jack, but she always held back.

However on this latest visit she had found Addie more subdued and one night she herself had heard sounds of sobbing from the room that Mother shared with Jack. It seemed terrible that in all these years Mother had sustained the sort of treatment she had received and yet she never complained or turned on her tormentor.

"You seemed worried about Cathy." Uncle Stanley looked concerned. "Would it be nice if we asked her here for a little holiday?"

"Oh, it would be lovely." Verity fervently clasped her hands together. "But Jack would never let her."

"But why not, just for a few days? There is room for the younger children; I suppose Addie would have to stay behind to go to school."

"Oh no, we could *never* leave Addie," Verity said aghast. "That is . . . she wouldn't like . . ."

Discomfited, not quite knowing how to proceed, Verity was aware of the concern on Uncle Stanley's face as he gently prompted her to continue, moving across from his desk and taking a chair next to hers.

"Verity, I can see something concerns you deeply, my dear. Tell me what it is."

"It is Jack." Verity hung her head. "He is not very nice to Mother. Sometimes we hear sobs from their bedroom at night." She looked anxiously up at her uncle. "And if you think we are imagining it I can assure you we are not. Jack is a violent and abusive man and I fear for Addie if she is left alone with him."

"You can't *mean* this!" Uncle Stanley's expression was horrified.

"I do . . ." Verity took a deep breath. "When I was younger he attempted a violent act towards me. That is why I visit the house so seldom and never let myself be alone with him. As far as I know he has never attempted the same thing with Addie. He never liked me, but he does like her. It is mainly . . ." she hung her head again, "you see, Jack drinks. It is when he is drunk that he mostly behaves like that. But on the occasion he tried doing what he did with me he was not completely drunk."

"But *where* were your mother and sisters?"

"They were out. Luckily they arrived home in time to prevent anything happening. That is . . . how I came to know the facts of life, Uncle Stanley."

"My poor dear." Stanley put an arm round her and gave her a hug. "This is a terrible thing to have happened."

"I was only nine but I have not forgotten it."

"And you never told anyone? Not even your mother?"

"I never could bring myself to mention it, certainly not to Mum. I'm sure you understand why. Besides, Aunt Maude and Granny never approved of Jack. They knew his reputation. I knew that if they got to know about this they would make a terrible fuss, maybe make things worse for Mum. But he does abuse her, he does ill-treat her and that is why she cries herself to sleep at night."

"Poor woman," Uncle Stanley murmured, stroking Verity's back. "Poor, poor Cathy. Your aunt, it is true, would be very upset if she knew. Besides, in a family situation there is nothing one can do and, thank heaven, you have been safe all these years with us."

"Safe," Verity confidently tucked her hand in his, "and *very* happy."

She looked up at him and once again her features were illuminated by that special smile. "I love you, Uncle Stanley, as much as I love Mother. You have been the perfect father to me and I am immensely fortunate to have you . . . and Aunt Maude," she added dutifully.

"Maude loves you as much as I do, like a daughter, and we wish only the best for you. Now," Uncle Stanley rose and returned to his desk. He opened a drawer and took out a folder in which were a sheaf of papers which he began to sort through. Then he turned to Verity again. "Your aunt and I have been thinking about your future. You are nearly seventeen and next year you will leave school where you have performed so well with excellent examination results. I wondered if you would like to consider a university education? Your aptitude for maths and the sciences is exemplary. I thought we might even consider the universities of Oxford or Cambridge?" Uncle Stanley became more animated as he went on. "Your aunt is afraid of you becoming a blue-stocking. I know she has a mind to marry you off as soon as possible, but in my opinion that would be a waste. We need educated women, well-educated women who can play a part in society. Now I wondered . . ."

Verity joined her hands in her lap and looked calmly at her uncle.

"Before you go on, Uncle, I should tell you that I have decided what I want to do. I have been of the same mind for a long time." She paused and studied his face. "I would like to be a nurse."

"A nurse!"

"I know that's not what you might have had in mind for me."

"But if a nurse why not a *doctor*? You have the qualifications, the ability."

"No I would like to be a nurse, to be near to people, to help them. You know that when Stella was born I helped to deliver her. It shocked Aunt Maude a good deal but it was then that I had an inkling of what I would like to do, be close to people, go into their homes."

"But as a doctor . . ."

Verity shook her head firmly. "I have not the stomach for years of study, or for the difficulties women doctors face in what is still a man's world. You have to be brave to do it and I am not brave enough. There are too many male doctors but no male nurses. That is women's work and it is what I would like to do."

For several seconds Uncle Stanley said nothing but tapped the top of his desk as if deep in thought. When he spoke at last his expression was grave.

"I do respect you, Verity, but I think you are mistaken. You have a fine brain and I think you would be wasted in nursing which is very mundane sort of work. Despite the deserved fame of Florence Nightingale and other fine women like her it largely consists of menial and domestic duties and I think you are made for better things. I must say that if this is your attitude and I can't change your mind I shall be very disappointed, but I wouldn't attempt to stop you. Now, my dear, will you promise to think about it? To take a long holiday with Aunt Maude on the continent; to visit France, Italy and Greece? I shall join you, of course. And maybe by the end of that time you will have changed your mind."

Verity, however, did not change her mind. She had thought about it too long, ever since Stella had come into the world.

The prospect of caring for people had started to appeal to her from that moment. When the time came, the delights of Paris, Venice and Rome instilled in her a love of travel, which she would keep all her life, a desire to see distant places and different people.

But when she returned she said goodbye to childhood and adolescence and applied to train as a nurse at one of the great London hospitals: Charing Cross.

Four

At first there had been enormous enthusiasm for the war, but as the papers began to fill with lists of casualties the fervour of 1914 evaporated.

Jack Hallam had not shared the general enthusiasm to take up arms and had been reluctant to volunteer. But as the need for men grew and his call-up papers came, he sought the help of Lord Ryland to intervene, but his request was treated with contempt by the peer who had, however, himself managed to avoid the draft on account of his age.

Lord Kitchener had said "Your Country Needs You" and Jack was needed as much as anybody. By 1916 the country could no longer depend on volunteers and conscription was introduced. Jack was thirty-seven when his summons to arms came. The Battle of the Somme had just created enormous casualties and the pages were crammed with names of the war dead.

Jack was sure he was going to die and all at once he was overcome with nostalgia, with love for his family, the countryside and the home he was about to leave.

Supper on his last night was a solemn occasion. Jack's suitcase was already packed and stood in the hall for collection first thing in the morning. The children were largely silent, not knowing what to say on this awesome occasion: Father prepared to fight and die for his country.

Besides Cathy and Jack the family now consisted of Peg, Edgar and Stella who were all at the local school. Verity who had excelled in her studies was now a theatre sister at Charing Cross Hospital, busy looking after the many wounded in the war. She was seldom able to get leave, but wrote regularly to her mother and Aunt Maude and Uncle Stanley.

Addie too had left home and was at teacher training college in Bristol.

Cathy had not had a happy life with Jack Hallam, but now that he was about to go away she realised that she was used to him. He was not all bad. He was evil-tempered and a drinker, but he was also capable of kindness and consideration. He was very good at his work and valued by Lord Ryland who overlooked his weakness for drink and the many days he had off on account of it.

Cathy wondered how long it would take the army to discover that Jack was an alcoholic and ignominiously dismiss him; and then he might find himself without a job with Lord Ryland as well.

Yet, though she did not love Jack, it was difficult to hate him on account of his good qualities. He was not a bad father, especially to his own two whom he adored. Addie had grown distant from him and Verity had never liked him, a feeling that was mutual. Whenever Verity came to stay, Jack contrived to find something to do that would take him away from home.

When you were in the kind of situation she was in, you made the best of things. You accepted life as it was, and if she got beaten regularly and forced to make love to her husband she at least had a roof over her head, enough to eat and five beautiful children. She had not the airs and graces nor the money that Maude had, but she had her own form of security and the family that poor Maude had longed for.

On this important occasion, Cathy sat pale-faced at one end of the table, Jack at the other.

"You must all be good to your mum while I'm away," he said looking sternly round at them.

"How long will that be, Dad?" Edgar asked, scooping up his meat, potatoes and gravy.

"I don't know, lad. They say the war will be over soon."

"They've been saying that since it started," Cathy scoffed. "If you ask me, nobody knows."

It was an awkward meal with many unnatural silences as if nobody knew what to say. Peg was especially fearful as several of her friends had already lost relatives in the war. Peg had grown quite close to Jack. Like the others she feared his drinking and the consequences for Mother, but he never harmed her. He was good with her and, as she loved nature she used to help him with the gardens, especially after several of the gardeners had volunteered for the front in the euphoria of 1914.

After supper Jack stood by the empty fireplace filling his pipe and made a little speech telling his son that he was now the man of the house and he should look after his mother and sisters.

To ten-year-old Edgar it appeared an onerous duty, and his shoulders seemed to sag with the weight of the responsibility.

After his little speech Jack went round the room solemnly kissing each child on the forehead. When he came to Cathy he took her by the hand.

"Time we were all in bed, Mother. There is an early start tomorrow."

Cathy and Jack lay facing each other their faces illuminated by the light of the moon. He put out his hand and stroked her face.

"You know I love you, Cathy."

She said nothing but her body trembled slightly. Sometimes she thought that the present was preferable to an uncertain future. What would happen to them all if Jack didn't return from the war?

"I know sometimes I have a funny way of showing it," Jack went on, "but that's when the drink takes hold of me."

"If you don't control yourself, Jack, they will dismiss you from the army," Cathy whispered. "You will receive a dishonourable discharge. And if that happens Lord Ryland will never have you back here."

"I will control myself. I'm a changed man, Cathy." He put a hand on her shoulder and began to caress her. "I am ashamed of myself for the violence I have shown towards you. I promise you that if I come back safely it will never happen again. I don't know why I do it but you provoke me. You never *give* yourself to me. I think it is because you never loved me."

Cathy lay quietly listening to him. It was true she never had. She had loved Billy but married Jack for security. She had never been wooed. He was a clumsy, inexpert lover from the beginning. He never ever knew how to treat a woman properly. Even now he leaned towards her and kissed her clumsily. He'd had a few at the pub before supper and his mouth stank of drink. As usual she stiffened and he held back.

"You see, Cathy, you never respond to me. It is very frustrating for a man to have to try so hard."

"It's because I'm afraid of you, Jack, and the violence. I would never have put up with it for all these years if it had not been for the children. What I can't understand is that you have it in you to be a good and kind man, but that is not a side of you I see much of."

"Just tonight, Cathy, in case I never come back, will you try to love me?" Jack said in a wheedling tone, tears of self-pity filling his eyes. "It may be the very last time I ever make love to a woman."

Gently his hand moved from her face to her breasts. She could feel the tears on his face and, instead of being rough and careless, he was trying to please her in a way he seldom had before. She thought that he was no longer a violent and brutal husband, a man overfond of drink, but a brave soldier going to the war.

Maybe it was relief that made her give herself freely, even lovingly, to him just in case it was for the last time?

Verity's lids felt very heavy and, momentarily, her eyes closed and quickly, guiltily, she jerked herself awake again. She looked round to see if anyone had observed her momentary weakness, but all eyes seemed to be on the patient on the table in front of them, the skilful surgeon tying the final stitches to close the gaping wound in his abdomen. She looked at the clock on the theatre wall and saw that it was nearly midnight. Besides being exhausted she felt light-headed and realised she had not eaten since a cup of tea and a piece of cake had been handed to her at about five o'clock in the afternoon.

The anaesthetist removed the chloroform mask from the face of the patient and looked at him critically. He had a fifty–fifty chance of survival, maybe less. His face with its thick stubble of beard was deathly pale. Two orderlies came to remove the body from the table on to a trolley and wheeled him away. The surgeon took off his mask and wiped his face with a cloth that Verity held out to him.

"Thank you, Sister. You look very tired."

The surgeon looked around at the nurses cleaning the instruments for tomorrow's list, or the night's emergencies. The hospital operated round the clock as patients were sent to London straight from the docks after having been repatriated from France. The more serious cases needed the skills of surgeons at the main London hospitals. Mr Colefax was the top man in his field dealing with abdominal injuries. The patient who had just been wheeled out of the theatre had had his spleen and half of his stomach removed. No one cared any longer to make a prognosis.

Dr Harvey, Mr Colefax's registrar, also removed his mask. He also looked exhausted as he stood talking to Mr Colefax, who was making notes about the last patient.

"I'll say "goodnight' then," Mr Colefax said, finishing his notes and giving those around him his cold, impersonal smile. There would be no word of thanks from him, however hard they worked, however many hours they spent round the table. They were people doing their duty, just as he was or the soldier on the table had been doing when part of a shell ploughed into his stomach and shattered his chances of surviving into old age.

Everyone stood back deferentially as the great man left the theatre. The junior nurses continued with sterilising the instruments and tidying up the theatre.

"Are you on duty tonight, Dr Harvey?" Verity asked the young man. "You look all in to me."

"I think Dr Jameson is on night duty. You look all in as well to me, Sister. In fact," he smiled sympathetically at her, "I think I saw you close your eyes."

Verity blushed.

"It was only a second . . ."

"Please," Dr Harvey put out his hand, "I meant no criticism. To be on duty from just after dawn until midnight is asking too much of anybody." He smiled kindly down at her. "How old are you, Sister?"

Verity flushed deeply. "Really, Dr Harvey I don't think that is any business of yours."

"I apologise." Dr Harvey looked contrite. "I didn't mean to be impertinent."

"That's quite all right, Dr Harvey," Verity said crisply. "Now if I were you I'd go and get a good night's sleep."

She then removed her gown and cap and went to the sluice room to wash her hands.

She stood at the door saying "goodnight" as the nurses passed by her, with a smile or a word of praise for each. They were all doing their duty, but they still deserved some thanks, which was something those great men, the surgeons, never seemed to realise.

Dr Harvey was the last to go and he stood back at the door to let her pass. "After you, Sister Barnes."

"Thank you, Doctor. Please don't forget to turn out the lights."

"As if I would. Let's hope there are no more cases tonight."

Dr Harvey turned off the lights, held the door open for Verity and then closed it as they passed through. In front of them stretched the long, badly lit, gloomy corridor of the hospital opposite one of London's main line stations through which most of the casualties came from the coast.

"I don't suppose you'd like a coffee, Sister, would you?"

"Oh, I'd *love* a coffee," Verity replied, "but where?"

"There's a place at the station that keeps open all night."

"Perhaps a sandwich too, or a bun." Suddenly the thought of food seemed the most desirable thing in the world.

"The Matron won't mind, will she?" Dr Harvey glanced at Verity.

"She won't know," Verity said and as they exchanged glances a sense of intimacy seemed suddenly to spring up between them.

Dr Harvey had only qualified the previous summer, yet already he was a registrar. The war had taken so many doctors to the front lines that promotion was rapid. He was not unattractive, a rather stockily built man with fair hair, slightly sparse, and spectacles. He had a cheerful, open face and at one time he'd broken his nose. She heard that he played rugger for the hospital and idly wondered what he did with his glasses.

As they strolled out into the night the streets still seemed alive with people scurrying into the station concourse or emerging from it with their coat collars turned up against the weather. Dr Harvey took Verity's arm as they crossed the Strand and she wrapped her cloak tightly around her, suddenly feeling rather vulnerable. Although she wore her nurse's cloak and, under it, her uniform, she felt somehow in mufti without her starched headdress, which she had left in her locker.

The garish lights of the station were dimmed by the smoke from the engines pulling the long trains. Already there were stretchers on the platform, and she thought it would not be too long before the lights went on in the theatre again and the night-time emergency team took over.

As well as the soldiers disembarking on stretchers, a line of new recruits, their heavy kit on their backs, was forming on one of the platforms. They were cheerful, rather rowdy young men who looked as though they were setting out on a great adventure rather than going to war, or perhaps the two were synonymous.

A tea-room was still open, crowded with people who had

either come to meet the wounded or were seeing loved ones off. Despite the gravity of the situation there was an air of almost frenzied jollity as if a party was in progress, except for the faces of some of the women, many of whom were showing signs of tears.

"You get a table, I'll get the coffee," Dr Harvey volunteered. "Or what passes for it." In wartime real coffee had become a luxurious commodity.

"As long as it's wet and warm," Verity said cheerfully. Espying a table about to be vacated by a couple holding hands, the man in uniform, the woman not much older than herself, she made for it giving them a sympathetic smile as she waited for their seats. But they had eyes only for each other.

Verity found that her tiredness had left her and she sat down, looking about her. There was something quite exciting, even exhilarating about the whole atmosphere, bustle and energy, that was similar to the one that was all pervasive at the hospital and which suited and stimulated her. She had, after all, not been wrong in her choice of career.

She watched Dr Harvey as he queued up for service and remembered that moment of intimacy they had seemed to share, as if their relationship had somehow deepened. She didn't know him very well. He had only been a short while on the firm as registrar. She thought he was about twenty-six or twenty-seven. As he came towards her carefully carrying a tray, he smiled across at her. She waved and then got up to help him manoeuvre the tray on to the table.

"No sandwiches I'm afraid. All gorn, ducky," he said imitating the cockney accent of the girl behind the counter. "No coffee either but there is hot tea and buns."

"Buns are fine," Verity said, eyeing them ravenously. Now she realised that it did all seem like a great adventure. "I'm starving."

"You should take more care, Sister Barnes," Dr Harvey said reprovingly. "The Sister in charge of theatre must not be permitted to starve. I say," he carefully put down the plates and cups and saucers and then stood the tray up against the side of the table, "aren't you very young to be Theatre Sister?"

"And aren't you very young to be a registrar?" Her hands around the warm tea-cup, Verity looked across at him and smiled, her irritation at his renewed familiarity suddenly evaporating.

"I'm twenty-six."

"I thought you were about that. I'm twenty-one. Yes I am very young but I have passed my exams and they need nurses. So many of them have gone to the front. I wish I could too."

She stirred her tea and put the cup to her lips. She thought it was the sweetest, most welcome liquid she had ever tasted: ambrosia. A fire seemed to shoot through her body with the first gulp.

"Did you volunteer?"

"Yes, but they wanted me here."

"Me too, but I hope in six months or so I'll get the chance to join up as a medic. The trouble is I'm short-sighted and they take the able-bodied ones first."

"I wondered about your rugger." Verity studied him over the rim of her cup.

"Oh you know about that?" Dr Harvey smiled as if gratified by her interest.

"I heard you played for the hospital."

"I can see well enough to play the ball but not enough to aim at the goal. Sometimes I manage to keep my glasses on."

"Not very wise." Verity shook her head.

"Tell me about yourself, Sister." Dr Harvey stirred his tea and handed her the plate of buns. "Go on, you said you were starving."

"So I am." Verity took a bun and sat for a moment eating it. It was rather stale but the taste was divine.

"Good," she said.

"About yourself?" Dr Harvey encouraged her.

"Nothing much to tell. I'm a Dorset girl. I have three sisters and a brother."

"Mother and father?"

"Mother." Verity frowned, reluctant to divulge too much about herself. "My father died when we were young."

"Leaving such a large family?" Dr Harvey looked surprised.

"No. My mother married again. I have a stepfather. They had two more children. In fact my stepfather was recently called up."

"He must be quite young."

"He is. It took him long enough to join up. He didn't volunteer." It was hard to keep the contempt out of her voice but she looked with a fixed expression at the man opposite her as if to discourage any further questions. "And you, Dr Harvey?"

"I wish you'd call me Rex."

"And you must call me Verity." She knew she was blushing slightly and was grateful for the heat of the cafeteria.

"Nothing much to tell about me either. My father is a country doctor in the Yorkshire Dales. He hopes that one day I'll join his practice. I'm not sure. I'm an only child so they depend a lot on me. I suppose we're lucky now that there's a war. Some families have several children at the front. I heard of one of my father's patients who has lost three sons in the past year. My father helped bring them all into the world. I don't know how people like that survive, but somehow they do."

There was a few minutes' silence while they finished their frugal meal. Rex Harvey suddenly yawned and his face seemed to turn grey.

"I think we must get to bed," Verity said, suddenly overwhelmed herself by a feeling of total exhaustion. "Do you live near?"

"Yes, I have digs in Clerkenwell."

"But that's some distance."

"I'll survive. I enjoy the walk. I'll see you to the nurses' home."

They rose together, their table being immediately taken by another couple, the man this time in sailor's uniform. The woman with him looked rather contemptuously at Rex and muttered under her breath. "It's amazing how some people escape being sent to the front." Rex turned, flushed and was about to proceed without comment, but Verity felt a sharp stab of anger and said:

"This gentleman is a doctor at Charing Cross Hospital. He saves many lives every day by his skills. You ought to thank God for him because one day your loved one may have need of him."

The woman who had spoken went scarlet. The man with her seemed about to reply, but his words were lost to them as Rex took hold of Verity's arm and propelled her across the room. Breathlessly they stood once more in the station concourse.

"You shouldn't have said that."

"I had to."

"It was very kind of you."

"I meant it."

The sense of intimacy deepened imperceptibly.

They walked out of the station and stood in the forecourt gazing towards the hospital, where many of the windows were still lit up.

They crossed the busy road and walked to the nurses' home in Chandos Street, stopping in front of the main door.

"Well . . ." Verity began, "thanks very much, Rex."

"Look," Rex said fumbling for words, "maybe we could do it again some time? I don't mean tea and a bun at Charing Cross Station but a proper meal, maybe a show. Would you like that?"

"I'd like it," Verity said. Her tiredness suddenly seemed to disappear once again.

"Well . . . I'll doubtless see you tomorrow in the theatre. We can talk about it then. Sleep well, Verity."

"And you too, Rex . . . and thank you."

As he turned away she lingered for a few minutes at the door and watched him walk into the night.

It was after one in the morning and she had to be in the theatre by eight.

As Verity entered the main hall the night porter came out from his box, his expression grave as he approached her.

"Sister Duckett would like to see you, Miss Barnes."

"Oh?"

"She is in her office." The porter pointed to a door off the hall.

"At this hour?"

The porter said nothing but accompanied Verity along the corridor and, after knocking at the door and hearing the command to enter, opened it for her.

Sister Duckett, who was in charge of the nurses' home, looked up from her desk at Verity and then gazed pointedly at the clock on the wall. "What time did you leave the operating theatre, Miss Barnes?"

"Shortly after midnight." Verity followed her gaze too and looked at the clock.

"And where have you been since then?"

"Dr Harvey invited me for a cup of coffee and something to eat. Neither of us had eaten since tea-time. We went across to the railway station."

"I see." Sister Duckett sat back as if considering how much of a fuss she should make.

"I trust that you don't see anything *wrong* in that?" Verity felt irritated and prickly at being treated like a schoolgirl, though the conditions under which the nurses lived did some-times resemble those of a rather strict boarding school.

"Not exactly *wrong*, but a little inconsiderate. As you had not checked in we were worried about you."

"I'm sorry. I didn't think of that." Suddenly Verity saw the sense of her superior's concern. The streets of London in wartime were no place for a young woman to be out alone.

"However," the expression on the face of the senior nurse softened, "it is not that I wish to see you about. I am sorry to tell you, Miss Barnes, that your mother is very ill in hospital in Sherborne and your presence is required immediately."

Verity's hand clasped her breast.

"What is wrong with Mum?"

"I don't know the details, I'm afraid, but I have made arrangements for you to be given leave and you have permission to take the first train home in the morning."

"Thank you Sister." Verity prepared to leave the room.

"Try to get a little sleep," the head nurse went on in a gentle tone of voice. "Oh and, Miss Barnes, try in future to have a little thought for others, won't you?"

"Yes, Sister," Verity said in a subdued tone, "and thank you."

When Verity got to the hospital in Sherborne the curtains were drawn round a bed in the corner of the ward to which she had been directed. A nurse sat at the table at the head of the ward and looked up enquiringly at the visitor.

"Mrs Hallam. I have permission to visit her."

"Oh," the nurse got up, "you must be her daughter?"

"Yes. I'm a nurse at Charing Cross Hospital. Is she very ill?"

"She is better, I am glad to say, than she was yesterday. She lost a lot of blood."

"*Blood?*" Startled, Verity looked at the nurse.

"A haemorrhage. I'm sure the doctor will explain the circumstances to you." Verity followed the nurse down the ward and stood aside as she drew back the curtain to let her through. Her mother's face was as white as the sheet tucked up to her chin. Her eyes were closed and her hands joined together on the counterpane made her seem already dead. But Verity was relieved to see that the even rise and fall of the bedclothes covering her chest showed she was still breathing.

She was overcome by the most tender love and concern for her mother, that strong bough of the tree on whom the whole family depended. Her mother might have given her away when she was young but she had done it for the best, and she'd been proved right. The younger children had been well looked after with money from the Carters, and so had she. Verity doubted whether she would be where she was now without the upbringing given her by Aunt Maude and Uncle Stanley.

She leant down to kiss her mother who moved slightly, but her eyes remained closed.

"She is sleeping," the nurse whispered. "Maybe you should leave her until she wakes up?"

Verity nodded. "Might I see the doctor?"

The two women walked back along the ward and Verity waited by the nurses' desk while she went to get the doctor. She returned in a few minutes without him.

"Dr Fletcher will see you in his room," she said, inviting Verity to accompany her back along the corridor where she knocked on a door. An authoritative voice called "Come in" and Verity walked towards an elderly man who went on writing at his desk.

Verity was not unfamiliar with the rudeness of some members of the medical profession, so she waited patiently until he had finished.

"I'm Dr Fletcher," he said leaning back in his chair and not attempting to shake hands, "the medical superintendent. Please sit down."

"Thank you, Doctor."

"And you are," the doctor studied a piece of paper on his desk, "Mrs Hallam's eldest daughter?"

"Yes; I'm a nurse at Charing Cross Hospital. Theatre Sister," she added, as if to emphasise her status.

"I see. Well, Miss Hallam, your mother nearly died here yesterday. She had a very severe haemorrhage. Did you know she was pregnant?"

"No, I had no idea!" Pale-faced and shocked, Verity shook her head.

"About three months. She was found in a pool of blood by, I believe, one of your younger sisters when she returned home from school."

"Oh!" Verity put her hands to her face. "How awful."

"The young girl had the good sense to call for an ambulance and we intervened to save your mother's life. She had a transfusion of five pints of blood."

"I see."

The doctor continued to look grave and a censorious note entered his voice. "The point is, Miss Hallam, your mother's miscarriage was not spontaneous. I believe it was the result of some intervention, either by herself or another person. There was substantial scarring and perforation of the uterus. She may well have to have a complete hysterectomy."

Verity stared at the desk in front of her saying nothing.

"You do realise," the doctor went on, "that this might be a criminal matter, abortion being illegal in this country?"

"You are quite *sure* there was intervention?"

"Quite sure. Some instrument was used to procure the abortion. However," the doctor rose and, coming across to Verity, perched on the edge of his desk. His expression remained stern but the tone of his voice changed. "I have no intention of informing the police. I understand your father is in the army and she has younger children to care for. When I heard that you were a nursing sister I thought I would speak to you in private. But I do want you to take care of your mother, talk to her and ensure that this kind of thing does not happen again."

"If she has a hysterectomy it won't be necessary."

"I take it that the baby *was* your father's?"

"My stepfather's. There is no doubt of it. He was here in July. My mother would never dream . . ."

"Quite so. That's what I thought." The doctor's rather stern features relaxed. "I don't want to come too hard on a woman who is already oppressed enough."

"Thank you, Doctor." Verity also rose. "I promise to do all I can to see that my mother is properly looked after, and warned about the future."

Cathy lay in her bedroom looking out of the window. It was so sad now that autumn was here and all the leaves were falling. It seemed to increase the sense of depression she felt. Tears began to trickle down her face and, as the door opened she attempted to brush them away.

Verity appeared round the door carrying a tray which she

placed on the table by the side of her mother's bed. Then she poured some liquid into a cup and handed it to her.

"Drink it all up," she commanded.

"Yes, nurse," her mother attempted a weak smile.

As Cathy took the cup Verity sat on the side of the bed and reached for her mother's other hand.

"Why did you do it, Mum?"

"I couldn't cope with another baby. Especially his. I have had enough of babies."

"I know, Mum." Verity squeezed her hand tightly. "There are ways of controlling conception, and when he comes back . . ."

"Jack is *not* a bad man," Cathy insisted, tears welling up again in her eyes. "I know you don't like him, but he has some good in him . . ."

"How can you say that when he beats you?"

"Oh," her mother's voice faltered, "you know?"

"Of course I know. We all know. These walls are very thin."

"The little ones know too?" Cathy looked both terrified and horrified.

"Everyone knows. I'm sure he forces you to sleep with him too, doesn't he? You can tell me. I'm a nurse."

"Yes, he does. But the night before he left was different. He was tender with me and I felt sorry for him. He told me he loved me, but I felt nothing towards him. I have too many bruises to remind me of how hateful he can be." Cathy rubbed her arm, wincing painfully as if the bruise marks were still there. "Much as I love Ed and Stella I didn't want another child by him, not at my age."

Verity leaned forward and gazed earnestly at her mother. "Mum, have you ever thought of leaving Jack?"

"I have often thought of it." Cathy, her face strained, looked up at her daughter. "But where can I go? To my mother, to Maude? What do you think they will say? My mother told me that I had made my bed and must lie on it. The times she's said that to me! She said the same thing about Billy. She never approved of the men I married. She was wrong about your father, but right about Jack. I would never demean myself with Maude. Besides, I have three young children. Peg is a little older now, but the other two – what would happen to them? A woman without other means of support is in no position to leave her husband. We are too dependent on them." She clutched Verity's hand. "You know I hate myself for saying it, but I can't help wishing – may God forgive me – that something might happen to Jack to prevent him returning from the war."

Five

E very day the toll mounted as the cases continued to pour
in from the Somme. The wounded waiting to be operated on flowed from the wards and into the corridors of the
hospital. Civilian cases had to take second place to the men
from the front line.

There had been no chance to talk, but from time to time the
eyes above the mask of the assistant surgeon seemed briefly to
glance at her and then quickly look down again towards the
patient on the table.

The team had been operating for several hours and, gowned
and masked, Verity went quietly about her task assisting the
surgeon-in-charge, handing him his instruments, occasionally
mopping his brow, staunching the blood inside the deep
wounds, keeping an eye on the activities in the rest of the
theatre staff who were her responsibility.

Rex finished stitching the massive gash in the leg of the
patient. Mr Peckham, the senior surgeon, stood back and
removed his mask. "Time to take a break, Sister," he said to
Verity. "I think eight hours is enough for anyone to stay on
duty. Go and have a cup of tea." He looked over towards Rex.
"You take a break too."

"How about you, sir?" Rex asked as he stripped off his
mask.

"I am going to my club in St James's for some lunch. I shall
be back here at half past two. Mr Harlow will take over in my
absence assisted by Dr Beck."

Removing his gown, Mr Peckham went to the scrubbing
room.

The patient was wheeled out and the table prepared for the next casualty.

"Care for a sandwich?" Rex asked Verity casually. She nodded without speaking and then for a few moments gave instructions to the nurses remaining behind.

By the time she joined him Rex had scrubbed, removed his theatre clothes and, wearing a tweed jacket and grey flannels, stood outside the door waiting for her.

"Same place?" he suggested with a smile.

"You mean the station? Why not?"

It seemed quite natural to be with him again, even if she hadn't seen him for a couple of weeks, and that after the briefest of acquaintanceships.

They left the hospital by the main door, crossed the road and were swept up by the crowds, which seemed larger than ever, entering and leaving the station. The whole place was a pulsating mass of people, stretcher cases still emerging from the trains stationary at the platform; groups of soldiers, heavily kitted out, waited in groups or said goodbye to loved ones.

But now faces were uniformly grim. All the excitement, the euphoria of patriotic fervour seemed to have gone. The expectations of surviving the war, even winning it, dwindled as bad news continued to arrive by the hour. The terrible haemorrhage of the Somme campaign continued unabated.

Once again Verity waited, watching Rex, a feeling of tension, of mounting excitement lurking beneath her calm exterior.

"I think this table is where we sat before?" Rex said as he put down two cups of tea and sandwiches made of grey-looking, almost black wartime bread. "Not very appetising, I'm afraid," he grimaced.

"It doesn't matter. I'm starving." Verity seized the sandwich with both hands, and bit into it.

"I wondered where you got to?" Rex placed the tray by the side of the table and smiled across at her. She thought how nice and sensible and ordinary he looked. Comfortable to be with. She thought Mum would approve of Rex.

"Oh! Didn't anyone tell you? I'm sorry. My mother was ill."

"I'm very sorry to hear that."

"After you left me that night in Chandos Street I got a message to leave at once for home. I took the first train in the morning."

Rex looked genuinely concerned. "How is your mother now?"

"Much better. You see it was not so much Mother as the smaller children who needed looking after. My younger sister, Adelaide, we call her Addie, has had to take my place as I felt I couldn't take any more time off from the hospital." Verity looked gravely across at Rex. "Mother had a miscarriage. Quite nasty for a woman of her age. She is over forty."

"Oh dear," Rex winced in sympathy. "And your father . . ."

"My *stepfather* is in the army."

"Oh yes, you told me." He paused and his expression brightened. "Look, I wondered about that meal and a show. Is it still on?"

"Of course. I'd like it."

"You see I may be going abroad."

"You've been called up?" Verity tried hard to conceal her emotion.

"I've volunteered for the RAMC, the medical corps. I may in fact be sent to the Balkans."

"The *Balkans*!"

"They have a desperate need of doctors. Hardly any doctors at all."

"And when will this be?"

"I don't quite know. I hoped to get my full surgical qualification first, but it seems there may not be time."

"I'm sorry." Verity looked at her half-eaten sandwich and realised that she didn't feel so hungry after all. Just having begun to get to know Rex made it seem somehow so much worse that he should be going away.

"We'll keep in touch, though," he reassured her as if reading her thoughts.

"I hope so."

"About that night out . . ." Rex reached inside his pocket and produced a diary. "Could you do Thursday? A friend of mine is having a party. He's being sent to France."

It was her first date and she tried hard to look nice for it. But she was not very fashion-conscious and she had never worn make-up. Few nice girls did. But she had lovely light brown hair which she released from its neat day-time bun for the night, so that it hung shoulder-length, showing a slight wave on top. The blue dress with magyar-type sleeves and a wide lace collar had been worn at several parties at the nurses' home. It was her best dress. Her only one.

Looking at herself critically in the mirror she decided that she looked rather young and, perhaps, a bit frumpish for her first date with a man. She frowned angrily at herself for the thought. She had always scorned feminine wiles, and so Rex must take her as he found her. In any event, he was soon going away and nothing could possibly come of this.

Looking out of the window she saw it was raining, and putting on a raincoat over her dress, she also took an umbrella.

Rex was waiting for her in the hall of the residence, pacing up and down smoking a cigarette, a raincoat over his arm.

"I'm afraid it's raining," he said. "Glad you came all prepared."

"I'm afraid I've nothing much to wear," Verity pointed to the dress under her open raincoat. "I'm not much of a fashion plate."

"You look fine." Rex studied her approvingly. "I thought we'd eat first."

"I can't be too late." Verity glanced towards the porter who was reading, or pretending to read the evening paper full of gloomy war news. "This is like a girls' school, you know."

"Midnight. I promise. No later."

"I shall be back round midnight," Verity told the porter.

65

"No later please, Miss. Sister Duckett doesn't like her young ladies to be out late."

"You see, I told you," Verity murmured with a smile as Rex took her by the elbow and steered her through the front door.

"We can walk. The party's in Bloomsbury. There's a little place near by that still does passable Italian food. You don't mind walking, do you?" Verity shook her head. "Not too tired?"

She shook her head again, gratified by his attention and concern. That afternoon two men, both young, had died on the table. There was no point in brooding; but loss of life was always tragic, and young life especially so.

There were a lot of men better looking than Rex, she was sure, but few she thought with a nicer nature. Thinking back to her stepfather and his treatment of her mother she decided that that was what counted, not looks. She could never imagine Rex beating a woman, forcing her to make love to him, or trying to hurt her in any way. She looked sideways at his robust yet homely features and felt an unexpected surge of emotion.

She determined on her first date to enjoy herself, have fun. Life, after all, was short.

The room was already crowded when they got to the party in Doughty Street close to the Gray's Inn Road. It was only nine o'clock but some people looked as though they had been there for hours. Many were clearly drunk. Several couples were already dancing frenetically to the reedy strains of a gramophone in the corner.

A lanky man, also bespectacled, red face running with sweat, a glass in his hand, came forward to greet Rex warmly.

"This is Tim," Rex shouted above the noise. "Tim, Miss Barnes. Verity. She's a nursing sister at my hospital."

"How do you do?" Tim enthusiastically pumped her hand as a woman with a glass in her hand and feathers in her hair wove past, pausing to lightly caress Rex's cheek. "Darling," she murmured, and passed on again.

"Come and have a drink," Tim commanded, ignoring the woman. "*Lots* of drink, for tomorrow we die."

"Oh, *don't* say that." Suddenly, vividly Verity recalled the two young men who had been wheeled out to the morgue from the hospital theatre a few hours before.

Tim, momentarily seeming to sober up, solemnly shook his head. "I don't expect to come back. No honest I don't. It's carnage out there. I've even sold my horse."

"Tim's parents live in the country," Rex volunteered.

"What will you drink, Verity?" Tim enquired, looking at her drunkenly. "Gin?"

"Er . . ." Apart from the rare glass of wine Verity didn't drink, had never drunk, but a glass was thrust into her hand and Tim went over to welcome some new arrivals who trooped through the door looking and sounding as though they'd already spent the evening partying.

"Mad," Rex smiled at her. "Not quite like parties at the nurses' home, is it?"

"No it isn't," Verity said severely, thinking of those decorous evenings when only the two-step or an occasional foxtrot was danced, lemonade was served and everything came to an end at ten.

Rex slipped an arm round her waist and placed his cheek gently against hers. Although she could scarcely hear the music they somehow managed to gyrate around the room, each still clutching a glass in one hand.

"Did you know that girl?" Verity asked as the music stopped.

"What girl?" Rex looked surprised.

"She called you 'darling'."

"Never seen her in my life before."

"Then why did she call you 'darling'?"

Rex laughed, a little uncomfortably it seemed to Verity.

"There are people like that. I don't think you've come across them before."

"Are they what you call 'a fast set'?" Verity asked mischievously.

Rex laughed.

"Tim was a stockbroker before the war. He and I were at school together."

"Is he married?"

"Divorced."

"Already?"

"Don't sound so shocked."

"I'm not, honestly." She realised that whatever her feelings, she should try and conceal them or else she would spoil Rex's evening, and probably change his opinion of her.

Rex finished the beer in his glass and put it down on a table full of empties. Verity put hers beside his though she had not tasted a drop. They'd had a glass of wine with their dinner and she felt she didn't want any more to drink. Looking round the room she thought there were going to be a lot of heavy heads the following morning.

The music started again and suddenly a tall man loomed up in front of her and put both arms round her waist.

"Do you mind?" he said to Rex, who smiled and moved away.

The man immediately put his cheek against Verity's and pressed his body close to hers. He was sweating profusely and stank of beer, some of which had split on his shirt front. She thought he looked and smelt disgusting, and tried unsuccessfully to disengage herself.

"What's your name?"

"Verity."

"You look very disapproving."

She didn't reply. He stuck his crotch up against her and his body gyrated suggestively. A surge of anger and revulsion passed through her.

"You look very chaste. I imagine you're a virgin." Her partner leered at her.

"I imagine you're *drunk*," she retorted, now frantically trying to pull herself away, but she was pinioned by his arms.

"Oh, don't be nasty. My name's Kit. I'm going to France next week with Tim."

Kit made a clumsy attempt to kiss her, but as she turned away the kiss landed wetly on the side of her neck.

"Come on," he said, roughly trying to turn her head round.

She felt as if her neck would break as she resisted, but he persisted, now using brute force. She could feel his saliva trickling down her neck, under her collar, down her back. Whether he was going to France or not she decided she didn't care. With a monumental effort she raised a knee and jabbed him hard in the groin. He released her immediately and doubled up with pain.

Verity saw his eyes redden with rage like a maddened bull and looking away for help, at least a way of escape, she noticed Rex dancing very close to the woman who had called him "darling", completely oblivious of what was happening to her.

Free from her tormentor, or would-be seducer, Verity rushed to the door and opened it without anyone seeing her. Her coat was among a pile on the hall table and she frantically sorted through it. Finding it she struggled into it when the door opened and Rex stumbled out and looked at her aghast.

"Verity, what are you doing?"

"I don't like it here," she cried hysterically. "I'm going home."

"But . . ."

"I'm sorry, and I don't want to spoil your fun, but I don't like it here and I don't like the people. It's not my sort of place."

"I'll come with you," Rex said as if he'd instantly sobered up.

"No, honestly. I'll be all right."

"Don't be absurd. I can't let you walk through the streets at this hour. Anyway I'm not enjoying it much either. It's like a sardine tin inside there."

"Well, if you're sure." A walk alone in the dark didn't exactly appeal to her.

"Sure," Rex said, going through a pile to find his coat. "Quite, quite sure."

It was blissful to be outside, to relish the cold night air. For a while they walked purposefully, side by side, not talking.

"I'm terribly sorry," Rex said at last. "I didn't know it would be like that."

"There are too many people and they were all horribly drunk. Even the women were drunk. I didn't like it and I think it's disgusting." Verity felt she didn't care what Rex thought. This had to be said.

To her surprise he stopped and nodded vigorously.

"You're right. It *is* disgusting. People have been made mad by the war. I shouldn't have taken you and I'm sorry."

"I enjoyed the meal." Verity suddenly felt sorry for Rex. Their first date had been a fiasco. She found she was trembling as much with humiliation as rage and delayed fatigue. It was as if she'd been physically and emotionally violated, which in a way she had.

Rex took her hand and they strolled through the empty city streets towards Southampton Row. She found the touch of his hand surprisingly comforting, that firm, capable surgeon's hand. She could visualise it skilfully using the instruments on the operating table.

They crossed Southampton Row and walked towards Covent Garden. One or two cafés were still open and Rex said:

"Look. It's not yet midnight. How about a coffee?"

"That *would* be nice." Verity gave him a grateful smile and for the first time since they'd left the party found herself beginning to relax.

The café was quiet. The owner had been about to close but brought them coffees, planting the bill firmly on the table beside Rex.

"Mustn't stay long," Rex said with a smile. He put his hand on Verity's. "I *am* sorry about tonight."

"I tell you it's perfectly *all right*," she insisted, attempting to smile. "I don't drink or go to parties, that sort of thing. I'm not used to it. I suppose I'm naïve. I don't like men I don't

know trying to kiss me. It's horrible." She wiped her mouth as
if from the memory.

"I know. It *is* horrible. We should have gone to the cinema.
They say *Birth of a Nation* is very good. Look would you like
to see it?"

"Well . . ."

"Tomorrow?" He looked at her eagerly.

"I can't get tomorrow off. In fact I don't know when I can
get a night off again."

"Is that the brush-off?"

"No, it's true. Having been away I must make up the time.
They've been very good to me."

Rex leaned towards her. "You *are* a very good person,
Verity. And I like you a lot. Compared to the crowd we've left
behind you're the genuine thing."

Abashed, Verity examined her nails. Was he really trying to
tell her she was a prude? A bit dull?

She studied his face carefully. "You know you said you
didn't know that woman who called you 'darling'?"

"I didn't."

"But you were dancing with her, very close I thought."

"Well," Rex looked at his coffee cup. "That is a party, I'm
afraid. Parties are like that. It didn't mean a thing."

Verity's expression was sad.

"I'm not . . . very worldly, you know. I suppose you must
think me very unsophisticated."

Rex responded with enthusiasm. "I do and I like it. There
are very few unsophisticated women around." He reached for
her hand again and gently squeezed it.

Addie rang the bell and the children obediently abandoned
whatever game they had been playing in the playground and
formed themselves into a neat line. She looked down at them
affectionately, at their eager, hopeful, trusting little faces
raised towards her. Both girls and boys wore brown smocks
over their day clothes and some were cleaner and less
crumpled than others.

71

They were all seven years old and Addie was their pupil teacher at a village school seven miles from Sherborne. Since Mother had been ill she cycled to school and back along the winding lanes in the rain and snow of winter, and through the balmy days of spring and summer.

She thought in many ways it was a perfect life, and yet . . .

The children marched past her in an orderly line into the schoolroom where the headmistress, Mrs Whitchurch, who was the only other teacher in the school, would take over for the afternoon while Addie got on with her own studies for her teacher's training diploma.

Addie followed the line into the schoolroom and had a word with Mrs Whitchurch before collecting her books, taking her bicycle out of the shed in the playground and, mounting it, set off on the road towards home.

It was a clear warm day in what had so far been an indifferent summer.

The combatant powers were still largely in stalemate with losses and gains on the part of one being offset by similar losses and gains on the part of another. Land only a few feet wide was being frantically fought over: inches, a few feet lost or won in a day, won, lost again the day after. The summer weather on the Continent had been atrocious and the troops were stuck in the mud of Ypres, a place that was to become synonymous with the whole misery of war. In parts of France the French troops had mutinied as a protest against the wretched conditions in which they fought.

At home the first real food shortages had begun to hit, but the Government had introduced only a voluntary scheme of rationing. Special food economy campaigns were held and even Government Control tea which looked, and tasted, like sawdust was hard to get. Addie, however, had a rather sanguine and optimistic nature. She felt, as the middle sister, she had no other option. She had to be adaptable.

Adelaide Barnes always felt a little eclipsed by her two sisters, Verity on the one side, Peg on the other. Verity was strong, clever, even formidable. Addie had never ceased to miss Verity, and yet partly to resent her because she had grown more distant with the years as the result of being brought up away from home and her real family. Verity was the eldest sister, one looked up to and both feared and admired.

Peg, on the other hand, was everyone's darling. Addie and Verity had Mother's large, wistful brown eyes and softly waving brown hair, but Peg was fair with China-blue eyes like their father and, like handsome Billy who in his youth had stolen the hearts of all the girls, Peg was a heart-breaker too: winsome, soft and loving, everyone's darling. This, to her shame, sometimes brought out the envious side of Addie – a side she tried hard to control – stuck as she was somewhere in the middle between the two.

She was shorter than Verity, not so striking and without Verity's direct, sometimes challenging gaze. She was not as cuddly or so appealing as Peg, but she had a peculiar innate charm of her own of which she was largely unaware, an almost feline grace and gentleness that endeared her to her pupils. She was soft and feminine, ready and anxious to please.

Addie, though not tall, was slim, with a lithe figure and the build and deportment of a ballet dancer, and had she not to some extent been eclipsed by these two very different sisters she could have developed a more decisive, incisive personality of her own.

Addie was a bit like a river into which all the tributary streams with their own peculiar idiosyncrasies trickled. She was solid and steady. People depended on her and to each she gave full measure to the extent that she was easily exhausted.

Addie had not Verity's interesting air of melancholy or Peg's exuberance. She was, perhaps, better balanced and receptive than the other two. She was a very happy young woman despite the cares of home, the worry about Mother's health, which still gave concern since her miscarriage the year before and, above all, the war which dominated the lives of everyone.

It was a rare fine day in that bleak summer of 1917 when soldiers drowned in the mud of Flanders' fields. Addie hummed a tune as she cycled along the lane towards home. The trees lining each side of the road inclined gently towards one another overhead, so that they resembled the vault of a church. Raising her eyes she caught glimpses of the sky between the green foliage and she felt a curious sense of exhilaration. She also felt guilty to be happy because there was so much that was wrong in the world, so much that was bad and evil; but happy at this moment in time she was.

There was a bump and Addie, brought back to reality from her blissful reverie, looked down. She had ridden over a sharp stone and there was an ominous wobbling of the bike. With a sigh she dismounted, and inspecting the damage saw that one of the tyres was completely flat. It was useless to continue to ride so, with another sigh, she started to wheel her bike towards home, another two or three miles to go on what was proving a very hot day.

Fearing that Mother would be worried Addie walked as fast as she could, but soon she began to tire. It was very hot and her long skirt and thin-soled shoes seemed to hamper her progress. Despite the heat she took off her hat and rested it on the pile of books fastened to the back of her bicycle. She felt hot and tired, suddenly irritated by this unexpected change in fortune and, hence, her mood.

Conscious of a rumbling noise behind her Addie glanced back and saw a large motor car driving slowly along the uneven road. She stood back to allow it to pass, but when the driver saw her he slowed down and finally stopped alongside her.

A cheerful freckled face looked out of the window.

"Need any help?"

Addie of course knew all about the dangers of talking to strange men. Hadn't Mother told them repeatedly as children so many times? But she soon saw that he wasn't a strange man. She had the sun in front of her but, peering closer, she recognised Lord Ryland's son Lydney, someone she had seen often, though usually from the respectable distance judged fitting for employer and employee: those who ruled and those who served.

"Isn't it one of Jack Hallam's pretty daughters?" he enquired gallantly.

Addie blushed.

"Adelaide, Mr Ryland. They call me Addie."

"And what is the matter, Addie?" Lydney Ryland jumped out and inspected the damaged wheel. "Oh dear," he grimaced. "This is a job for Frank. I think you'll need a new tyre." Frank Carpenter was the man to whom everyone on the estate turned when something went wrong. "Look, hop in and I'll give you a lift."

"But the bicycle?"

"We'll tuck it in the side of the bank and send Frank with his cart back to fetch it."

"Oh, but I couldn't."

"I'll ask him then," Lydney smiled. "I'll run you back home. How's your mother? I heard she wasn't well."

"That was last year. She's fully recovered, thank you Mr Ryland."

"You're the middle one. The schoolteacher."

"Yes, I am." She settled back admiring to herself the sensuous softness of the leather upholstery, the gleaming chrome of the finish of the interior of the car. She had never been inside one before.

"And how is your sister the nurse?"

"Verity. Busy. She got engaged in January."

"Really, who to?"

"A doctor called Rex. He's with the RAMC in the Balkans."

"Do you like him?"

"Oh, very much." Addie smiled at the memory of the time when they had first heard the news about Verity's whirlwind romance, and how much they'd all liked Rex when she'd introduced him to the family. Somehow, because Verity was so serious, they had never associated her with an interest in men, but had thought her married to her career and, perhaps, a confirmed spinster.

"And how are *you*, Mr Ryland?" Lydney had been invalided home after a gas attack at the battle of Arras.

"I am much better. But until my lungs are clear they won't let me return to the front. I'm still very short of breath." Lydney coughed obligingly as if to prove his unfitness for action. "And please call me Lydney; or even better, most of my friends call me Lydd."

His smile was infectious. He was not much older than she was and she had always been attracted, though at a distance, by his boyish charm. There had been the annual cricket match between staff and Lord Ryland's family and guests; the staff Christmas party at which the family distributed largesse, but stayed no longer than half an hour; the summer opening of the house and grounds for a good cause. Oh, those halcyon days that seemed now so long ago! It was incredible to think that Lord Ryland's handsome heir had been in battle, seen unspeakable horrors in which men had died. She looked at him with respect.

"Was it awful?" she whispered.

"What?" Lydd, who had been making the cycle safe out of sight of the road, climbed into his seat and started the car.

"The war."

"It is absolutely awful," he nodded gravely. "You cannot imagine what it is like: the cold, the mud, the lack of proper provisions, the cries of wounded men. The sight of the dead and dying." Addie saw how his knuckles, clenching the wheel, whitened as he spoke. He grimaced as if in pain at the memory. "But we are all in this together, and I want to be back with my battalion as soon as I can."

"It's very hard for me to imagine." Addie sat hugging her books on her knee. "I was thinking today how lovely it was and how lucky I was and now, you know, I feel selfish because of all the brave men like you out there."

"There is no need to feel selfish," Lydd said gently. "What

we are doing is so that people like you – and that England – may survive, proud and free."

Lydney started the car and drove slowly along the road trying to avoid the pitfalls that had destroyed Addie's bicycle tyre.

"So where are you teaching, Addie?"

"At the school in Minster Parva. I'm doing my teacher training there to help Mother. She won't admit it, but she is still weak."

"And your father?"

"He is in the north somewhere. He hasn't yet gone abroad and doesn't know if he will." Addie pursed her lips in silent disapproval. They were all secretly a bit ashamed of their stepfather who had not wanted to enlist and now had escaped being sent abroad, yet still seldom found the time to visit the family or Mother. According to him his duties, though unspecified, were essential.

"Lucky man," Lydd said grimly.

"Oh I think he wants to be in the thick of it," Addie lied loyally. "But his regiment is to do with training and supply."

"Of course someone has to do it and Jack's quite old."

"Not yet forty."

"Really?" Lydd looked surprised. "Younger than your mother?"

"A little." Addie bridled defensively.

"He's not your real father, is he?"

"No. My father died."

"He's a nice chap. I like Jack." But now they had come to the end of the lane and in sight of the gates of Ryland Castle. Lydney drove through and stopped outside the door of the lodge which was their home.

"I'll go and see Frank and ask him to fetch your bicycle."

"It's awfully *kind* of you Mr Ryland . . . Lydd." Addie jumped out and smiled gratefully up at him.

"See you again, Addie, soon I hope."

He waved at her and Addie turned to watch as he continued his journey up the drive.

There had seemed something really special, quite thrilling about that short journey and the proximity of the dashing, glamorous Lydd.

If only he wasn't Lord Ryland's son, she thought as she walked slowly into the house, and thus quite, quite out of reach.

Six

A ddie took her books out of her locker, slipped on her raincoat and went out into the school yard to fetch her bicycle. It was a cold summer's day with the threat of rain, and she looked nervously up at the clouds scudding across the sky as she wheeled her bicycle to the entrance of the school and prepared to mount it.

There was the toot-toot of a horn and looking across the road she saw Lydney Ryland waving to her, a broad smile on his handsome face.

"Can I give you a lift, Miss?"

As she wheeled the bicycle across the road, he opened the door and got out, stood looking down at her, still smiling. "Can't you leave the bike here?"

"I shall have nothing to come to school on tomorrow."

"That's all right. I'll bring you."

Nonplussed, Addie stared at her bicycle and then at Lydd. "I think I ought to go home on the bicycle in the normal way."

"But why?"

"I just think I'd better."

"Is there something wrong, Addie?"

She shook her head vigorously. "Oh no, not at all. It's just that I don't know what Mum will say."

"But why should your mother say anything? You're quite grown up."

Addie shook her head again and shyly studied her feet. She knew Lydney would think her childish, and perhaps despise her, which was the very last thing she wanted.

"I'll drop you off before we get home if you like."

"Mother will wonder where my bicycle is."

Addie began to blush until it totally suffused her cheeks.

"Let's go for a spin then," Lydd suggested, "and you can come back and collect your bicycle. Is *that* all right?"

Lydd gently took the bicycle from her and wheeled it back inside the school yard. She followed him, showed him where to put it and he pushed it into the shed and closed the door.

"Where would you like to go?" he asked as he opened the car door for her.

"Anywhere you like."

Addie settled against the rich-smelling upholstery, suddenly feeling happy and strangely carefree.

Lydd reversed the big car and drove slowly along the lane away from the school towards Sturminster Newton, in the opposite direction to home. When they came to the main road he put his foot down on the accelerator and the car leapt forward.

"I love this car," he cried above the noise of the engine.

"I can see," Addie smiled.

"You know you look really very pretty when you smile." He glanced at her. "You should do it more often."

"Are we going anywhere particular?" Addie ignored his remark. "I shouldn't be too late home or Mum will worry."

"We won't be late. I thought we'd drive up Bulbarrow and walk through the woods above Milton Abbas."

Addie nodded contentedly: "That will be nice."

Past Sturminster Newton bridge and going up the rise towards Fiddleford, Lydney slowed the car down. "Why are you so worried about what your mother thinks?"

"Because I am. That's the way we were brought up."

"To be afraid of your mother?"

"I'm not *afraid*," Addie said indignantly. "I just don't want to worry her."

"You're very nice, Addie," Lydd said gently. "Very good."

He turned the car off the main road and drove through the village of Okeford Fitzpaine, then up the winding slope of Bulbarrow with its dominating view of the Dorset countryside. The sun peered through the clouds and the whole valley was bathed in a golden light.

Lydney stopped the car at the top and looked at the scene before them.

"I always feel terribly moved by this view. I would remind myself of it when I was stuck in some goddamned trench and think of the bluebells in the wood."

"It must be terrible." Addie's eyes brimmed with sympathy. "I can't begin to imagine how bad it must be." She looked up at his grave face and realised that the mood between them had somehow changed, grown closer yet also more sombre. "No wonder people don't want to go back."

"You've no idea what fools our leaders are," Lydney said bitterly. "They hurl men into the slaughter without a thought. For a few feet of land we sacrifice thousands of lives. And yet, you know, if I had the chance to stay here I would refuse it. There is something very ennobling about the war that I can't quite explain. Apart from feeling a coward if I didn't go back I enjoy the camaraderie of the men. They are a bunch of such good blokes. The nation really should be proud of them. But when the war is over a lot of questions will be asked. Men, and the bereaved, will demand answers."

He turned to her and his arm slid along the back of her seat.

"I like you a lot, Addie. I keep on thinking about you. When I come back I want to see you again."

Addie stared thoughtfully at the floor of the car. She felt his finger flutter lightly across her cheek.

"What is it?" he asked as she flinched.

"You know what it is," she raised her head and her eyes met his. "You are the son of Lord Ryland and my stepfather is the gardener."

"Such attitudes are old fashioned. The war has done away with them all. I have seen on the battlefield the equality of all men. When it comes to bravery there is no one better in the world than the British foot soldier. And women now are participating in the war. They're taking the place of the men at home and working in munition factories. Whether I am the

81

son of Lord Ryland or Frank the odd job man isn't important, nor is it who or what you are. The world is changing out of all recognition." His face was so near hers that she could see the faint blond stubble on his chin. His blue eyes looked intently at her. A ray of sun caught his ash-blond hair and turned it to gold.

Addie thought he was wonderful and as his face came even nearer to hers his features blurred and all she saw was his lips.

His kiss was very firm, yet warm and loving, not frightening as she thought such a thing might be. She had never been kissed by anyone before. She moulded herself into his arms and returned his embrace, so that their kiss lasted for some seconds.

They parted with reluctance. Lydd brushed the hair from his eyes and smiled tenderly at her. Then he straightened himself, briskly reversed the car out of the lay-by where they were parked and drove towards the extensive woodland near by, which was bisected by a long narrow, winding road covered with greenery which formed a thick roof over their heads.

Lydd drove off the road, down a track through the woods and out on to a field which formed a platform overlooking a deep valley filled, now that the rain had stopped, with the late afternoon sun.

They sat for a moment looking at the scene then Lydd got out, walked round the car and opened the door for Addie.

"Let's go for a walk."

Addie got out and he took her hand. Not knowing what to expect she felt apprehensive, yet excited, very grown up. It was as though her girlhood had ended and she found herself precipitated on to the verge of womanhood.

They walked for some time in silence, but it was a comfortable, companionable silence, not one born of unease or not knowing what to say.

"It isn't as though we haven't known each other a long time," Lydd turned to her as if trying to explain himself. "I mean I'm not a stranger."

Addie agreed. "No, but I don't know you, either. Your mother and father aren't strangers, but I wouldn't say I *knew* them. For instance what would they say if . . ." she paused, suddenly feeling awkward and embarrassed, "if they could see us now?" she finished lamely.

"I don't know," Lydd shook his head. "My parents belong to a generation that has grown apart from mine. I think before the war perhaps I was like them. Now if I see a pretty girl whom I like and she likes me, it doesn't matter who she is." He looked at her intently. "Do you know what I mean?"

"I think I do."

"You said your sister's fiancé was a doctor. But she is a gardener's daughter too."

"No," Addie shook her head. "Verity had a different upbringing from us. She was adopted by an aunt who had married well. Uncle Stanley is an engineer, an entomologist. Verity went to a private school."

"So this makes a difference that you think is important?"

"Yes," Addie nodded her head firmly. "It is a matter of class and Verity is a better class than we are. There is no doubt about it."

"You're a very silly girl." Lydd shook her hand and, sitting on a grassy bank, pulled her down beside him. "After the war everything will change. There will be no class barriers. Everyone will be equal." He released her, joined his hands and gazed at the sky. "I think I would like to go into politics to help bring this change about, as a Liberal of course, though the Labour Party is making great strides and one day there will be even more members as MPs. I'm sure of that. Maybe I'll be one of them, though what my father will say I can't think."

Lydd smiled at the thought and leapt up, and they continued their walk to the end of the field where it joined the woods again and then turned back. "I must get you home," he said solemnly, "or your mother will be very cross."

Cathy looked angrily across at Addie as she came through the door unpinning her hat.

"And what time do you call this?" she asked pointing meaningfully to the clock.

"Sorry, Mum." Addie glanced at the faces of the three children who sat gawping at her.

"You better have your tea, Addie." Mother's voice was still tense, "and then I want a talk with you."

Peg made a face as her elder sister sat down beside her, and Stella gave a nervous chuckle. Ed seemed less interested in the proceedings than his food and got on with his tea of cold ham and baked potatoes.

Addie, too excited by the events of the afternoon, found she had little appetite but, with Mother's eyes grimly upon her, she went through the motions. She was usually starving when she came home from school, but not today. Mother, seemingly preoccupied, had very little to say and left it to Peg and Stella who were never short of words. After tea they scrambled off their chairs and the girls began clearing away.

Mother told Ed to begin his homework and then beckoned to Addie to accompany her to the sitting-room next door. She closed the door and turned to her daughter who stood facing her nervously.

Was it possible that Mother could know about Lydd?

"Mrs Whitchurch came to see me on her way home," Mother said. "She said your bicycle was left in the shed and she was worried about you. I told her you hadn't returned, but as soon as you did I would ask for an explanation and then send word to her. I can tell you I was worried sick until you came through the door. Where is your bicycle now?"

"Outside, Mum."

"So where did you go from the time you left the school until the time you picked it up again?"

"I went for a walk." Addie hung her head, suddenly realising how worried her mother must have been. How untypical this behaviour was of her.

"By yourself?" Cathy looked incredulous.

"No. Lydney Ryland was passing and offered to drive me home."

"*Again?*" Cathy knew all about the puncture the previous week.

"Yes. I said I needed my bicycle to get to work tomorrow so he suggested we had a drive."

"I see." Mother's eyes narrowed suspiciously. "Is that all?"

"Yes, Mum." Addie felt herself blush again at the memory of that long, passionate kiss. She knew her features must give her away and blushed even harder.

"Where did you think you're going to get with Mr Lydney?"

"I don't think at all, Mum. He's a nice young man and we talked about the war and about class—"

"*Class!*" Cathy exclaimed. "What do you mean about class?"

"About the difference between the classes, us and his. He doesn't believe in them."

"Oh, doesn't he indeed?" Cathy snorted. "Well, I'm sure his father does."

"That's what I told him." Addie's eyes were downcast.

"Did he make a pass at you?"

"In a way," Addie smiled shyly.

"But that was all?" Suddenly Cathy looked apprehensive.

"Oh yes. That was all."

"You expect me to believe it? A young man home from the war, eager for a bit of fun with a woman of a lower class?"

"Mum that is a *horrible* thing to say," Addie protested. "Lydd is *not* like that. He is an absolute gentleman."

Cathy's expression softened and, going across to her daughter she took her by the hand and drew her gently down on to the sofa.

"I'm sorry, Addie, but you do know, don't you, that a young man can lead a girl on? I'm sure, however innocent you are in the ways of the world – and I believe you still to be – you know that? He can say things he doesn't mean and that will lead you to do things you shouldn't do . . ."

Addie's hand tightened in her mother's grasp. "Oh, Mum, you don't *think*—?"

85

"No, I don't," her mother reassuringly squeezed her hand. "I know you and I trust you; but this is the second time you have seen Mr Lydney in a week. It can't be coincidence that he was passing the school today?"

"I don't know." Addie looked perplexed. "I really don't know." She put her face between her hands. "Oh, Mum, I feel so confused. He is such a nice man and, yes, he said he did like me, because I also wondered what his parents would say. He said that things would be very different after the war and all class structures would be abolished. He said he'd like to be a Member of Parliament and fight for equality. I think he is very fine."

"And did he ask to see you again?"

Addie nodded. "Yes, tomorrow. He said he would pick me up again and that I should tell you – so he's not secretive, Mum – and that he would tie the bicycle to the back of his car."

"Then my advice to you, Addie, is to decline his offer. Tell him you cannot accept it and come back home at the proper time on your bicycle. I must remind you, Addie, that you are still not yet of age and until you are I expect you to do as I say."

As Addie got up Cathy raised her eyes. "Will you do that, Addie? Do that for your own sake as well as mine? If Lord Ryland had any idea that his son was interested in the gardener's daughter, he might tell me to pack my bags and leave. His lordship has been very good at letting us stay on here rent free while Jack was away. All that might change if he had any inkling of what was going on. Mr Lydney may not believe in class, but his father most certainly does."

Addie looked at her mother and impulsively went over to her and kissed her. For a moment she took her hand and held it tight. But she said nothing more and, letting go of Cathy's hand, she turned and left the room.

Cathy sat back and looked reflectively for a few moments after her daughter. She felt very weary. The war and her

abortion had taken their toll on her. It had taken her a long
time to recover. She had the sole responsibility for the children
and little money to live on. Sometimes she felt much older
than her years, and today was such a day. She was proud of
the success Verity had made of her career and thankful she
was engaged to a nice, good man. But she had often felt that
Verity was no longer her daughter. Much as she loved her she
had been brought up by someone else and, consequently,
Cathy was closer to the other four. Verity she had seen a few
token times a year, the others she saw every day.

Addie was especially precious to her. She was proud of her
too. She was a good scholar, an example to the younger ones,
a credit to her mother. She had never put a foot wrong in her
life, always been hard working and obedient without being
shamelessly docile. Got on well with Jack. She was a resourceful girl, full of character. Now she was all set on a worth-
while career as a schoolteacher.

How terrible it would be if Addie fell for the wrong man, as
Lydney Ryland undoubtedly was, and had her heart broken
by him.

Addie heard the car coming after her as she pedalled home
from school on the last day of term. She heard the "toot-toot"
of the horn but she didn't stop, only pedalled faster. She was
almost in sight of home when she heard the car stop, the door
open and footsteps running after her. She put a foot on the
ground to steady herself and stopped just as Lydd caught up
with her.

"Addie—"

"I can't see you!" she cried. "I can't see you *ever* again."

"But why?"

"My mother says. And she is right. Whatever you think
about class and how things should be that is not the way they
are now."

"It's *ridiculous*, Addie . . ."

"I know, I *know*. But she says if your father got to know
about us seeing each other he might throw her out. Now she

87

pays no rent and he is very good to us. We get produce from the farm, butter and milk, occasionally meat."

"My father would never throw out a woman with four dependent children. He is not that sort of man."

She rounded on him. "*How* do you know, Lydd? *How* do you know? You said that his ideas and yours were not the same. You respect him for it, and I respect my mother. I cannot risk the future of my family just to have a few hours with you . . . much as I enjoyed them." She lowered her eyes, feeling suddenly self-conscious.

"I think it's very unfair of you. Look I shall tell my father . . ."

Addie stared at him aghast.

"Oh no. Please, please not. Besides, there is nothing to tell *him*."

Lydd seized her by the shoulders and gently shook her.

"Look, I think about you all the time, Addie. Can't you realise that I'm serious?"

"But you hardly *know* me."

"I know enough. You don't have to know a person well to fall in love, and I think I am in love. I have seen you often about the place, always been attracted to you. I tell you I am quite serious about you . . ."

"Oh no, no!" Addie put her head into her hands. "Please no."

She drew away, resumed her seat on the bicycle again and furiously pedalled off, hot tears stinging her eyes.

Lydd in love with her? Surely it was impossible?

Term had come to an end and Addie busied herself with her tasks in the house. Now she was able to devote more time to helping her mother with the household chores, with looking after the children. Every day was devoted to some fresh idea for an outing, to some amusement or educational task to keep them occupied.

But everything she did, however well done, was mechanical. She could only think of the young man up at the house and what he had told her. It was surely quite impossible that he could mean what he said, and yet, why not? She felt the same about him but she had imagined it was one-sided, a crush on the part of an immature young woman for a worldly exciting man, a soldier bloodied in war.

Besides, what could come of love for Lydd? There couldn't possibly be a happy ending. But every day she hoped that somehow, as she went about her tasks on and around the estate, or took the children for their walks or boating on the lake, she might catch sight of him.

But she never did. And then she learned that he had gone up to London, and she imagined he would forget all about her there with the sophisticated young women he would be sure to meet, the dances he would go to and the good times he would undoubtedly have.

August was a dismal month, the days seemed to creep by. There was no improvement in the weather which was the same across the Channel, and its effect on the progress of the war was disastrous. There were heavy losses and the prevailing mood was one of gloom.

Between rainstorms Addie did her best to amuse the children, but she was oppressed too by the weather, the news from the front and the fact that Lydd had taken her at her word and made no contact with her.

Every day she hoped, and then she despised herself for being so silly. She knew that her mother kept a watchful yet sympathetic eye on her, but nothing more was said.

Then she heard that the family had gone to Scotland for the shooting. Lord and Lady Ryland had been joined by Lydd and his brother Hubert and sister Violet.

In a way it helped to ease her pain. If he was not here there was no point in hoping to see him.

September came, the weather went from bad to worse and there was no improvement in the news from the front as the opposing armies fought with great loss of life over the same small strips of ground in and around the decimated town of Ypres, over which two battles had already been fought.

It had needed all of Addie's ingenuity and skill to keep the young people occupied during the long school holiday and now she looked eagerly to the resumption of term both for herself and her siblings. She would go back to Bristol to resume her course of studies and with so much to do all day there would be less time to think about Lydd and what might have been.

Addie was at a table in the sitting-room helping the children with their drawing when her mother called her from the kitchen.

"Mrs Capstick is right out of baking soda. She sent down to see if I had any, but I couldn't find it. Now I have." Her mother got up from the kneeling position on the floor where she had been rummaging through the cupboard and held up a jar. "Run up, like a love, and take it to her."

"Yes, Mum." Addie was glad of a respite, even on a wet afternoon.

"You'll be pleased when term starts," her mother said, a sympathetic gleam in her eye. "And Addie . . ."

"Yes, Mum?"

"I shall miss you. You have been such a comfort to me, and a help with the children."

"I'll come home every weekend, Mum."

Cathy put her hand on her daughter's arm.

"Thank you for being so good, you know what I mean? I do understand, believe me I do, but I think you've done the right thing – you know, about Lydney. He was not the right man for you. One day you will meet one who will be."

"Yes, Mum."

And better suited to me, Addie thought bitterly. He will be a farmer or a servant at the castle and there will be no argument about class *then*! She took the jar and went into the hallway where she put on a waterproof and her hat, called into the sitting-room to tell the children she wouldn't be long. She went out of the back door and, feeling more cheerful because it was nice just to get away, took the path that led from the lodge to the castle perched on top of the hill.

Despite the rain Addie took her time, relishing the freedom, the fresh air on her face, the luxuriant green of the fields and the surrounding woods enhanced by all the rain, even the familiar sight of the sheep peacefully grazing on the slopes of the meadow.

She went round to the back entrance of the castle and into the kitchen where she handed the baking soda to Mrs Capstick, the cook, who thanked her for it, said she didn't know how she had run out and promised to return the amount borrowed when she had replaced her own store.

"There's no hurry," Addie said with a smile. She lingered for a moment in the warm kitchen, familiar to her from so many visits over the years they'd been at Ryland. Various staff were busy at their tasks: cooking, clearing up or polishing, for even though the family were away there was the staff to feed and a hundred and one chores to perform like cleaning all the silver and polishing the glass.

"When does the family return?" Addie asked.

"Lord Ryland doesn't say. They are having a very good season. Oh, and Addie . . ." Mrs Capstick, busy over a pot on the stove, took an envelope from her apron pocket and handed it to her. "On your way out, be a dear and give this to Mr Matthews, who you will probably find in the hall or one of the rooms off. It's a letter came for him. I do hope it isn't the call-up." Cook examined the envelope with a worried expression then handed it to Addie who climbed the stairs from the kitchen that led into the body of the castle which she had hardly ever seen.

At Christmas there was a staff party, but the ballroom was approached from a side door, so she took her time inspecting the vast deserted hall with portraits of past Rylands on the wall; the men mostly in military uniform, the women looking elegant, aristocratic and arrogant too, poised, beautifully gowned – and all ancestors of Lydd.

There was no sign of Matthews, the under-butler, in the hall or in any of the rooms into which Addie nervously peeped. She was preparing to go down to the kitchen and return the letter to Mrs Capstick when she heard her name called.

"Addie!" She turned and there stood Lydd on the stairway dressed in jodhpurs and a hacking jacket as though he was about to go riding.

The two stood looking at each other as if it were a moment encapsulated in time. Addie's heart seemed to turn a somersault as Lydd sped down the rest of the stairs two at a time and, as he extended his arms, she spontaneously flew into them and was engulfed in his embrace.

"Addie, Addie . . ." he murmured, nuzzling his face in her hair. "You don't know how much I missed you."

"I missed you too," she said.

"But why are you here?"

"I came to find Mr Matthews. Cook had a letter for him. She thinks it may be the call-up." Lydd took the letter from her and glancing at it said, "I think she's right. I'll give it to him. He's in the gun room." He held up a hand in a warning gesture. "Don't you *dare* run away. Wait here for me."

He was soon back and taking her by the hand led her, unprotesting, up the stairs.

"Now that you're here I'm not going to let you go," he said. "We must go to my room where we can be undisturbed."

"But I can't—"

"And you can tell your mother you saw me. I've something to tell you." Lydd hurried her along the corridor that ran the entire length of the castle. He turned a door handle and drew her into a room, a large room, a man's room, a boy's room really with trophies on the walls and shelves full of books. In the middle was a single bed and from the window, towards which he took her, a magnificent view of the lake and, beyond that, the lodge.

"From here I can see where you live." He put his arms round her waist and pointed. "You don't know how many times I've stood here thinking about you and wondering what you were doing, if you were thinking of me."

"Lydd . . . what are you doing here? I was told you were still in Scotland."

He drew her over to the bed and sat down beside her, still

holding her hand. "Addie, I have been recalled to my regiment. I am fully fit now and I am needed at the front."

"Oh, Lydd." She put her head against her chest. "And the war going so badly."

"It will go better once I am out there," he said lightly, smiling reassuringly at her, but his expression was tense.

"When do you go?" she whispered.

"Tomorrow."

"Oh Lydd . . ."

He started to caress her and then put his mouth on hers and they kissed passionately. All the time she knew that she was yielding and when he began to unfasten the buttons on her dress she didn't resist him.

"Addie, I do love you. I want you so much and when I come back, when the war is over, I want you to be my wife. Do you understand?"

"Yes."

"And will you?"

"Yes."

Her dress fell to the floor, off came her under-garments, her stockings, until she was naked, stretched out on the bed, to be adored, worshipped by the man she knew would one day be her lawful husband. And that made it right. This act of homage, of mutual love that would unite them for ever.

PART II

The Sixth Child

Seven

Anglo Russian Hospital, Petrograd, 27 December 1916.

I had a very busy day today. I hear that one of the doctors is going through the lines so he is taking my letter through with him, so luckily I started to write to you. I should keep all these postcards, they will be nice to look back upon later on.

There were some letters and then:

21 January 1917.

A picture of St Petersburgh and this is a very nice wide street.

5 April 1917.

Russia is a wild place, a seething mass of revolt and discontent. Now that the Czar is deposed the troops at the front don't want to go on with the war. Kerensky does all he can to restore law and order but they say he won't last the year.

4 September 1917.

Can you understand the Russian language yet? I can't. (A picture of a building in a town whose name was written in Cyrillic and which Verity couldn't understand.)

There were lots more often with a scribble on the back:

Kischinew (no date).

One of the Russian towns that we passed through on our way here. Stayed about four hours.

Dear Rex was usually a man of few words. His letters, however, were longer but rather stilted as though he was dealing with an unfamiliar medium.

Perhaps this was understandable. They had not really known each other very well when that hurried proposal was made a few days before he was sent overseas. It had taken her by surprise, and sometimes she thought it had also surprised him. Maybe he had wanted an anchor, the thought that there was a sweetheart to come home to. And even now she wasn't sure whether she really loved him, or whether it had seemed at the time rather nice to be engaged when so many women were losing husbands and fiancés.

But gradually Rex and his memory had become more precious. She slept with his latest letter or card under her pillow for several days after it arrived, like some soppy sentimentalist she would normally despise. And still, despite the upheaval in Russia, the cards kept coming with a few words hurriedly scrawled on them whose very brevity seemed so like Rex.

And now this latest one:

27 November 1917.
    Sent you a telegram to say I am now nearly in the Arctic Circle. Leave tonight at 8 p.m. Fondest love, Rex.

The postmark was Sweden.

Verity sat back from the table on which the postcards from Rex lay scattered as, looking through them, she had tried to put them in order. She gazed out of the window at the patch of blue sky visible above the high buildings. Thank God he was safe.

The postcards had been coming all year as Rex moved round with his detachment from the RAMC, attending as best they could to the thousands of wounded among the Allied troops sent back from the front. He had been stationed for months at the hospital in Petrograd but with the collapse of the Russian army in the autumn and the defection of the common soldier to the Revolution it had become dangerous and they had been forced to move on.

Russia in revolution was now too unstable a place in which to linger.

It had been a very worrying year for those left behind in England. As casualties poured into the wards from the conflict in France and Flanders, Verity had little time to think of her fiancé far away in one of the most dangerous theatres of war: Russia and the whole of the Balkans were in flames.

Thank God he was safe, she thought again, picking up all the postcards and putting them in order, and thinking ahead to the time when they would be together united at last and able to go through them, Rex giving an explanation, commenting about his adventures. By that time they might be married and well . . . she knew they both wanted children. She could imagine Rex as a country doctor like his father, and she thought they would have rather a large family, and maybe a nice house like Aunt Maude and Uncle Stanley's, only perhaps in a village or a market town, hopefully in a county like Dorset.

Soon perhaps, now that Russia was out of the war and the Balkans on the verge of collapse, he would be home.

And then what? Possibly their marriage. She pictured the little church at Norton Magna bedecked with flowers. With any luck it would be a glorious summer's day – dared one hope for next summer? She allowed her fantasies to roam freely. Uncle Stanley would give her away and perhaps Lord Ryland would allow a reception to be held at the castle as he did for favoured employees. Or, perhaps, Uncle Stanley's house would be more appropriate with a marquee on the lawn? One didn't like to rely too much on the patronage of Lord Ryland. There was something demeaning about it.

Verity was already preparing her trousseau, embroidering sheets and tablecloths, soft silk or muslin nightdresses, light, rather daring confections for her honeymoon. When she had finished each item it was carefully wrapped in tissue paper and placed in a drawer.

She sighed and looked at her watch. She had to be on duty in an hour but the prospect of such happiness ahead seemed to lighten the load of the work, which she loved but at times found oppressive. After this war she would be ready to retire, to marry and start a family.

There was a tap on the door and she called "Come in" and turned round in her chair to see who it was. Although she had a few close friends Verity was not gregarious by nature and an unexpected caller was unusual.

She was startled to see Addie standing in the doorway and with an exclamation she leapt up and went across to welcome her. To her absolute astonishment Addie leaned against her chest and broke down in tears.

"Addie, what *is* it?" Verity asked in alarm. "Is something wrong at home?" Addie shook her head and after a minute seemed to recover.

"Sorry," she said, brushing the tears away from her eyes and attempting to smile. "That was silly of me."

However, noting her pale face and dishevelled appearance, Verity knew something must be gravely wrong and leading her to a chair made her sit down and began unfastening her coat.

"Where did you come from? Bristol?"

Addie nodded.

"You look as though you've been travelling for days."

"It seems like it. Because of all the troop movements the trains are slow and frequently delayed, or don't run at all."

"Where's your case?"

Addie gave a despairing gesture and started to cry again. Verity swiftly got to her knees on the floor beside her and took her hand.

"Darling, I can't help you if you can't tell me what the matter is. Are you in trouble?"

Addie nodded and vigorously blew her nose.

"Deep, deep trouble," she said and her eyes, awash now with tears, looked piteously at her sister. "I think I'm going to have a baby."

"You think . . ." As the enormity of what her sister had

100

said sank in, Verity got to her feet and stood looking down at the crumpled figure huddled in the chair.

"In fact I'm sure." Addie went on. "I've missed three periods. I feel sick in the morning . . . you know, just like Mum."

"I see." In a detached, professional way Verity seemed to absorb the news as if she was talking to a patient and consulted the fob watch on her apron once more.

"Look, I have to go on the ward soon. I want you to have a bath and then get into my bed. I'll try and get you a room here, say you aren't well. I'm sure they'll understand."

"Oh *don't* tell them . . ." Addie's expression was terrified.

"Of course I shan't! Don't be silly. I shan't say a word. I'll say you're staying with me for a few days. However if what you tell me is true I want you to be seen by one of our doctors."

"Oh but I can't . . ."

"Oh but you *must*. There is no question about it. I am not going to let happen to you what happened to Mum. Don't be alarmed, there are some nice women doctors and you will see one of them. You must be properly taken care of and then . . . we shall see."

Despite her shock at the news Verity smiled at her stricken sister tenderly and stroked her brow. "Now don't worry. You're with me and you're safe. Does Mum know?"

"Oh no!" Addie shook her head. "I daren't tell her. Oh Verity, what shall I do . . ." She began to weep again and Verity could see just how tired and distraught she was. She became practical once more.

"I'll make you a cup of tea and then you must go to bed and have a good sleep. Now promise you'll stay here and you won't run away?"

"Oh, I promise," Addie said with a pathetic smile. "Besides, I have nowhere to go."

Cathy sat for a long time staring out of the window, her chin cupped in her hand as though she was deep in thought.

Then she turned to Verity, standing behind her, anxiously waiting to see her mother's reaction to the shattering news she had brought her.

"Why couldn't she tell me herself? Am I so frightening?"

"It's not *that*, Mum." Verity drew up a chair and sat down next to her mother. "You can understand she's very nervous."

"But I had to know some time."

"You mustn't take it to heart, Mum. With all the implications, and the Ryland family, she had to tell someone else first. Who but a sister she was close to? I can see her point of view. Perhaps she thought I'd do it better, temper your justifiable anger and distress. Besides there would have been so much emotion involved, as there was for me. We could hardly talk about the situation without Addie dissolving into floods of tears."

Cathy removed her hand and sat upright in her chair, her chin squared in her customary expression of determination, a resolve to overcome all odds. It was this stance that had got her through life so far, and doubtless would continue to do so.

"Maybe you're right," she said at last. "What are we to do?"

"Addie need not come back here until after she had had the baby. Then, I suppose, adoption?"

"But you said Lydney Ryland had asked her to marry him. If that really is the case, at some point I suppose he must be told."

"Don't you believe that Lydney offered marriage?" Verity looked hesitantly at her mother.

"I don't know what to believe, and that is the truth. It is not like Addie to lie. On the other hand she might, so as to cover up what she has done, which is shocking. But then again, I can't see Lord Ryland's heir proposing to the gardener's daughter. He must have known what a scandal it would cause. Things like that don't happen outside story books."

"I believe Addie. I don't believe she'd tell a lie."

"Then why didn't *he* tell his father? He has been away three months and we have heard of no plans for a marriage."

Cathy's tone was heavy with sarcasm. "If he did propose, then in my opinion it was to encourage a young, impressionable woman like Addie to misbehave herself, with no intention of keeping his word."

Cathy ruefully shook her head. "Oh, dear, I blame myself. I forbade her to see Lydney and of course when people are told not to do a thing invariably they do it. I wouldn't have thought someone like Addie would disobey me and do anything so foolish. She knew the facts of life. I made sure you were both told before you went for your training."

Inwardly Verity smiled at the memory of Mother painstakingly attempting to tell her the facts of life when all the time she knew them so well as a result of accompanying Uncle Stanley on his many entomological expeditions.

Unaware of Verity's thoughts Cathy suddenly jerked her head. "I know. Addie must go to Maude until she is confined. By that time we might know what Mr Lydney Ryland has in mind and if he is indeed prepared to make an honest woman of my daughter whom he has wronged."

"What an excellent idea." Verity sounded pleased. "Aunt Maude is just the person."

"You don't think she'll mind?"

"I don't think she'll be pleased at the situation poor Addie has got herself in, but I'm sure she'll do it. She would not want her to go to a home. None of us would, would we, Mum?"

Aunt Maude and Uncle Stanley accepted with good grace the task of giving shelter to a niece of whom they were extremely fond, even if deploring the circumstances. They had a large house well sheltered from the road and there was no need for Addie to venture outside the garden. So her shameful secret could be kept from a world too anxious to hear scandal.

The college she was attending was told that she had an illness that needed prolonged rest but, hopefully, would be able to return for the session beginning the following autumn.

Verity took Addie to their uncle and aunt and stayed with her for a few days, having taken leave from the hospital. She was desperately tired and worried herself because she hadn't heard from Rex for a long time and had no idea where he was. Addie, still bemused by everything that had happened to her, valued the company of her sister and was reluctant to be separated from her.

"I wish you could stay," she said as they sat together in the drawing-room on the last day before Verity had to go back. Aunt Maude had gone to the shops and Uncle Stanley was, as usual, at work.

"I wish I could," Verity leaned over and pressed her hand. "But I can't. I will come and see you often and Mum . . ." She paused. "Mum will come and see you too."

Addie and her mother had not yet met and this was an interview that Addie dreaded, however much Verity tried to reassure her.

"Mum doesn't believe that Lydd asked me to marry him, does she?"

Verity chose her words carefully.

"Mum doesn't believe that you would deliberately tell a lie, but she thinks you might try and explain your . . . what happened by somehow justifying it. You know what you did was wrong, but if you thought you were going to marry and Lydney was going away . . ."

"You think I made up the whole thing?" Addie's expression suddenly became angry.

"No, I don't. Not for a minute. On the other hand Lydney might have said that he loved you in order to seduce you."

"Lydney would *never* do such a vile thing," Addie retorted. "He said he loved me and I believe him, or I did then . . ." She paused and looked doubtfully at her sister.

"Did you with . . . Rex? I mean he was going away too."

Verity didn't reply immediately. For some reason her younger sister's question had shocked her, as had Addie's pregnancy, hard as she tried to conceal it.

No, she hadn't gone to bed with Rex but sometimes she wished she had. He had been very persistent and they were, after all, engaged. But it hadn't seemed right and she couldn't do it, so he went away to the war frustrated, and she was left without an experience she craved. She was sure that Rex had respected her for her stand against anything more intimate than a few kisses but, still, she often wondered how she'd feel if she never saw him again.

She shook her head.

"No," was all she said.

"I wish I hadn't." Addie hung her head. "Particularly as he never wrote. Not a word," she lifted pain-filled eyes, "in all this time."

"It must be very difficult to write from the front."

"But people do it. I'm sure he writes to his mother and father, but not to me." Addie lowered her head. "That's what makes me sometimes think, as you suggested, that although I'm sure he loved me perhaps he didn't *really* mean it about marriage. He said it in order that I shouldn't feel bad. And now I do. I feel awful. I feel wicked and ashamed and dirty . . . and I think Lydd must despise me for giving in to him. That's why he doesn't write." And she threw herself against her sister's bosom and wept.

Silently Verity stroked her, murmuring comforting words, but in her heart she thought Addie was right. Maybe if she had given in to Rex he would feel the same way about her too.

Cathy went to the front door and looked impatiently towards the castle. She already had on her coat and hat and Frank would be here any minute to take her to the station to get the train to Bournemouth. She was fidgety and ill at ease, nervous about her first meeting with Addie, the prospect of leaving Mary Capstick, the cook up at the castle, in charge of the children despite the fact that Peg was fourteen and nearly grown up.

Mary Capstick was a friend of Cathy's and had offered to stay the night that Cathy would be away. She would give them lunch and supper up at the castle and the children looked forward to this with some excitement, as if to a big adventure.

If Frank didn't come any minute, Cathy decided, she would

miss the train, but just then she saw the pony and cart emerge from the stables by the side of the castle and trot briskly along the road towards the lodge.

Cathy ran inside to get her case and give Peg her final instructions. There were a dozen dos and dont's and if she was in any doubt about *anything* she was to go straight up to the castle and see Mrs Capstick. In any case they were to be there at one o'clock for their lunch, and . . .

"Mum, we will be perfectly all right," Peg said firmly, trying to stem her mother's flow. "We are going to go for a walk this morning . . ."

"And you are *not* to go too far . . ." Cathy wagged a finger at her.

"We won't go outside the estate, I promise, and then in the afternoon we are doing drawing." Peg, who was taller than her mother, stood up proudly. "I have already made all the preparations, Mum. I am looking forward to being in charge. Oh, and Mum, give love to Addie."

Peg looked at her mother with concern. It was disconcerting being told that Addie was ill, but not knowing what was the matter. And why couldn't she stay here and be looked after by them? Was it *catching*? Time and time again she had asked her mother and as many times got no satisfactory reply. She kissed her mother as the cart clattered to a stop outside the door. "And tell her . . . we'll see her soon."

Waved off by Stella and Ed, finger in his mouth, in the background, Cathy held tightly on to her hat as she climbed into the cart beside Frank, while Peg handed up her case.

"Take care, Mum. Safe journey," she cried as the cart moved off, Frank flicking the pony lightly across its back to get some movement out of him.

"Sorry I'm late, Mrs Hallam. We had some terrible news up at the castle. I didn't know until the last minute whether or not I'd be able to come. Still," he shrugged his shoulders, "there was not much I could do."

"News? What news?" Cathy, still feeling agitated, not

paying much attention, peered forwards as if that would make the station come in sight more quickly.

"Mr Lydney has been killed in action. Terrible news it is."

"*Mr Lydney* . . ." Cathy's heart seemed to stop. "Oh, how terrible."

"There was a telegram this morning. There's been a big battle at Cambrai in France. He and all his men manning a machine gun post were killed. His bravery was mentioned in despatches. Maybe he'll get a medal."

"Oh that *is* terrible," Cathy repeated, not knowing what else she could say. "So Hubert is the heir?"

"Yes. Still it don't make up for losing Mr Lydney. Such a nice young man. Never any trouble. A proper gentleman."

Maude opened the door and embraced her sister. The two women had not seen each other for months. Negotiations about Addie had been conducted by Verity.

"How is she?" Cathy asked immediately.

"She's very well. A little quiet, but I suppose that's to be expected under the circumstances."

"It's very *good* of you to have her." Cathy unpinned her hat, put it on the hall table and shook out her hair.

"It's no trouble and *she* is no trouble. But have you thought, Cathy, what to do afterwards?"

"You mean after she has the baby?" The women were speaking in whispers. "I have no idea. Adoption I suppose."

"I think she wants to keep it."

Cathy looked at her sister in alarm.

"But that's out of the question."

"That's what I thought. Do you know who the father is? She never speaks to me about it."

"Perhaps we could talk later, Maude? And maybe I could see Addie on her own to begin with, if you don't mind."

"Of course I don't mind. I'll get some coffee and ask Doris to bring it to you. I'll take you up to Addie. She's in her room. She spends most of her time there. We are very fond of her, of course, but she is not the company that Verity was."

107

"The circumstances are very different, aren't they? I expect she'll take some time to settle down."

"I expect so."

Maude showed Cathy to Addie's room, knocked on the door and then left her. There was no answer.

"It's Mum," Cathy whispered while giving another tap. "Can I come in?"

The door opened and Addie stood looking at her, her face pale and apprehensive, and somehow defensive.

"Addie," Cathy said, attempting a clumsy embrace. "There is no need to look so worried. I am your mother and I *do* understand."

Addie, feeling cold and unresponsive, allowed a peck on her cheek and then walked back into the room. Cathy, after closing the door, followed her. Addie sat on the side of the bed and Cathy, trying to compose herself, undecided as to what to say, walked to the window and gazed out.

"It's a miserable day."

"Yes," Addie said.

"What do you do all day?"

"Sit about. Read. Think. Not much else to do."

"Peg and the little ones send their love."

"What did you tell them?" For the first time Addie showed some sign of animation.

"We say you are not well. It seemed the best thing to do. It is very kind of Maude and Stanley to have you."

"I know, because neither of them approves." Addie sounded bitter.

"Addie you can't expect people to *approve*. What you did was . . . silly."

"Mum, if all you've come here to do is to tell me off you might as well go home again." Addie's expression was stormy.

Cathy felt a sense of despair at her daughter's intransigence. She wished now that she'd seen her sooner, but everything had happened so quickly: Verity's hurried visit, the consultation with Maude and Stanley, also undertaken by Verity, and her installation at the Bournemouth house. It all happened almost in a matter of a week or two.

"I didn't come to tell you off. I just said that you can't expect people to approve. The fact is that they have given you a home and they are very kind. It was the only thing we could think of. Better this than in an institution, isn't it, Addie?"

"I suppose so. I'm quite sure that when Lydd comes home things will be all right. Oh I wish . . ." Addie gazed despairingly at her mother, "I *wish* he'd write."

Cathy turned again to the window and looked out on to the desolate wintry scene in the garden which seemed an echo of the bleakness in her own heart, as if everything there was frozen over. She had absolutely no idea what to do for the best. Maybe she should leave it, but then wouldn't Lydney's death be in the papers and being a Dorset man, the son of a prominent family, Maude and Stanley were bound to see it and would certainly tell her? Steeling herself she turned and faced Addie, feeling that this was one of the hardest things she'd had to do in her life.

She sat down beside her, put an arm around her waist. "Addie, I have something very difficult to tell you."

"What is it, Mother?" Addie gazed anxiously at her.

"I heard just before I came away today from Frank – there seems no gentle way of telling you this – but I'm afraid Lydney Ryland has been killed in action in France. I'm terribly sorry." Her arm round Addie's waist tightened, but there was no response. Addie just stared straight in front of her. Then, as though she had been struck on the back of the head with a brick, she fell forward and, without trying to save herself, slumped on to the floor.

It was nearly midnight, but the three older ones remained downstairs sitting round the fire. Stanley had a large whisky in his hand, Maude a smaller one.

The doctor had been and after examining Addie to make sure she was all right, he had administered a sedative; but even that didn't seem to work and she remained in a highly agitated state until at ten Cathy gave her another left by the doctor and, finally, she fell asleep.

"I had to tell her," Cathy said. "It will be in the papers. Him being the son of Lord Ryland."

"Oh you had to tell her. No question," Stanley concurred. "What a terrible tragedy for her and the family."

Cathy had spent the evening telling her sister and brother-in-law the story which they too seemed to find hard to believe. Now Stanley said:

"Do you believe Addie?"

"What, that Lydney is the father? Oh, yes."

"No, that he said he would marry her."

"Yes, I do. Addie has always been a very truthful girl. She is also very religious, that's why I found the whole thing so difficult to believe. That she would do it . . . you know."

"But if he said he was going to marry her that would make it all right in her eyes?"

"I suppose so."

"I hope Verity wasn't so silly," Maude said disapprovingly, "before Rex went away."

"At least Verity didn't get pregnant," Cathy retorted.

"She *is* a nurse," Stanley murmured.

"Really, Stanley, I don't know what you think my girls are. I would never have expected either of them to behave like this, but there is *some* excuse for Addie because she is young. Lydney Ryland made a play for her and he was a very attractive young man. I'm quite sure that Verity and Rex, being that much older and more responsible, behaved properly."

"Are you going to tell Lord Ryland?" Maude asked.

"I hadn't thought about it."

"It is his grandchild."

"If he believes her." Cathy looked across at her sister. "He could say she made it up. I'm sure he never mentioned the relationship to his father, or we'd have heard about it before. We'd probably have had notice to leave by now." Cathy pursed her mouth grimly.

"You mean you are *never* going to tell him?"

"I had no plans to."

"What does Jack say?"

Cathy shook her head dismissively. "Oh, Jack doesn't know."

"How many times have you seen Jack since he was called up?"

"Twice."

"Twice in two years. That's strange, isn't it, as he has never been further away than Blackpool?"

"I don't miss him and I don't expect he misses me. We write as seldom, too. He can stay in Blackpool for the rest of his life for all I care."

"I see. It's like that." Maude joined her hands on her lap. "You *have* got a lot of problems haven't you, Cathy?"

"I suppose I have. But once Addie has the baby it can be adopted and that will be one problem solved."

Maude glanced at her husband.

"As I told you earlier on, Cathy, Addie seems to have no intention of having the baby adopted. In so far as we've discussed the matter, which isn't much, and she refused to tell me anything about the father, she has said one thing quite firmly: she will not give the baby up.

"However . . ." Maude paused, "now that she knows the father is dead perhaps she will be sensible and change her mind. Then she can start her life all over again."

Eight

V erity stood on the platform, one of a vast crowd, mostly of women of all ages – mothers, wives, sweethearts – who, like her, were waiting for their men to return home. Yet unlike some of them she felt perfectly calm, though a little apprehensive. Rex had been gone eighteen months and she wondered how much he would have changed. Sometimes she thought that if it were not for the framed photograph of him she kept by the side of her bed she would have difficulty visualising him.

Charing Cross was as busy as ever even at midnight, with trains pulling in full of wounded and going out again with fresh fodder for the German guns or, as they were known, "the sausage machine" – fed in with live men to spew out dead ones. There was little enthusiasm now for the war. Gone for ever was the patriotic fervour of 1914 and now there was an overall air of weariness and despondency yet a determination, on the part of the Germans as well as the Allies, to slug it out to the bitter end.

There still seemed no end to the war. In fact at times the German Army appeared to be on the ascendant. The Allied forces were now deprived of the Russian Army which had disintegrated in the face of the revolution and whose leaders had been forced into a humiliating peace settlement with Germany at Brest-Litovsk.

Debilitated by revolution, famine and now civil war Russia seemed finished as a great power, an easy prey to German aggression.

Verity, huddled in her nurse's cloak, had fled over to the

112

station after being in the operating theatre most of the day. The atmosphere was yellow with thick, acrid smoke from the engines, filling her lungs and making her choke. The cries of people greeting one another or saying tearful goodbyes, the noise of the huge steam engines punctuated by the whistles of the guards, all contributed to create a scene of such confusion that when the train puffed alongside the platform on which she was standing she hardly realised that it was the one which Rex was supposed to be on.

With difficulty Verity held her ground as it came to a halt, doors flew open and the crowd surged forward, many women on the verge of hysteria as they sought out their loved ones.

It was an ambulance train. The wounded came off first with their accompaniment of nurses or orderlies. Some men appeared close to death. One looked as though he had died already and, on seeing him, a woman had thrown herself across the stretcher as it was lowered to the ground and let out a piteous wail.

Verity decided it was hopeless to try and find Rex in all this so she moved slowly to the barrier where she turned and watched as the melancholy procession passed by, mostly stretcher cases, although there were many walking wounded as well.

Then she saw half a dozen officers emerge and huddle together at the end of the platform as if having a discussion. One turned to one side and lit a cigarette and as he looked up he saw her. Immediately he dashed his cigarette to the ground, said something to his companions and hurried towards her.

"Rex!" she cried. But how changed. He was leaner, he seemed taller and he'd grown a moustache. As he removed his cap she saw he'd lost even more hair which now receded well back from his forehead.

"Verity," he said and, cap in hand, bent to kiss her cheek. "How nice of you to come."

It sounded very formal. She didn't know how to reply. She

113

felt awkward, ill at ease as, obviously, did he. Men and women were flinging their arms round one another and embracing, and here she and Rex were greeting each other as at a formal social gathering of some description. Behind him a soldier appeared with a suitcase and some military bags. Rex's batman.

"Where shall I put your kit, sir?"

"I'm going to try and get a room here in the hotel."

"Are you hungry?" Verity asked. "I've only got cocoa back at the home and . . ."

"No men allowed," Rex smiled. "Nothing has changed, has it?"

"I'm afraid not." She smiled too, but still that awkwardness was there. They seemed to have become complete strangers.

"Look, I'll see if I can get a room at the hotel and they're sure to provide a meal of some kind. But you . . . you look dead on your feet."

"I am," Verity admitted. "But you must be too."

"I've been dead on my feet for months. It's amazing how you can get used to it." He spoke in a sort of brisk staccato as if he were giving orders. She felt that, in some ways if not all, Rex had changed completely.

The batman hovered and as Rex set off towards the hotel he picked up the case and bags and followed him, Verity trailing behind them both.

She wished now that she hadn't met Rex, but as she saw the other officers claimed by various of their womenfolk she was glad she had, even if the initial meeting was strained. After all it was bound to be. Only letters and postcards to keep the light of love alive for nearly two years.

Love? Were they in love? She wasn't sure.

Rex was lucky. The hotel had a cancellation. His batman took his bags up to a small room which overlooked the platform, thus probably guaranteeing him a sleepless night.

Rex gave the man his instructions and, as he saluted smartly and went off, turned and smiled at Verity.

"Thank you for coming. You look absolutely exhausted. I am too. Not much sleep for nearly a week. I think we should both turn in, don't you? What is your rota for tomorrow?"

"I don't know, we're very busy."

"I'll look in." He smiled and pecked her on the cheek. "It is simply lovely to see you again. We'll have lots of time to talk. Can you find your own way down?"

"Of course," Verity said. "Goodnight, Rex. I'm so glad you're safe home."

Despite her exhaustion Verity found it almost impossible to sleep that night with the thought of Rex just across the street in the station hotel. He was so near and yet so far.

Somehow it didn't seem an auspicious homecoming.

They hadn't greeted each other like lovers. Well, they weren't. They were an engaged couple who had been separated for many months. Rex's letters, though informative, had never been passionate. Nor, of course, were hers. They were mostly about the hospital. Little about the family. Nothing about Addie, not a word.

Maybe if, like Addie, she and Rex had made love their relationship would have been different. They would have felt a closeness that was absent tonight. But then they might not have. She didn't know. They had become quite intimate on one or two occasions before he left. She had gone to his room where she yielded to impulse and they lay on his bed and embraced. They had come very near to full intercourse but at the last minute she always held back, feeling ashamed the next day of having gone so far. She was quite glad when Rex went off to the war and the importuning, this feeling of pressure to do something she didn't want to do, stopped. She was sure he respected her for it.

A lot of nurses had slept with their boyfriends and regretted it. One had had a baby like Addie. Her boyfriend rejected her, her family threw her out and the baby was adopted. She was now back on the wards, having lost seniority, respect and determined never to have anything to do with men again.

No, Verity thought as dawn came streaking in through the window, she had definitely done the right thing.

She was a gorgeous baby. Over eight pounds of her, strong and sturdy with Lydney's ash-blond hair and bright blue eyes. She was his baby all right. There was nothing of the Barnes family about her. Cathy peered over the crib and took one of the tiny hands which clenched firmly over hers.

"Isn't she a darling?" she said gazing at Maude who was also drooling over the crib.

Maude nodded and sighed.

"So difficult to give her away, and yet . . ." she dropped her voice in case Addie came into the room, "we have to. There is no alternative, not if Addie wants any sort of life, never mind a career."

Little Jenny, as Addie had called her, was just two weeks old and this was the first visit from her grandmother. Not that she hadn't wanted to come, but the two younger children had been ill with influenza and she had not dared leave them.

Perhaps because of her youth Addie had had an easy labour and a swift delivery. She came home two days later having no wish to be patronised by the nurses, as she was in the hospital, and be taunted by the other women, most of whom had husbands to visit them and bring them flowers.

Aunt Maude had been a reluctant visitor and hadn't stayed long in case she should be seen by anyone she knew. She'd worn a hat with a half-veil over her face.

Appearances were important to Aunt Maude and she had no wish for it to get around that a niece of hers had had an illegitimate baby.

Jenny's birth didn't seem an occasion for rejoicing as it did when the other babies were born, yet Addie's baby was the prettiest in the ward and one kind nurse gave her a lot of attention and helped her to breastfeed, although it was not encouraged when babies were being put up for adoption, as they all assumed Jenny would be. It was some surprise, therefore, to learn that Addie intended keeping the baby, and the adoption authorities were unceremoniously turned away. After two days Addie discharged herself and, with Jenny carefully wrapped in a shawl, requested a cab to take her home.

Addie didn't care about anybody except the baby with whom she had immediately formed a strong bond. Even before she looked into those bright blue eyes, so reminiscent of Lydd's, she knew she loved her as she loved no other, and whatever happened she would never part with her.

Addie quickly recovered from the birth, the baby was strong and well looked after and even Aunt Maude and Uncle Stanley came to regard her with affection, though sighing sadly about the time when they would have to part with her.

But, as in many families, little was said. The matter was seldom referred to for fear of upsetting Addie, and now Cathy had been asked to talk firmly to her daughter and try and get some common sense through to her in a way that Maude and Stanley had failed to do.

Cathy took the baby from her cot and sat her on her lap and was rewarded by open eyes and what looked like a smile, but could have been wind.

"She is *so* advanced," Cathy said admiringly, taking her hand and flapping it about. "I'm sure my children never smiled at that age."

Maude sat next to Cathy and took the other hand which she also flapped up and down, making cooing noises as she did.

"Coo coo," she said, "coo coo." Then, more practically, "Cathy, what are we to do about Addie? You must talk to her. There is no sense in her hoping for something that cannot happen. The child is only just twenty. This baby would ruin her life. What decent man would want to marry her? What school would employ her?"

Cathy looked for a long time at the baby, and then at Maude, smiling mysteriously at her. She thought how Maude and Stanley had yearned for children, and how that had made them adopt Verity. The thought had occurred to her before, not once but frequently during the long period of Addie's sojourn with them during which they agreed they had become very fond of her, but never as fond as they had been of Verity.

There was always something that Addie held back, as if she did not wish to, or could not give herself entirely. Verity had been reserved in the way that they were reserved, but she had a warmth towards them, undoubted affection for them, which Addie lacked perhaps because of the circumstances and the feeling that, however kind they were, she was only there on sufferance.

Cathy put Jenny back into her cot, tucked her up and gave her a kiss.

Then she settled back again next to Maude and carefully examined the single ring on her wedding finger. Maude had a mass of diamonds as well as her wedding ring on hers, but Cathy had never had anyone rich enough to give her diamonds or other jewels and there was just the solitary gold band which she thought had belonged to Jack's mother, so there was nothing he had had to make a sacrifice for.

"Maude, I wondered if you and Stanley . . . you know how much you longed for children."

Maude gave her a startled look. "Go on," she encouraged her.

Cathy threaded her fingers into one another.

"Well," she paused not quite knowing how to go on.

"You can't possibly mean," Maude's voice rose, "that *we* should adopt Jenny?"

"Why not? You say you love her."

"I didn't say we *loved* her." Maude spoke precisely. "We have been very careful to keep emotion out of it for Addie's sake as much as ours. Of course we did discuss it, knowing how averse Addie was to adoption, but we were never in any doubt as to what our decision would be. Jenny is a dear little thing, but we don't think it is in Addie's interests, and it's certainly not in ours. We're far too old and set in our ways. Besides it would look very *odd* for us to adopt a young baby. People would talk and ask all sorts of questions."

Maude patted her lap firmly. "It is much much better if Addie says 'goodbye' to the baby and makes a clean break. Why don't we do it while you're here, and then you can take Addie back with you and she can make a fresh start?"

"You mean . . . in the next day or two?"

"Why not?" Maude spoke briskly as if enjoying a surge of confidence. "I can ring the people at the children's home today."

"And what if she never finds new parents? I hear there are a lot of unwanted children as a result of the war, unfortunate cases of men being killed in battle and wives and sweethearts deserted and abandoned, just like what happened to Addie."

"That won't be your worry, dear," Maude said in a kindly tone. "She will no longer be your grandchild. But I'm sure she will be well looked after. These places are very good."

"But she *will* always be my granddaughter," Cathy said indignantly. She stood up and brushed her skirt. "I think I had better go and talk to Addie."

"Yes, do talk to her," Maude pleaded, entirely misreading Cathy's mood. "Try and make her see sense. Why, by tonight or tomorrow at the latest it could all be over."

Cathy went along the corridor and gently pushed open the door of Addie's bedroom. She lay on the outside of her bed fully clothed though without shoes, her hands resting on her stomach. She was still fast asleep. She looked so young, so quiet and tranquil that Cathy's heart turned over. Addie had not the beauty of Peg or the strength of character of Verity, but she had her own special qualities of steadfastness, charity and fidelity that endeared her to everyone, especially her mother. It was Addie who had assumed the mantle of the eldest child when Verity went away, had lovingly yet firmly looked after the younger ones, who was so quick and dependable. She would, in fact, make a splendid mother.

How typical, yet how foolish of generous Addie to give herself to Lydney when he was about to go to war, and then to refuse to blame him for the consequences.

And how guilty Cathy had felt when she heard that her daughter turned to her remote elder sister, who she had not grown up with, rather than herself, when she was in trouble. She felt she'd failed her as a mother.

Tears stung Cathy's eyes as she sat by Addie's side and tenderly stroked her arm.

Addie's eyes immediately flew open, an expression of alarm on her face.

"Is everything all right, Mum?"

"Everything's fine," Cathy smiled reassuringly. "Aunt Maude and I have just been with Jenny. I think she's now fast asleep."

"Oh that's good. I must go and feed her soon." Addie clutched her mother's hand and smiled. "It's good to have you here, Mum. Aunt Maude and Uncle Stanley are not quite the same."

"I'm glad of that. I want you always to feel that. I am here when you need me. I don't think you always felt that in the past."

"I was afraid," Addie said simply. "You had told me not to see Lydney. I didn't think you'd understand."

"Well I do now and I'm here to help you. Addie," Cathy's hand remained on her daughter's arm, "I want to tell you something and I don't want you to speak until I've finished."

Addie nodded. "Go on," she encouraged her.

"I have talked to Aunt Maude about Jenny's future. I had hoped that Maude and Stanley might offer to adopt her, but they say they're too old."

"Besides which," angrily Addie sat upright on the bed, "I do *not* want them to adopt her. She is my baby. I don't think you'd any right to do that, Mum."

"I was only thinking of you. Addie, you must be practical. How can you possibly keep Jenny? What will you live on? You can't work if you have a baby and I can't afford to keep you. You must also think about what people will say and your chances for the future. An unwed mother is an object of derision and scorn in our society and your child is at a disadvantage. I'm sorry but she is. You will have very little

chance in life and will be an embittered old maid, and Jenny
may give you little thanks for it."

Addie glared at her. "Is that what you really think?"

"I have to put it to you to give you a final chance to think
about the future, your future and Jenny's. Maude would like
to inform the authorities while I am here and then I can take
you home . . ."

Addie's hand crashed firmly down on the bed. "No, no,
no," she cried. "No, no, no. I will never, ever part from Jenny,
whatever happens. Never."

Dinner that night was a very strained affair. Maude hardly
said a word. Stanley, unusually for him, seemed to drink a
little too much and started slurring his words. Cathy felt
dejected and also friendless. There was no one really in whom
she could confide. She and her sister had grown too far apart.
She didn't wonder that Verity had grown up to be so self-
controlled in the company of these two worthy citizens who,
although kind and compassionate, seemed lacking in imagi-
nation.

Addie didn't come down to dinner but stayed with her baby
as if fearing that, if her back was turned, someone would come
and take her away. Cathy felt that, instead of gaining Addie's
confidence, she had lost it while she was only trying to help
her make an informed decision.

"So you think Addie has said her final words?" Maude
murmured as the last course was cleared away. They didn't
like to speak of the matter in front of Doris.

"Her mind is firmly made up," Cathy said. "She wants to
keep Jenny and I can't stop her. In a way I agree with her, and
I must make room for her and her child in my home as I
confess I have already in my heart."

"So you will really take her home with the baby?" Maude
looked incredulous.

"Yes, if I must. She is my daughter – Jenny my granddaughter."

"And what will you tell people?"

"I won't tell them anything and you can be sure they won't ask. I *might* tell Lord Ryland but not, of course, that the child is his granddaughter. That wouldn't be fair. Also, as I told you before, he wouldn't believe it. I think his lordship will be fair to me as long as I don't make a scandal, and I shan't. Addie will go back to college and complete her training. That way she can contribute to the upkeep of her baby and the family home. We shall be pressed but we shall manage."

"And what will Jack say?"

"Jack can do as he likes. He can't throw the child out of the house because if he does I will go with her. Anyway Lord Ryland would never allow it.

"In time, you will see, people will think the child is mine. Stella is only ten." Cathy smiled a little coquettishly, showing something of her former attraction as a young woman. "They will think that I had a baby late in life, when my husband came back from the war."

Uncle Stanley took Addie, Cathy and baby Jenny to the station in a cab and made sure they were comfortable in their carriage before awkwardly bidding them goodbye.

It had been an emotional morning, the haste with which Cathy had announced her decision and Addie's joy on hearing it. Maude and Stanley had made another attempt to dissuade her, pointing out the many pitfalls she would have to overcome: the possible stigma, the unknown reaction of Jack, Lord Ryland and the castle staff whose tongues would wag. Mrs Capstick had been in the know about Addie's pregnancy and had a reputation as a gossip.

Not one word, however, had been said to her or anyone about the identity of the baby's father. Cathy had murmured something about a young man Addie had known in Bristol, who had promised her marriage and had abandoned her.

Even Mary Capstick, however, would not have expected her to arrive home with her daughter's bastard.

Now that she was to be liberated and keep her baby Addie was generous to Aunt Maude and Uncle Stanley. Generous in her praise for their kindness, and for all they had done. She promised to write to them and come and see them. Aunt Maude even had tears in her eyes as she said "goodbye" from the front door and Uncle Stanley looked a little sad now and kept on gazing at Jenny as though he knew he would miss her, and may have wondered if they had made a mistake in not offering to adopt her. After all their bond with Verity now was not as strong as it had once been.

Blood, as they say, is stronger than water, and Verity spent most of her free time with her natural family and only made rare visits to the house where she was brought up. He and Maude faced an increasingly lonely old age.

The guard blew his whistle, Uncle Stanley removed his hat and kissed Cathy and Addie on the cheek and Jenny on the top of her little head poking out from her shawl.

He jumped on to the platform and closed the door of the train just in time, stepping back quickly as it began to pull away. He looked rather a sad, isolated figure as he stood there in the breeze waving his hat to Cathy and Addie who stood by the window waving back at him. Then, when he was out of sight, they sank back in their seats, making sure that Jenny, fast asleep in her crib and oblivious of all the fuss going on around her, was all right.

Addie then tucked her arm through that of her mother and put her face against her shoulder. She felt content, closer to her mother than she ever had before, and knew that she had done something very brave.

"Thank you, Mum," she whispered, squeezing her arm. "I will never forget what you have done for me and Jenny."

"I had no choice," Cathy said smiling tenderly at Addie. "I think from the moment I saw her I knew that I would never be able to let go of my granddaughter. I fell in love with her at first sight." She patted Addie's arm comfortingly. "We have done the right thing, Addie. We *will* be all right. We'll get by. For one thing I could never let my granddaughter be brought up by a stranger. She's part of us, part of our family and that's how it should be."

Nine

The occasion was a doubly festive one: Germany had surrendered, and the war to end all wars, which had cost so many millions of lives and changed the balance of power in Europe, was at last over. Flags flew over Appleburn, the picturesque village in the heart of the Yorkshire Dales, where Rex's father had his practice.

The Harveys' house, set back from the village green, was a solid, substantial dwelling built of grey Yorkshire stone. Next door was the surgery and a few yards away, beyond the green, flowed the River Wharfe from its source high up in the Pennine range on its journey towards the sea. Dr Harvey had met them at the station in Leeds in his newly acquired motor car which was a rarity in that remote part of the country where pony and trap or horse and cart were still the norm.

The journey had been exciting and unusual, literally up hill and down dale through some of the most beautiful, heavily wooded countryside that seemed at times to rival even Verity's native Dorset for its grandeur.

Appropriately it was wet and misty when they arrived and the celebratory flags hung limply from their poles or the lines criss-crossing the village. Inside the house a huge fire had welcomed them and the smell of newly baked cake, reminiscent of Aunt Maude and Uncle Stanley's house in Bournemouth and the welcome when she came home from school in time for tea.

Verity had met Rex's parents shortly after they had become engaged. They came to London to be introduced to her and say goodbye to Rex before he left for the Balkans.

That was two years ago and she hadn't seen them since. Dr Harvey was stocky like Rex, who much resembled him. He too had been a rugby player, wore spectacles, was bald and had a forbidding expression as though he could be rather grumpy towards patients whom he suspected of malingering or wasting time. When she first met him Verity had thought that she would never like to have to take any intimate problem to him requiring intuition and understanding of the feminine psyche.

However, there was another side to Dr Harvey who seemed more relaxed in his own home, and in the short time she had been there Verity had warmed to him. He was clearly devoted to his only son and relieved to have him safe.

Mrs Harvey was tiny and rather plump, exuberant, excitable and friendly. She complemented her husband and must have been popular with his patients.

If Rex was to be believed his father was much respected in the district as a good doctor, which was what counted in rural areas with poor communications. What was needed was a man who could stitch a gaping wound caused by some accident on the farm, or safely deliver a farmer's wife caught with a breech birth in the middle of a snowstorm. A good bedside manner was of secondary importance.

Rex spent much of the first two days closeted with his father either in his surgery or accompanying him on his rounds, leaving Verity and his mother to get to know each other better. But Verity soon got to know not only her prospective mother-in-law but everyone in the village. It was a small friendly place where everyone had known everyone else for generations.

"I'm so glad Rex is going to settle down," Mrs Harvey said as they had coffee in the kitchen after a trip to the local store. "I'm hoping he's talking to his father about joining the practice." She looked anxiously up at Verity. "Would you like that dear? Has he spoken to you about it?"

Verity nodded. "Vaguely. It is what his father wants."

"I hope he wants it too. James's father was the Rector here. We have a very long association with the village." Mrs Harvey had a worried expression on her face. "But I feel Rex is restless. He seems so fidgety to me, as if he can't settle."

"I do think he has been through a very bad time," Verity said gravely. "I found him much changed after he came back."

"He is certainly not the Rex who went away," his mother said sadly.

"At first I thought we were like strangers; but it has improved. I think he was just re-adjusting. We both were."

"And is it all right now?" Mrs Harvey looked at her anxiously.

"Oh, much better," Verity nodded reassuringly. "You know, we've hardly seen each other since he came back. There's been so much work for him to do at the military hospital and, of course, we are now treating influenza cases as well as the war injuries at Charing Cross."

"Not for much longer!" Mrs Harvey raised her eyes heavenwards. "Thank God this dreadful war is over and our loved ones are all spared." She looked enquiringly across at Verity. "Your stepfather is all right, isn't he?"

"He never left the country. He was one of the lucky ones."

"Then your mother will be glad to have him back again."

Verity rather pointedly didn't reply.

Mrs Harvey's next question was more practical. "Have you decided on the date of the wedding?"

"I think that's what Rex is talking to your husband about. Perhaps the spring?"

Mrs Harvey clasped her hands together in rapturous anticipation. "Oh I do *hope* so. A spring wedding would be so lovely. Of course it will be in Dorset, but the countryside is lovely there too isn't it?"

Verity nodded. Spring wedding? As soon as that? Leaving the hospital and assuming the role of the wife of a country doctor? Probably the following year their first child? It was all very difficult to imagine now, but that was how things were meant to be, and it was what she wanted. As if reading her thoughts Mrs Harvey went on:

"Would you like it here dear? I mean if everything works out? Actually there is a house for sale in the village. We thought it would be ideal for you and Rex, or are we perhaps going a little too quickly for you?"

"No, no," Verity assured her. "I'm sure Rex wants to be settled after his demobilisation and of course I want what he wants."

"What a sensible attitude." Mrs Harvey looked approvingly at her. "I'm so pleased. I thought that as a modern young woman with your own career you might not feel that way. The war has changed a lot of things hasn't it? There are so many new ideas about the role of women. In my opinion it is the only way to deal with men. Want what they want and give them what they want. You can always get your own way by other means. Let them think they thought of it. It is the secret of a successful marriage and James and I have been married thirty-five years. Mind you a woman needn't be supine or spineless, but I don't expect you need me to tell you all this, one of a large family."

"I was adopted by an uncle and aunt. My mother's sister and brother-in-law."

"Oh really? I didn't know that."

"My father died when I was young, just after my youngest sister was born. My mother found it very hard to look after us and her sister Maude was very fond of me. Of course I didn't want to go, but I had no choice."

Mrs Harvey looked concerned, her expression one of motherly concern.

"And were you able to see your mother and the rest of the family?"

"Oh yes, but not as often as I'd have liked. I also felt isolated from my sisters Addie and Peg."

"And how old are they?"

"Addie is twenty. She's training to be a teacher. Peg is still at school. I have a half-brother and sister who are still quite young."

Mrs Harvey smiled sadly. "How lucky you are. Unfortunately I had complications when Rex was born and couldn't have any more children. Which is why he's so precious." She reached across and took Verity's hand. "And how lucky we are to be having you as a daughter-in-law, my dear. We love you already."

She kissed Verity on the cheek and Verity hugged her, conscious of her good fortune in having a future mother-in-law who seemed to be cast in the same mould, the same stuff as her own mother and Aunt Maude.

That night at dinner there was a feeling of celebration in the air. Rex was in an especially good mood. He had been up the dales with his father who had also shown him the house for sale in the village, and Rex was full of this. He seemed to have lost the drawn look of the permanently tired: a pale haggard face, the weariness about the eyes of someone always expecting disaster. The flippancy of his letters and postcards had disguised his real feelings about the war.

Verity had found Rex much changed in the few times she'd been with him since his return. Usually he came up to London on an afternoon train and returned in the evening leaving time for a walk along the Embankment and tea at Lyons Corner House. Rex had had many terrible moments during the war, making his way across the Balkans and Russia often in the wake of atrocities carried out by both sides and, as a medical man, he had been expected to deal with them unhesitatingly. But he had seemed unable to talk to Verity about them. He tried to carry on as if nothing had changed, but it had and one day she'd asked him if he still loved her and wanted the engagement to continue?

This had appeared to jolt him, to make him realise how distant he had become – how, if the truth be told, rather selfish.

When he got back to his unit he wrote her a long letter trying to explain himself, asking for understanding and suggesting a holiday with his parents.

Yet even in the train he was solemn and uncommunicative as if he still lived in another world.

However, gradually he had unwound. He spent a lot of time with his father. He was obviously close to his mother. He began to seem more normal, more affectionate towards her and, tonight, he seemed transformed and optimistic, his slightly rubicund face pink with pleasure.

"We saw the house," he said to Verity, "and tomorrow we're both going to see it. Your approval is most important."

"I'm sure I'll approve." Verity could sense that she was already falling naturally into the wifely role. She saw Frances glance approvingly at her.

"The house is to be our wedding present to you," James Harvey announced. "We thought it was a practical gift."

"It's very generous of you, Dad."

"Very, very kind." Verity could hardly believe her ears. A house of their own!

"We want you to be happily settled and I know young people haven't much money. I want you to make a fresh start here and I can't tell you how I shall value having a partner in Rex. I shall be able to put my feet up, perhaps do a bit more fishing."

Rex turned eagerly to his fiancée.

"You could help in the dispensary. Would you like that, dear?"

Taken unawares Verity carefully put down her knife and fork.

"It's a splendid idea. I'd like to be of help in any way I can."

James Harvey sat back and contentedly joined his hands across his stomach.

"Now for the important decision. The date of the wedding. Any thoughts on the subject?"

The ensuing silence was broken again by James. "Well, Rex and I have discussed it. He has to get his discharge. Verity too will have to give notice to the hospital. The house has to be got ready. But we did wonder if by the spring . . ."

129

"We'd thought next spring too!" Frances Harvey beamed excitedly.

"Is that settled then?" James looked round the table.

"Fine by me." Rex raised an eyebrow at his fiancée.

"And me," Verity returned his glance, but nevertheless she felt rather overwhelmed by the speed of the change in Rex who had never once discussed the wedding since his return.

"Spring it is!" Dr Harvey rose and went round the table to kiss his future daughter-in-law. "I can't tell you how pleased we shall be to have you in the family. I couldn't have made a better choice myself."

The following day the couple went round the house which was at the end of the village, half-way up a hill overlooking the Wharfe. It too was built of grey Yorkshire stone, double fronted, with a large garden back and front. It had four bedrooms, various outbuildings, even stables. In summer the front would be covered with roses and wisteria.

The Harvey parents had tactfully decided the lovers should look at the house on their own and they now stood by the window of the sitting-room, bare of furniture because the owner had died, overlooking the valley.

It really was a magnificent view and the house itself had a happy, lived-in family kind of feel. Verity could imagine raising a family here, growing old and, like James and Frances, never wanting to leave. Maybe if they had a son, or sons, one of them might be a doctor and carry on the family tradition.

She'd become part of the village, like Frances, perhaps with an expanding waistline like her too. She'd fret and worry about the children – with any luck there would be more than one – their schooling, their little illnesses, hopefully few of these, and when they grew up she'd worry just as Mum and Aunt Maude had worried about her, though without much cause.

But compared to her mother's, it seemed a very rosy future, one with security and no shortage of money.

Really she felt blessed. Only too recently she had wondered

if Rex still loved her and now the wedding was only a few months away. It seemed an almost miraculous transformation from doubt to certainty.

Rex saw her expression and murmured:

"Happy?"

"Very."

He took Verity in his arms and kissed her. It was a deeply passionate kiss, far from the chaste expressions of affection they'd shared since his return which had helped to reinforce the idea she had that a barrier had been erected between them. He gently inserted his knee between her crotch.

"I do want you, you know."

She nodded, but her expression was a tease. With her free hand she pushed his knee away and whispered:

"When we're married. Not long to go now."

Hands entwined they continued their exploration of the house. Despite her rebuff Rex seemed excited, almost elated.

"We'll have children," Rex said. "You do want them don't you?"

"Of course."

"Four maybe."

They were now on the top floor and he flung open one of the windows and gazed out of it. Then his expression grew sombre and almost perceptibly she could feel his mood change once again.

"Sometimes, you know," he said, "all this seems unreal to me." He gesticulated towards the surrounding hills. "I don't want to exaggerate the effect of what happened to me because millions of men went through the same thing, but the war has changed me."

"I know, Rex. It has changed us all." She clasped his hand tightly.

Rex went on. "I couldn't believe there was so much evil, so much cruelty, a denial of God and all that is good. Somehow it made me doubt that He exists. I feel I am struggling to regain not only my faith but my belief in humanity. I felt that in church on Sunday, and coming home here with you and being with my parents, who like you so much, has somehow chased the demons away. This timelessness, this land of England is, after all, what we fought for."

Rex perched on the window-sill and, hands shaking, lit a cigarette. "But you know, that's only part of it. You see Verity I don't really *know* what we did fight for. We were never in danger of being occupied by an enemy. Why were we there? Why didn't we let the bloody continentals fight it out for themselves? The Serbs and the Boche and the French? Why did we get involved? We were in a war that had nothing at all to do with us. And what were we doing in Russia? What business was it of ours?"

"You said it was humanitarian," Verity reminded him, "because they were short of doctors."

"That was then. I was an idealist. I am no more. I saw humanity at its worst – dreadful deeds. I questioned the competence of those over us and I wasn't alone. You've no idea how often parts of the British army came close to mutiny."

Verity was shaken by this change in Rex's mood. Even his face had darkened, and the haunted look had returned to his eyes as if he was suffering from shell-shock. Maybe this was a form of it. Some soldiers had committed suicide on their return. Anxiously she reached for his hand and pressed it hard.

"Don't think about it now, dear. Don't let it spoil the day. It's all over."

"But it isn't," Rex insisted. "It's still all there, not only in my mind. I can even smell it: the stench of some of those hospital units where we operated round the clock. Some were crawling with cockroaches, the men covered with lice, their wounds horribly infected and suppurating. I wake up at night and I can still see it all."

Verity drew him away from the window, an arm protectively round his shoulders. He leant his head against her breast as if he was too weary to go on.

"You're all right now," she murmured tenderly. "It's a bad dream. It will all go away."

But Rex shook his head. "No, no," he said, "it won't. Ever."

Tears suddenly coursed down his cheeks and he clung to her as a child clings to its mother. This was a new Rex, one she had not known before: vulnerable, all his confidence gone.

Verity pressed his head against her bosom, but her erstwhile sense of happiness and security was replaced by doubt and uncertainty but also, more disturbingly, by a feeling of foreboding as if a cloud had suddenly obscured the sun and darkened their future together.

Jack Hallam paused as he came in sight of the lodge. He was slightly out of breath from carrying his heavy suitcase the couple of miles from the station. He was in two minds whether it was good to be home or not and had not notified anyone of his arrival. He had only been away two years, but it seemed much longer and but for a couple of brief visits he had almost forgotten his family and, as a consequence, he suspected, had been forgotten by them, especially the younger ones.

Well this was what happened in wartime, even if you'd been no further than Blackpool where his regiment had been stationed recruiting and training for the 8th Dorsets. Jack Hallam had been very lucky. He had had a happy war. Not for him the trenches with the perpetual bombardment and small chance of survival once you went over the top. His age had been in his favour, enabling him to secure a cushy job at home. He had never had the slightest desire to be a hero so he could have asked for nothing better.

Jack lit a cigarette and resumed his walk with his suitcase, pausing again as he stood at last outside the front door.

It was a year since he last stood here and then he knew he was going away again. This time he wasn't.

He didn't feel so happy to be home.

He tried the door handle and pushed open the door. It was

mid-afternoon and nearly dark on a late December day. In his case he had carried presents for the children at Christmas.

Jack put down his case, took off his overcoat and put his hat on the hall stand, checked his hair in the mirror, his neat, new, carefully waxed moustache.

He wore an obviously new suit, rather a loud check, complete with waistcoat, a white shirt with a stiff collar and a brown-and-yellow tie. His hair parted in the middle was thick with grease. He had put on several pounds in weight, and looked fleshy.

The house was silent and in semi-darkness. Calling for Cathy he pushed open the door of the sitting-room and looked round. In a chair, half asleep, was a young girl nursing a baby. She looked up, startled, as the door opened and stuck the tip of her finger in the mouth of the baby who had started to cry.

"Goodness me," the girl cried. She was no more than sixteen or so and not one of his brood. "Who might *you* be?"

"I be the master of this house," Jack said half humorously, "and who might *you* be?"

"I work at the castle." The young girl lowered her eyes. "I'm baby-sitting for Mrs Hallam."

"Baby-sitting." Jack stared at the infant in his arms. "This is not your baby?"

"No sir. It's Mrs Hallam's." She then appeared to realise the importance of what she'd just said and her mouth fell open.

"Then it's your baby, sir, if you are Mr Hallam."

"*I* have a baby?" Jack could not hide his amazement.

"It seems so, sir. Shall I go and tell Mrs Hallam you're here? She went up to the castle."

"No, wait until she comes back," Jack said with a nasty edge to his voice. "I'd be interested to hear what she has to say."

He then left the room and went upstairs inspecting the bedroom where he'd last slept over a year before. Of course it was possible that the baby was his, but wouldn't he have been told? Wouldn't even Cathy, the worst of correspondents, not that he was much better, have told him that?

Jack suspiciously examined the bed, turning back the bed-clothes and looking carefully at the sheets, opening drawers and cupboards for evidence of a strange presence but detecting none.

Then he went downstairs into the kitchen and was filling the kettle when the back door opened and Cathy came in lowering her umbrella because it had begun to pour with rain.

"Jack!" she gasped when she saw him. "When did you get here?"

"Oh, not long ago." Jack put the kettle on the hob and gazed insolently at his wife. "Quite a little surprise I had."

"Oh?"

Jack jerked his head in the direction of the sitting-room. "A baby."

"Yes." Cathy took off her hat and tidied her hair scraping a loose piece back behind her ears. "I meant to tell you about that. I hadn't expected you home so soon."

"The war is over, you know."

"Of course I know, but I thought you'd have written."

"Why didn't *you* write, Cathy, and tell me about the baby?" There was an unpleasant note to Jack's voice and Cathy looked at him in surprise. She called to the young girl that she could go, thanked her and waited.

"It's not *mine*, Jack, if that's what you're thinking," she said as the door closed.

"The girl said it was your baby."

"She doesn't know. She hasn't been long at the castle, and that's what we tell people."

"Whose baby is it then?" His voice was thick with suspicion.

Cathy looked at the kettle on the hob, waiting for it to boil. Then she put tea in a pot and got two cups out of the kitchen cupboard. She got a cake from a tin and put it on a plate, cutting two slices from it. When the kettle boiled she made the tea and stirred it. Her heart felt as heavy as lead.

Jack sat at the kitchen table, like a cat, watching her, a mean expression on his face. She was reminded how familiar this was and how much she loathed him.

When so many men who had been loved had been sent to the front and didn't return, why had Jack, whom she didn't love but positively hated, been given a safe job at home?

She sat opposite him and drank her tea. "It's Addie's baby," she said as she put down the cup. "Addie had a baby and wouldn't give it up. Some people think it's mine. We thought it best that way."

"And why didn't *I* hear about this?"

"I didn't know how to tell you."

"You knew last year when I was home?"

"That she was expecting, yes."

"Addie wasn't here then?"

"She was at Maude's. I didn't tell you because I knew how you'd create, and I thought you need never know because Addie would have the baby adopted." Cathy poured herself a fresh cup of tea. "Anyway she wouldn't."

"You should have made her."

"I couldn't."

"But why let her come back here with all the scandal? It might cost me my job with Lord Ryland."

"Because I love her. She is my daughter and the child is my grandchild."

Jack got up and, rounding the table, leaned over Cathy and shook his fist at her. For one moment she thought he was going to hit her and she cowered in her chair holding up her hand to protect her face.

"Now look here, Cathy, I'm not having any bastard child of Addie's in my home. Do you understand? I'm a respectable man with a respectable job of work to do. Does Lord Ryland know about this?"

"Yes." Cathy lowered her head.

"He knows about the baby?"

"Yes." Cathy met his eyes. "But not that it's Addie's. He

has been told she's the daughter of a relative whom I've adopted. Which is true."

Jack looked at her despairingly.

"But someone must know Addie is the mother."

"Some do know and I am telling the truth. Mary Capstick knows. Frank Carpenter knows. But they are sworn not to say a word."

"But the children know!" Jack shouted at her, getting more and more angry.

"Peg might *guess*, but she says nothing. She believes what I tell her. I said the baby is a relative's and that's all I will say to her. She won't argue with me. I couldn't say it was her sister's for goodness' sake! The younger ones naturally accepted that I went away for a few days and came back with a baby. They are too young to understand."

"Well I'm not standing for it," Jack shouted. "I am going straight up to Lord Ryland and I shall tell him that child is a bastard. I won't have it or the girl in my house."

"In that case I will leave you, Jack." Cathy rose and gazed at him across the table. "I shall take the children and leave you."

"And where will you go?"

"I'll find somewhere. Addie is working. Verity is working and they will help support me." She looked at him contemptuously. "You will then have to explain to Lord Ryland why your wife has left you and I don't think his lordship, who is a kind and just man, will think much of you on account of that! He will think less of you than Addie if you insist on telling him the truth. As I have had to bring three children up by myself during the war and never asked for an extra penny beyond the measly amount I got from you, I don't think you will come too well out of it Jack, and you might well find yourself looking for employment elsewhere."

As Peg lay in her bed listening, memories came crowding back of the times before Dad went away and Mum seemed always depressed and unhappy, and sometimes had bruises on her face, and there were those noises in the night. Father had gone out to the pub immediately after supper, had returned very late and then lurched up the stairs crashing into the bedroom where Mum had gone hours before.

There were the thumps and bangs from the grown-ups' bedroom, a creaking of the bed which seemed to follow a rhythmical pattern, and then the sound of weeping. Only now it appeared much louder than it had been before.

Mum weeping loudly as if crying for help.

Peg, making sure that Stella was still asleep, crept out of her bed, peeped in on the baby whose crib was in their room, quietly opened the door and stood listening to the weeping which was much louder now. Then she heard the sounds of slapping start again and Mum crying:

"Please Jack, please, please . . ."

"I tell you," he roared, "I'm not having Addie's bastard in my house."

"And I tell *you*," Peg heard Mum mutter as though she was under pressure, "I am keeping her here. If she goes, I go."

There was the sound of a scuffle, more slaps, more whimpering and then the rhythmical creaking started again so violently that the house seemed to shake. Peg could only surmise what must be happening to Mum. Terrified she put her hands to her ears and rushed back to her room, flinging herself into bed and covering her head.

It was awful to think that after the years of peaceful harmony at home Dad had come back bringing with him violence and discord, a return to the bad old days.

He wasn't her dad, but he had treated her well and she'd been quite fond of him, fonder than Verity or Addie. She had come to think of him as her father as she was so young when her real one died. But she knew he didn't treat Mum well, so they were all frightened of him.

So Dad's return wasn't altogether a good thing and, now, it was even worse to learn that Jenny was Addie's baby. Could it be true?

It was a question that Peg had never liked, never dared to

ask. Mum had never told her and she had learned not to ask questions. Mum could be quite severe when she wanted to administer a reprimand.

But how could Addie possibly have had a baby without being married? It was something that Peg couldn't comprehend, couldn't understand, but would dearly love to know.

Ten

"For she's a jolly good fellow,
For she's a jolly good fellow,
For she's a jolly good fellow,
And so say all of us!"

"Hip hip . . . hurray
Hip hip . . . hurray."

Verity, blushing, laughingly held up her hand for the noise
to stop. But it went on for some time until, with the help of
one of the doctors, she climbed on to a chair and, still
breathless, held up both hands until the room fell silent. It
had been decorated with streamers and banners, ribbons in
the shape of wedding knots and cut-out hearts pasted on the
walls of the nurses' dining-room. A two-tiered cake with white
icing had tiny plaster figurines of a doctor and nurse in
uniform at the top.

"I just want to thank you all for this wonderful party," she
said. "It has literally taken my breath away . . ."

"Send for a doctor," quipped a man at the back of the room
to the sound of renewed laughter.

Verity's expression grew solemn. "I shall miss you all terribly. I shall miss my work here. I shall even miss . . ." she
turned and smiled at a woman standing in the front of the hall,
"Matron!" Renewed laughter. "And I'm sure Matron won't
miss me. You will all be in my heart and thoughts . . . always,
and particularly the experiences we've shared during the war."

Verity blew a kiss and stepped down from the chair to be

140

succeeded by the woman she had addressed. The room grew silent again as Matron held up her hands.

"As you all know," Matron began in her calm, sensible voice, "Verity is completely wrong in thinking I shan't miss her. She knows she's wrong. I, like the hospital staff with whom she has worked so devotedly and tirelessly through these trying years of war, will miss her very much. She is a wonderful woman, a wonderful nurse, an inspiration to many. Her care for her patients has always been paramount, but her loyalty to the hospital and the staff here has been a very close second. Verity's devotion to duty has been inspirational and I know what help she has been to many an uncertain, insecure probationer nurse." She turned and looked at Verity who stood watching her, fighting back tears. "I know that in your new life you and your husband-to-be will continue to give yourselves to the community: Rex, whom we all remember and whose surgical skills we admire, as the general practitioner he has decided to be, and Verity, I believe, as assistant to him and his father in the dispensary."

"Choose the right poison!" came a cry again from the wag at the back of the hall and once again there was laughter.

"It is a very bright future you have, Verity, with your beloved Rex in a beautiful part of the country, the Yorkshire Dales. And don't be surprised if some of us contrive to cadge a holiday up there."

Matron looked towards a nurse who came forward and gave her a box which Matron presented to Verity. "This is something for your new home, a memento of your time at Charing Cross Hospital, from your colleagues and patients whom you have served so well."

Almost in tears, deeply moved, Verity stepped forward and carefully accepted the box. Matron, also rather emotional by now, got down from the chair and the two women embraced.

"Thank you, thank you all," Verity cried from the floor. "And you are all, all of you welcome any time you care to come . . . but not all at once," she added to fresh laughter.

Now that the formal part of the evening was over the crowd

of about forty women and ten or so men split up into small groups and Verity was surrounded by well-wishers who wanted to kiss her or press her hand.

It had been an emotional evening, the climax to an emotional week as the moment of departure drew near, and Verity began to make preparations for that momentous day: her wedding in two weeks' time.

It had, after all, been decided to have it in Bournemouth and to be married from Aunt Maude and Uncle Stanley's, a decision which had given them great pleasure. There had been fittings for the wedding dress, the bridesmaids' dresses: Addie, Peg and Stella. Ed was to be a page. Uncle Stanley would give her away and there was to be a reception in a marquee on the lawn. After that she and Rex were to honeymoon in Scotland before going to Yorkshire where they would live with his parents until the house was ready.

The banns had been read in church where she had been joined for one weekend by Rex, also busy coping with the influenza epidemic among soldiers, as well as preparing for his discharge from the army.

It had been such an exciting three months that it was a wonder there had been any room for work at all, but there had. The influenza epidemic had killed thousands, including two of the hospital staff, and people with respiratory problems and complications were still being admitted almost hourly into the hospital.

The party broke up before midnight. As she left, Verity was given the figurines from the top of the mock wedding cake carefully wrapped up in a napkin as a souvenir and, carrying these and the unopened present, she made her way back to her room with a couple of her close friends, Fanny Rice and Hilary Crabshaw, who had trained and served with her for the past four years, both of whom were to attend the wedding.

She would miss them a lot. Those late night chats after a day in the theatre or, in their cases, the wards where Fanny was a ward sister and Hilary, who had come a year later, a Staff Nurse.

Once in her room she removed the packing to reveal a beautiful cut-glass bowl on which had been engraved the words:

To Verity Carter-Barnes
on the occasion of her
marriage
from her friends and colleagues at
Charing Cross Hospital.

"Oh, isn't it *beautiful*," she exclaimed, holding it up to the light. "Oh it's *lovely*." She put it down carefully on the table in her room and they all stood back to admire it.

"I must be *very* careful of it," she said picking it up and examining it again. "It will have pride of place."

She gently replaced it on the table and flopped back on the bed.

"What a wonderful evening, a marvellous send-off. Thank you all so much."

She lay back on the bed and gazed at her two best friends who were looking at her mournfully.

"We shall miss you terribly, Verity."

"I'll miss you."

"You'll be too excited even to think of us."

She probably would, but she said loyally:

"I shall think of you every day. Don't imagine I don't have some misgivings about what I'm embarking on . . ."

"Oh, but you love Rex . . ."

"Of course I love him. It's not that. But I have enjoyed my career. I shall miss it. I am glad that Rex suggested I should help in the dispensary because I would lose touch completely. I should hate to be idle."

"I can't *ever* imagine you being idle, Verity," Hilary said with a smile. "That isn't you at all."

No she wouldn't be idle. There would be so much to do, plus a course in dispensing at the infirmary in Leeds which Dr Harvey had arranged for her.

"It will be your turn soon," she said slyly, but their only responses were downturned mouths.

"Some chance," Fanny said. And soon after that the girls left to retire to bed.

Verity, though tired, still felt restless. She wandered round picking up things and putting them down again, looking at her half-packed suitcase, examining the tiny figurines and the bowl, and imagining it filled with fruit on a sideboard in the pretty dining-room in their new house in Appleburn.

She thought about her friends and their prospects for marriage and she knew that, in many ways, the girls' final grimaces might have some justification.

So many men had been killed in the war that there would be a shortage for years to come. Many women of marriageable age would miss out altogether. She realised how lucky she was that Rex had come back safely. At least three of the nurses in the home had lost fiancés, one a husband and several had boyfriends who were missing or killed. If what had happened in the nurses' home was reflected throughout the country what hope had the masses of unmarried women who were left?

The next day was her last one on duty as Theatre Sister and every moment seemed precious and important to Verity, each act significant as she handed the instruments to the surgeons, or checked that the swabs had all been removed before the patient was sewn up. At the end of another tiring day she shook hands with the consultants and interns, also with the theatre staff, many of whom she embraced.

She removed her gown and mask and put them in the laundry bag for the last time.

She waited until everyone had left the theatre and, with a deep feeling of nostalgia, she wandered around making sure that everything was in place, as it should be and always had been during her tenure as Theatre Sister, ready now for her successor. She took a last glance round before she turned off the lights and closed the door behind her.

Verity walked across to the nurses' home thinking that by

this time tomorrow she would be on the train for Bournemouth. In a little over two weeks' time she would be a married woman. There was something very exciting about the prospect, now that it was so near, now that the die was finally cast and, yes, it *was* what she wanted. This evening she was spending packing and some of the girls would come to her room after supper for cocoa and a chat.

As she entered the hall a man standing with his back to the door, his hat in his hand, reading the notice board suddenly turned and she saw it was Rex. He came towards her with a diffident smile on his face.

"I see I startled you." He kissed her gently on the cheek.

"I wasn't expecting you . . ."

It should have been a nice surprise but somehow it wasn't. His smile didn't seem natural. It looked forced.

"You look tired," he said, then faltered. "Verity, is there somewhere we can talk?"

"Is something wrong?" she wanted to know, but he shook his head.

"Nothing wrong at all."

"We can go into the common room, but there's usually someone there."

"How about a walk along the Embankment?"

"If you like." She felt awkward, apprehensive, ill at ease. "I'll just go upstairs and take off my uniform."

Rex nodded and resumed his perusal of the notice board. She knew something was wrong. His attitude was artificial, diffident, apologetic. She quickly changed, put on a skirt and blouse and a coat on top, ran a comb through her hair and hurried downstairs.

Rex was waiting at the door and took her arm.

"I know there's something wrong," Verity protested as they crossed the Strand. "Tell me now."

"There is *nothing* wrong," Rex insisted between clenched teeth. "Just a change of plan."

They reached the Embankment, crossed to the river side and started walking in the direction of Cleopatra's Needle.

The atmosphere between them was strained and unnatural, reminding Verity of the time when Rex first came back from the war. Suddenly she stopped and searched his face.

"Tell me what it is."

Rex grasped her arm and, drawing her to the wall, leaned over it and gazed into the deep waters of the Thames.

"The wedding's off," Verity said in a flat, frozen voice.

Rex vigorously shook his head.

"No, the wedding is not off. It's not that at all. I'm merely suggesting we postpone it."

"*Postpone* it? And it is in two weeks' time!"

"The point is, Verity, that I am not ready to settle down." Rex ran a hand through his hair. "I am too restless. The thought of holing up in Yorkshire for the rest of my life appals me." Then, seeing her face, "Oh, don't misunderstand me. I will go there sometime, at least I expect I shall, but not yet. I am going to South Africa. I've booked my passage and I sail next week. There," an expression of relief flooded his face, "I've said it. Don't think it wasn't difficult and, Verity, I do love you and I hope you can try and understand."

"I find it very hard to understand." Verity, hands in her pockets and suddenly feeling desperately tired, sank back against the wall. "This must have been in your mind for some time Rex."

"No, it wasn't. It was quite recently. As I got my discharge and had my things forwarded to Yorkshire I thought 'I can't go through with this. I need to get away'."

"We could be married and go together, or is it me too?"

"Oh, no. It's not you, Verity. Definitely not you. I love you and I want you to be my wife. But I have to get away by myself first."

"And how long will you be away?"

"A year, two years. I'm going to travel in Africa."

"Don't you think you did enough travelling during the war?" She tried to keep the sarcasm out of her voice, but it was hard. "You told me you had had enough of wandering and wanted to settle down."

"Well, that's what I thought; but as I told you I'm not ready. I couldn't face it. Perhaps I'm not well. I don't know." His hand closed over hers. "I am very, very sorry, but it is not the end. If you still want me in two or three years' time then we can go ahead."

"It's three years now, is it?" Verity said bitterly. "I don't suppose you thought of me in all this? I'm leaving the hospital tomorrow. I've had a farewell party, a wedding gift."

"I'm sure they'd have you back."

A sense of real anger finally overwhelmed her.

"*That's* not the point, is it Rex? You may have worked all this out in your mind, but I haven't had the chance. Until a few moments ago I thought that in two weeks' time I would walk down the aisle as your wife. We would honeymoon in Scotland . . ." To her chagrin she began to weep, hot tears scalding her cheeks. "I really think you're the most *selfish* man . . ."

Rex awkwardly seized hold of her hand and tried to put an arm round her.

"I didn't think of it like that," he said contritely. "I am selfish, but I was also very confused. I have not recovered from the war. I came back a changed man. You saw it. My parents did. I should have said then how I feel now, which was that I didn't want to be trapped, not by you, not by marriage, but by force of circumstances. I just long to get away to a country which has no association with the war. There is no other woman in my life except you and I still want to share the rest of that life with you." He looked into her eyes but all he could see was burning resentment. "Please forgive me."

Verity angrily brushed the tears away from her cheeks, but forgiveness was not in her heart. Not at the moment. Maybe in time she would see things Rex's way and begin to understand. All she was conscious of now was that a crushing blow had been administered to her.

She thought of her friends at the nurses' home who, somehow, she had pitied because they had no man and she had. Now, whatever Rex said, she was in the same boat as they

147

were. Perhaps worse because they would think she had been jilted and feel sorry for her. Perhaps now she was being selfish too and rather petty.

"Your parents will be disappointed," she murmured.

"I've already told my father. It's the hardest thing I've ever had to do, apart from telling you. You know how he was looking forward to semi-retirement, fishing and so forth? But I think he did understand and I hope you will too. My darling . . ." he moved closer to her and let his lips linger on her cheeks. "I do love you and I want you. Before I go abroad . . . maybe?" He moved away and looked searchingly into her eyes.

Verity remembered what had happened to her sister. She had been cajoled into making love to a man who was to go away. Even if she was tempted to be as foolish as Addie, which she was not, Verity knew it would be wrong. It would also give the wrong message to Rex.

Instead she said with an edge to her voice:

"You could have had what you wanted in two weeks' time." With the tips of her fingers she gently pushed him away. "Now I'm afraid you'll have to wait a little longer."

The mêlée at the Tilbury Docks reminded her of Charing Cross Station during the war. There was the same noise, bustle and confusion, the cries of the porters, the groups of people clustered together saying tearful goodbyes. Even the smoke pouring from the funnels of the liner resembled the haze produced by the engines entering and leaving the station.

Verity was late and she looked round desperately for Rex, but he was nowhere to be seen.

Perhaps he had already gone aboard? She examined the faces peering over the rails, but it was impossible to make out one among so many. Then, in the distance she espied his father and mother and behind them came Rex, almost casually lighting a cigarette. As he threw away the match he looked up, saw her and waved, running ahead of his parents.

"I didn't think you were coming! I'd already gone aboard, but we came down looking for you."

"I was afraid I'd miss you. The train was late in at Waterloo."

He was smiling and cheerful and she thought he had never looked so well, certainly since he returned from the war. She gazed searchingly into his eyes and then said what had been locked up in her heart for the past week. "I feel I'm never going to see you again, Rex."

"Don't be silly," he said pecking her cheek. "As soon as I'm settled I'll send for you. Now that's a promise. How about it?"

"You never talked about 'settling' before."

She felt bitter and resentful as he had spent the past week with his parents not with her, yet still she had to come and see him to say "goodbye".

Rex looked behind at his parents standing tactfully a few yards away. "Verity I don't *know* exactly what I want. This is the purpose of the trip; to find out. But I'll write to you and—"

The liner gave a long blast and all those aboard could be heard being ordered to leave. People started pouring down the gangway and Rex turned to his father and mother and embraced each in turn. He and Verity again became separated by the crowd and there was no chance for a final kiss, but as he started to mount the gangway, making his way through those who were disembarking, he turned again and waved at her.

"I promise," he cried, barely making himself heard, "I promise."

Rex had scarcely got on board when the gangplank was raised and, as passengers lined the decks, the mooring ropes were cast adrift and the great liner began slowly to edge away from the dock.

Verity stood with Frances and James Harvey scanning the decks, but there was no sign of Rex.

However, they waved. Desperately they waved, and hundreds of fluttering hands waved back.

They stood for a long time as the liner, pulled by its tugs, slipped further downstream. Then, as the dockside crowds began to disperse, they turned away too.

"I'm sorry I was late," Verity said. "My train was late."

"Never mind, dear." Frances Harvey looked close to tears. "You saw him and that's the main thing." She put a hand on Verity's arm.

"I'm truly sorry. It must have been a shock for you. It was for us."

"I don't think he'll ever come back," Verity said, aware of a feeling of exasperation taking the place of resentment and grief. "Just now he talked of 'settling'. I thought he was going to travel?"

Dr Harvey had been lighting his pipe away from the breeze and now turned back to them. "I don't think Rex knows his own mind. I think it is best that he goes away for a while. The war has affected him too much. Once he's gone he'll realise his mistake and he'll soon be back."

They walked slowly towards the platform where a train was already standing by ready to take them back to London. Despite the crowds who had been there to see the boat off it was half empty as many still stayed behind to wave at the ship, even though the passengers could no longer see them and they could see nobody.

The three took seats in a third-class carriage and Verity thought how worn James and Frances looked, and how affected they too must have been by Rex's decision.

For a while each sat preoccupied with his or her own thoughts until the train steamed out of the junction.

James was the first to speak, looking at her kindly.

"What are you doing when you go back to London, Verity? Would you like a meal with us? We're staying at the Charing Cross Hotel. Are you going back to the hospital?"

Verity shook her head.

"I've left Charing Cross."

"You've *left*?"

"I'd handed in my notice. I thought you knew that. The day

150

Rex broke the news was my last day there. I couldn't face going back again and telling everyone."

"Then what are you going to do?"

"I'm applying for another post at another hospital. I've been at home for the past week busy cancelling all the wedding arrangements. My uncle and aunt were extremely upset. We had to write to all the guests who had had invitations, and send back all the presents . . ."

"But it is only a *postponement*."

Verity thought that from her tone Frances Harvey didn't sound very convinced.

"The guests still had to be told and the presents returned. The caterers had to be contacted, the vicar informed. I can't tell you what trouble it has caused. Naturally we said it was a postponement. But we don't *know* do we? Do we *really* know what is in Rex's mind?"

James Harvey, looking out of the window, sadly shook his head.

Verity realised then how devastated he must have felt and, leaning over, she touched his hand.

"I'm sure in time he *will* come back. He could have broken off the engagement and he didn't. After he has been away for a while he will see sense and want to come home. You're right. It's like a kind of brainstorm."

But his parents seemed as little convinced as Verity was in her heart, and for the rest of the journey she and James Harvey sat staring out of the window while Frances, who had looked very tired, appeared to doze.

When they reached London they once more stood on the platform looking a little lost and not quite knowing what to do.

"You're *sure* you won't come back to the hotel?" Frances enquired anxiously. "You'd be very welcome."

"No, I told my uncle and aunt I'd go straight back. They'll be expecting me. There's still quite a lot to do."

Frances impulsively seized her by the hand.

"We're very fond of you, you know, Verity. We do realise

how upsetting this must be for you, as it has been for us. But we know it's not the end and whether Rex returns here or stays in Africa he will, we are quite sure, always want to marry you." She leaned across and kissed her. "We wish you had been our daughter-in-law now, and that things had turned out as planned, but we remain hopeful for the future. We *must*." She squeezed her hand. "Please, please keep in touch, and come and stay."

"Oh, I will," Verity said and, realising she was once again on the point of tears and dreading making a fool of herself, she turned sharply away and walked quickly out of the station.

Eleven

C athy folded the paper on the kitchen table, removed her glasses and, leaning back in her chair, sighed deeply. The end of the war seemed to have solved nothing and left only chaos in its wake. Countries had been devastated and now they reckoned that as many people had died from the flu as had been killed in the war which had been over for nearly a year. One read about the Peace Conference in Paris and all the quarrelsome statesmen without understanding a word of it.

Cathy wondered how many people's lives had been blighted by the war, including hers, and for what?

She rose to make a cup of tea, enjoying the peace of the summer afternoon. Jenny was asleep in her pram in the garden and Cathy kept peeping out of the kitchen window to be sure she was all right.

Jenny who, despite Jack's threats, was still here, was her consolation. She was a laughing, bubbly, happy baby already toddling and had captured the hearts of everyone except Jack. Addie, who was teaching at a school in Bristol, made sure that her stepfather was out whenever she came to visit.

Addie now seemed quite happy for her daughter to be brought up by Cathy because it did give her more freedom and the chance she would not otherwise have had to pursue her career.

Cathy heard the sound of horses' hooves approaching the lodge and then stopping outside it. "This will be Miss Violet," she murmured to herself and, glancing out of the window, saw Lord Ryland's daughter dismount from her horse and go and take a peep at Jenny in her pram.

She bent down and gazed at her intently and then, looking up, saw Cathy and waved.

Wiping her hands on a cloth Cathy came to the door smiling.

"Nice afternoon, Miss Violet."

"It's lovely isn't it, Mrs Hallam? I was just admiring the baby. Is it yours?"

"Yes, Miss."

"I didn't know you had another child, Mrs Hallam." Violet looked surprised.

"She is the daughter of a relation, Miss, who couldn't afford to keep her. We have adopted her."

"How sad." Violet gazed at the baby in the pram. "But how lucky to have *you* as a mother."

"Kind of you to say so, Miss Violet. Not often we see you about, especially since . . . your fiancé was killed."

Momentarily Violet's face clouded. "Ted was killed just after Lydd. It was a double blow to the family."

"I'm very sorry, Miss Violet." Cathy gestured towards the kitchen. "I was just making a cup of tea. Would you like one?"

"I'd better get on with my ride. Beauty, my horse, is restless because I've been away so much and she misses me. By the way, how is Verity? I was sorry to hear that her marriage was off."

"Only postponed, Miss," Cathy said sharply. "Her fiancé has gone to Africa. He too was very affected by the war and didn't feel like settling down."

"But Verity's all right, is she?"

"Perfectly all right, and busy at work on her trousseau. Her fiancé thinks he might settle in South Africa and as soon as he sends for her, she'll be off."

"You'll miss her."

"I will, Miss Violet. We all will. They say it will only be for a while, but you never know do you?"

"And Addie?"

"Addie's teaching at a school in Bristol."

"I scarcely see anyone now," Violet said in an abstracted manner. "Without Lydd and Ted, my fiancé, life sometimes seems so purposeless. I keep moving around."

"You'll soon find a nice young man again," Cathy said comfortingly. "A pretty woman like you."

Violet smiled wistfully, shrugged her shoulders and returned to her horse, which was eating the grass by the side of the road then leaning over the fence and helping herself to the heads of the late delphiniums.

"Goodbye Mrs Hallam," she said as she remounted.

"Give my best to his lordship," Cathy replied. "And her ladyship, of course." Violet acknowledged her with her riding crop and rode on, and Cathy returned to the kitchen and finished brewing her tea, reflecting that when it came to grief and sorrow the nobility were affected as much as anyone.

It was no secret that Violet Ryland, who seemed so energetic and sporty and full of life, was said to have made an attempt at suicide after her fiancé, a lieutenant in the Guards, was killed, and had spent some time in a clinic.

She didn't look the sort to try and kill herself, Cathy thought, so brisk and practical, and very beautiful too, very like her brother Lydney. But now there was a sadness about her that had not been there before. She would surely find some other suitable man to marry before very long.

Cathy made her tea and took it into the garden where Jenny was still asleep. She had some time to herself with the baby until the children came home from school.

Jenny was stirring as Cathy came out and held out her arms to be picked up.

Cathy took her out of her pram and cuddled her for a few moments on her knee, but Jenny struggled to be put down and crawled away on the lawn, from time to time making awkward attempts to stand up. Then she would overbalance and fall down again.

Cathy was so preoccupied and amused by Jenny's struggles that she didn't notice a woman standing watching her until she coughed politely and Cathy looked up.

155

She was a good-looking woman of about thirty, dressed for travelling with a tight fitting two-piece costume and a large straw hat. She looked hot and tired as though she'd come a long way, and her body seemed to sag as she leaned against the garden fence.

"Excuse me," she said, "I wonder if you could help me?"

"What can I do for you?" Cathy asked politely, keeping an eye on the baby.

"I'm looking for Ryland Castle. Is that it?" She pointed up the road.

"That's it," Cathy said. "Is anyone expecting you?"

She could tell by the woman's clothes and her accent that she was not the class of person who would be a guest of the Ryland family.

"I'm seeking a Mr Hallam. He said he worked as a gardener to Lord Ryland."

"Then you've come to the right place," Cathy said, mystified. "This is his house."

The stranger looked startled and then from Cathy to the baby and back again.

"I'm his wife," Cathy went on. "Is there anything I can do for you?"

"His wife?" the woman gasped, attempting to stand upright.

"You'd better come in." Cathy opened the side gate. "I've just made a cup of tea."

Cathy went into the kitchen, followed by the woman who, however, remained in the doorway watching her.

"Is that your baby?" she enquired.

"Yes." Cathy turned to her, eyes narrowing. "Who are you?"

"Could I sit down?" The woman swayed and without waiting for an answer took the chair at the table where Cathy had sat reading the paper.

"My name is Blanche Thompson," she said. "I come from Blackpool."

"Ah!" Cathy turned and studied her intently. "Which is how you know my husband."

"I didn't know he was married." The woman shook her head, clearly on the verge of tears.

Keeping a careful eye on Jenny through the open door, Cathy sat down facing her by now unwelcome guest.

"Something went on between you in Blackpool, I suppose, during the war?"

Blanche Thompson nodded, dabbing at her eyes. "He said he'd send for me and I waited and waited. It's been over eight months and I began to feel desperate." Blanche gazed fearfully at Cathy. "We have a little boy, John. I was expecting, you see, to get married."

Cathy slumped on the table and put her head in her hands.

"The swine," she muttered. "The pig."

"How long have you been married?" Blanche asked in a broken voice.

"Fourteen years. We have two children of our own. In fact the baby isn't ours. It belongs to a relative and I'm bringing her up."

"Oh, I see." This seemed to relieve Blanche.

"It's just easier to say she's mine," Cathy said by way of explanation. "Stops people asking awkward questions."

Blanche nodded as if she understood.

"Jack will have quite a surprise when he sees you," Cathy said looking at the clock. "He should be home for his tea quite soon."

"Oh, I must go." Blanche got up, quickly swallowing her tea.

"No, please don't go," Cathy said pleasantly. "I think Jack should know you're here and we can find out what he's going to do about you and your son. It's only fair. Now you look all in, you're in no state to go anywhere, so why don't you go and have a little rest in one of the children's rooms and I'll tell Jack you're here? I will be very interested to see his reaction."

Blanche looked puzzled. "You're a very funny woman," she said, "the way you've taken this. It's as if you didn't care."

"Oh, I care," Cathy said grimly. "I care about you and your son, both of whom he seems to have shockingly neglected."

There was an enticing smell of freshly baked cake as Jack, wiping his feet and removing his cap, stepped into the kitchen and attempted to put his arm around Cathy who was standing at the stove preparing the evening meal. She gave him a sharp tap with her heavy wooden spoon and with an oath he removed it.

"There seems no pleasing you," he grumbled.

"There's someone to see you, Jack," Cathy said in an even voice without turning. "A lady."

At that moment there was a movement by the door and, looking over her shoulder, Cathy saw Blanche who, on seeing Jack looked as though she was about to retrace her footsteps. She had removed her hat and combed her hair and looked less stressed, but at this moment her expression was one of terror.

"What the hell are you doing here?" Jack said angrily going towards her and, as she turned in the doorway, he grabbed hold of her arm and dragged her back into the room. She put up a hand to try and defend herself as he struck her several times across the face and shoulders. "How *dare* you come here and disturb my peace?"

As the unfortunate woman cowed beneath his blows Cathy rushed over to him and began to hit him with her wooden spoon, whereupon he turned on her, leaving Blanche to fall on the floor.

Cathy dropped her spoon and she and Jack began to fight with each other like wrestlers when Peg appeared at the door holding a hand to her mouth in horror at the sight confronting her; one adult on the floor, two fighting like alley cats scratching and clawing at each other.

"Stop, stop," she cried plunging into the mêlée while behind her Ed and Stella watched the proceedings with grim fascination, eyes as round as saucers.

Peg tried to disentangle the warring pair as her mother was clearly getting the worst of it, though she was clasping Jack's hair as if with the intention of pulling it out by the roots and he was yelping with pain.

Finally the sight of Peg vainly tugging at her parents, and in danger of getting hurt herself, seemed to bring both adults to their senses and they stopped, drawing apart with grunts and moans and retreating to their corners like wounded gladiators.

By this time Blanche was lying face down on the floor sobbing hysterically.

"Your father," Cathy panted pointing to Peg, "is a liar and an adulterer and don't you forget what you saw and heard here today."

"He is *not* my father," Peg said robustly.

"Well you treat him like a father. You'll know better now."

At that moment Cathy appeared to notice for the first time the younger children standing by the door, looking lost and bewildered. She ran up to them and putting an arm around each led them from the room, telling them to go upstairs and not come down until they were called.

Jenny, who had been lying peacefully in her pram while Cathy got the tea, started to bawl and Jack roared "get the bastard out of here".

"Who are *you* to talk about bastards?" Cathy snapped briskly, applying a wet towel to the side of her face where a large bruise had started to swell up. "You've a bastard of your own I hear. That's what she says."

"How do I know it's mine? She was a whore when I met her."

Blanche painfully drew herself to her feet and looked as though she was about to try and summon the strength to start hitting Jack all over again. Instead, overcome with weakness, she was scarcely able to stagger across to a chair on which she flopped.

"I was *not* a whore," she protested, "and you were the only man I went with after you started courting me. You know full well that John is your son and you promised to marry me. You said you'd send for me after your discharge and all you did was

159

tell lies and make promises you never intended to keep. And I hate you Jack Hallam, and wish to God I'd never met you."

It had seemed a long winter, Verity thought, as she sat by her bedroom window looking out at the desolate garden still partially covered after a light fall of snow. It was now nine months since Rex had sailed away from Tilbury and an adventurous life he'd led since, travelling through Africa. But now he had finally arrived in Nairobi, according to him a bustling, thrusting town much beloved by Colonial expatriates and apparently in need of more doctors.

He had told her he had decided to settle there and wrote enthusiastically about the place, hoping she would approve. The climate was wonderful, the scenery spectacular and there was lots of good company as ex-service officers like him had decided to go to Africa in search of adventure and some had settled. Many had wives or fiancées who were about to join them, as he hoped Verity eventually would.

Rex had told her he was in the process of buying a house and in no time would be sending for her.

It was February 1920 and a lot had happened since the previous spring. Verity had got a job as a ward sister in the American Hospital in London and, having worked over Christmas, now had a fortnight's leave.

There had been letters with Rex's accounts of his travels, much more animated than his missives from the war, which had made her dare to hope he was recovering. They were not intimate letters, and he never said he missed her. They were rather like travel guides full of descriptions of places. But that was Rex's style and always had been. He was no romantic.

However, this was positive, and therefore good. On the bad side there had been chaos at home when an ex-girlfriend of Jack's had turned up and there had been a free-for-all at the lodge which Lord Ryland got to hear about.

The result was that Jack had been summarily dismissed and had gone north with his paramour. As the lodge was needed for the new head gardener Lord Ryland had lent Mother and the children a small cottage on the estate until she could find something permanent.

It was far from satisfactory and a worry to know what to do about Mum who had the burden of a small child as well as the older ones, and very little money apart from what she made helping out at the castle. Lord Ryland's bounty didn't extend to letting her have the cottage rent free.

Verity sighed. If only he knew it was harbouring his grandchild – what would his attitude have been then? But no one dared tell him. Mum had too much pride and, besides, she needed somewhere to live. In any case, the chance was that Lord Ryland would not believe her, although Jenny's colouring was exactly the same as his son's, and the probability was that as she grew older she would resemble him more.

There were imponderables to reflect on here, always a nagging concern at the back of her mind, coupled with the fact that one day she would no longer be near Mum but thousands of miles away, with no knowing when she would see her again.

With these worrying thoughts on her mind Verity cut the threads of silk on the sheet she had been embroidering for her trousseau. Already she had sent some parcels to Kenya so that there would be a chance they would be there before her arrival: bed linen, tablecloths, napkins, runners, antimacassars, beautiful lawn nightdresses.

It gave her something to do during her off-duty hours, and she would think about the future and wonder what sort of place it was in which she and Rex seemed destined to settle, and just when that would be.

The door opened and Aunt Maude popped her head round.

"Shall I bring you tea, dear, or would you like to have it downstairs with me?"

"I'll come and join you," Verity said jumping up. "There," she spread her hands across the beautiful linen sheet on which she had been embroidering blue forget-me-nots. "Isn't that pretty?"

"Very pretty, dear," Aunt Maude nodded approvingly. "You are a very clever girl and you never waste a moment. Rex is going to be a very lucky man."

She bent forward to kiss her and Verity put her hand against Aunt Maude's cheek for a moment.

"I am very blessed in every way," she said, "to have Rex and to have you and Uncle. But," she got up and looked rather sadly at her aunt, "I am so sorry the wedding is not to be here. Both you and Rex's parents will be so disappointed."

"We are, and I hate thinking of you going into something as important as marriage with no one close to you by your side."

"Rex says he has made some very good friends. There are lots of British expatriates there, all dying to meet me, he says. But, Aunt, to come back to England is such an expense and he has so much to do."

"I know, my dear. I know." Aunt Maude looked at her watch. "Uncle Stanley is a bit late. Let's have our cup of tea without him, shall we?"

In the winter Uncle Stanley, who was getting on, usually left the office early and came home for afternoon tea. Then he would spend a few hours before dinner in his study with his specimens and sometimes when Verity was home she would help him.

"I'm dying for a cup," Verity said with a smile and, her arm round her aunt's waist, they went downstairs into the sitting-room where Doris was putting out the tea things.

"I envy you going to Kenya in a way," Aunt Maude said as she began to pour from the large silver teapot. "I am going to try and persuade Stanley to let us have a holiday there next year. It will be most exciting."

Verity's eyes lit up. "Oh, do you think he would? That would be *wonderful.*"

"I only wish we could be there for the wedding."

"But why not?" Suddenly Verity sounded excited. "You could sail out with me. Oh, that's an idea!"

Maude's expression was one of doubt. "I don't *think* that will be possible, dear, not to arrange at such short notice. I mean Rex does say this spring, doesn't he?"

"Or the summer." Now it was Verity's turn to look doubt-ful. "He's not quite sure."

162

That was the trouble with Rex. He would keep on changing his mind.

Seeing her worried expression Maude looked at her with concern.

"You are *sure*, dear, aren't you?"

"Sure?" Verity blinked at her.

"About Rex. He has led you a bit of a dance."

"Rex got off relatively lightly in the war, Aunt," Verity said defensively. "You have no idea how many men have been mentally as well as physically maimed by it. We see scores of them in the hospital. Rex was a very different man when he came back from the war to the one who went off to it. I don't think he did know his own mind, but I'm sure he does now." She looked boldly at her aunt. "And so do I. I have no doubts at all about his love for me or mine for him."

Stanley Carter's feet seemed to drag as he walked up the long tree-lined road towards his house, getting slower and slower as he neared the gate where he stood for some time gazing around at the wintry, snow-covered garden and thinking about all the larvae incubating for the winter. He opened the gate at long last and walked slowly up the garden path towards the house, which was set well back from the road so that this took some time. When he arrived at the front door he delayed again in producing his key, fitting it into the lock and pushing open the door.

The warmth of the house hit him, as well as the fragrant smell of cake baking and bread making, inviting a sense of well-being that he was far from feeling.

It seemed like the happy, cosy intimate homecoming he was used to, and the fact that Verity was spending her leave with them would have made it just perfect, were it not for . . .

Uncle Stanley shook his head, sighed, removed his coat, threw his hat on the hallstand and, picking up the paper which he'd carried in his hand, opened the door into the drawing-room. There he was greeted with relaxed smiles by the two women sitting in front of the fire drinking tea.

"Stanley, dear," Maude said rising from her chair to pour him a cup, "you're a little late." She looked at him curiously. "Is all well, dear? You seem a bit down."

Stanley didn't immediately reply but looked round carefully as though to find just the right place to sit, and then he sank into a chair next to Verity who was also gazing at him with some concern.

"Don't you feel well, Uncle?"

"Verity, my dear," Stanley glanced up at Maude who was handing him his tea, and took the cup with murmured thanks, "there is no point in beating about the bush. I'm afraid I have something rather unpleasant to tell you." He produced the newspaper which he had carried into the room with him and folded it.

Both Verity's hands flew to her breast. "Uncle, don't say something has happened to Rex!"

"Rex is perfectly all right," Stanley said hurriedly, "I do assure you of that. There is nothing wrong with his health as far as I know but, my dear, you must prepare yourself for a shock." And he thrust into Verity's hands *The Times* newspaper opened at the social page.

"If you look under 'Forthcoming Marriages', you will see what I mean."

Stanley kept his finger on a place in the paper and after Verity had taken it from him she scanned the lines indicated. She then read them over and over again as if she couldn't believe her eyes.

DR R. E. HARVEY AND MISS E. M. HANCOCK. The engagement is announced, and the marriage will take place shortly in Nairobi, between Rex Edward, only son of Dr and Mrs James Harvey of Appleburn, Yorkshire, England and Esther Mary, elder daughter of Mr and Mrs Reginald Hancock of Trafalgar Road, Seapoint, Cape Town.

Verity put the paper on her lap and leaned towards the fire holding out her hands to warm them. Meanwhile Maude gently removed the paper and also read the contents that had caused such consternation.

"Had you *any* idea?" Stanley asked at last.

"None at all."

"It *is* Rex," Maude murmured as if she too couldn't believe her eyes. "I mean *our* Rex?"

"Oh, it's our Rex all right," Verity said bitterly. "There can hardly be two Dr Rex Harveys with parents living in Appleburn."

"When did you last hear from Rex?" Uncle Stanley held out his cup for more tea.

"About a month ago. The post does take some time from Nairobi. I was expecting another letter."

"And there was no . . ." Maude finished lamely, not liking to put the exact question.

"No there was no mention of another person," Verity said sharply. "He told me the purchase of the house was progressing satisfactorily and . . . she stopped and choked, kneading her hands together. "I think perhaps I'd better go to my room and try and compose myself."

As she got up Maude held out her arms and Verity fell into them.

"Don't hold back your tears," Maude commanded gently. "Have a good cry. We don't mind, do we Stanley?"

"Of course not," Stanley said gruffly, looking on the verge of tears himself. "I can't believe it of someone like Rex. Always so honourable."

"Not always *so* honourable," Verity burst out, violently blowing her nose. "Rex has always used the war as an excuse for his behaviour; but what excuse does he have for *this*? How can he possibly explain putting an announcement in the papers before letting me know? Shell-shock? I think not. Maybe I should call it cowardice without the excuse of being under fire?"

The letter was waiting for her when she got back to the hospital a few days later. In fact it had probably arrived the day she left. There were several other letters with it, and

165

after she got to her room these she opened first of all, but they were unimportant.

The really important one she hesitated to open, studying it with some care, turning it this way and that between her fingers. The postmark was well over a month old. Perhaps he had thought it would get here more quickly, that and the two weeks she had been away – six in all – would seem like enough time before the announcement in the papers. It was the only way to excuse him.

Swiftly Verity slit the envelope and drew out a single page written in Rex's typical doctor's scrawl.

> "My dear Verity," he began (no change there. It never had been "Darling" or "Dearest").
>
> This is a very hard letter to write, so I will make it brief. I have met a young woman with whom I have fallen instantly and madly in love. Her name is Esther Hancock and I have asked her to marry me. I met her at the house of some new friends I've made in Nairobi with whom she was staying. She is South African and was holidaying with them.
>
> I know how upset you will be about this and I can't tell you how sorry I am, Verity, and there was no easy way to tell you this. I think that with Esther I can begin a new life in a fresh country. In many ways you were too much part of my past with its unpleasant associations, though of course you couldn't help this. I do assure you of my continued high regard of you, and hope you will forgive me. I wish you all the best for the future.
>
> Yours sincerely,
>
> Rex.

Somehow it was the detached nature of the letter, the sense that she was being blamed ("you were part of my past", in other words lumped together with the destruction caused by the war), the lack of any real feeling, above all the impersonal "Yours sincerely" that hurt most of all.

It was then in the privacy of her room that all the rage, all the anger, resentment and sadness came cascading to the fore in a gigantic explosion, and she did what Aunt Maude had suggested: at long last she broke down and wept.

Twelve

The small group huddled around the grave, their eyes following the progress of the coffin as it was gently lowered into the ground. The vicar, prayer-book in hand, tossed a handful of earth which landed on the brass plate inscribed with the words:

Joseph Matthew Swayle
1841–1921

Grandfather had been a good age, Verity thought as she took her place in the line and, in turn, cast her handful of earth on the coffin.

Ashes to ashes, dust to dust.

As the vicar had said, there was a time for every purpose under heaven, a time to be born and a time to die.

Verity had always been religious and took the practice of her duties as a Christian seriously. She felt that her deep faith had helped sustain her during the war when she had had to help deal with so many terrible injuries, especially to young men, many of them teenagers, who would never again lead normal lives.

It had also helped her to survive the shock of Rex breaking off the engagement, the practical realisation that with the shortage of men it could mark the end of her hopes of marriage and family. It might be pessimistic to feel this way but it was sensible too. She had known she was lucky to have Rex, and common sense told her he would be hard to replace. Maybe that was why she had put up with his excuses, his changes of mood and, finally, she realised, his lies, because she was frightened of losing him.

Having lost him she had spent no time in self-recrimination, mourning for a lost love, wondering what might have been, but had resolved to fill her life with work. The part of the trousseau which had not been packed off to Kenya was carefully wrapped in paper and placed in a trunk which was put in Aunt Maude and Uncle Stanley's lumber room to await – who knew what? Would it ever again see the light of day?

If she was not to be married, now or ever, she was resolved to become a very good nurse. She had applied to train as a midwife so that even if she never became a mother she could help to bring children into the world. She had not worked it out that way but, she supposed, broadly that was the logic behind it.

Above all, her religion had given her stoicism because she genuinely believed that whatever happened it was according to God's plan.

This air of detachment, even serenity, instead of attracting people helped to keep them away, and now at the reception after the funeral of her grandfather she was rather a lonely figure in a room full of people, knowing very few of the mourners. There were relations there whom she scarcely knew either, mainly Swayles, as her grandmother had been an only child: Swayles, who mostly had come in from remote farms and whom she only knew by sight. There were younger members of the family there whom she didn't know at all.

Verity had never been very close to her grandparents, apart from a few dutiful visits a year when she lived with Aunt Maude and Uncle Stanley. According to her grandmother, ever since her marriage to Uncle Stanley, Maude had developed airs and graces, forgetting that she was a farmer's daughter, and considering herself to be a cut above farming folk. Grandma spoke with a broad Dorset accent whereas only a trace remained in Maude's cultured tones, and Verity's speech had no dialect vowels in it at all.

They were not a united family, Verity thought. The two daughters had not been close to their mother and father, or each other. Had it been a mistake for Aunt Maude to have adopted her? Did she regret it now?

Sometimes she did, for one of the results had been that there was a distance between her and her siblings. It was true that Addie had confided in her about the baby, but she felt she scarcely knew Peg, Stella or Ed, who was now a tall, good-looking youth of fifteen, and apparently a first-class scholar who had won a scholarship to the grammar school. Ed was there in a dark suit, with a mop of black curly hair, looking very like Jack. It seemed that was where the resemblance ended, because he was considered a boy who was thoughtful and conscientious, attributes that could never be ascribed to Jack.

People were taking their seats at the tables for the proper sit-down lunch that Grandmother had insisted upon. The room was filling up, men coming back from the bar with tankards of beer in their hands.

"We're on the top table," Aunt Maude, looking very severe in black, hissed in her ear. "I put you next to Peg because you hardly ever see her."

"Good idea." Verity smiled at her aunt. "I see she doesn't lack admirers." Peg had been in a corner of the room entertaining, or being entertained, by a group of young men dressed in their best with shining smooth-shaven faces and sleeked back hair.

"I think she's having too good a time to want to sit with me."

"Peg needs direction," Aunt Maude said crisply. "Else what happened to Addie might well happen to *her*. I worry about Peg, she's too pretty for her own good."

Cousin Arthur Swayle, who was one of Grandfather's many nephews, made an announcement from the middle of the floor inviting the guests to take their seats. Once everyone had sorted themselves out, the immediate family on the top table, the vicar said grace and waitresses appeared from the wings and started to serve a substantial and nourishing meal.

At the last moment Peg sidled into her place next to Verity and gave her a shy smile.

"I see you're popular," Verity smiled back shaking out her napkin. "Did you know all these young men?"

Peg shook her head. Maybe Aunt Maude was right, Verity thought, and Peg needed guidance. She was indeed a very pretty girl, tall and willowy with her long fair wavy hair and china-blue eyes, just like Billy, her mother had always said, and with Billy's temperament too: happy-go-lucky, a heart stealer.

Peg looked beautiful even in funereal black with her hat squashed well down over her head. On her other side sat Ed and next to him a young Swayle cousin. Next to Aunt Maude sat Addie, also looking quite forbidding in black as she now wore spectacles and her expression remained severe.

Peg felt rather shy in the presence of her elder sister, shy and a little tongue-tied. To her she was this incredibly romantic figure who had been crossed in love. She had been studying her surreptitiously across the room while pretending to be absorbed by the young men surrounding her, and was secretly pleased to be sitting next to her.

Peg was a romantic who scribbled stories in her room at night. She harboured a dream of being another Charlotte Brontë, the author of some powerful tale of passion and adventure. To her, her elder sister was a perfect subject for a tale of doomed love; the handsome doctor who sailed away eventually to find someone else, leaving his abandoned fiancée to mourn.

Only, somehow, that picture didn't quite fit Verity who had shown few outward signs of grief if, indeed, she felt any at all. Peg, with her writer's curiosity, would love to have known what exactly was behind her sister's impenetrable mask.

"Will you be coming home tonight?" Peg asked Verity, "or will you be staying with Aunt Maude?"

Verity looked at her sister's eager young face and caught her breath. Really she saw so little of her she felt she hardly knew her. It was quite wrong when only eight years separated them. In her excitement about her new life, the prospect of living overseas, she had neglected her family. There was something solemn and touching about the expression on Peg's face, her obvious desire to be with her.

"I *was* going to stay with Aunt Maude, but would you like me to come and stay with you?"

Peg nodded her head enthusiastically. "Mum is staying with Gran. We have to go to school tomorrow."

Verity looked concerned. "Then how are you getting home?"

Peg pointed to a man with a red face tucking into an enormous plate of food at the next table.

"Frank is taking us. He's now Lord Ryland's chauffeur. He lent us his car for the day."

"That was very nice of Lord Ryland."

"Frank is very nice too. I think he likes Mum."

"Oh, really?" Verity looked amused.

"He said he'd do anything for her. Mum says he's a foolish fellow. But I think she likes him too."

Verity laughed. She felt suddenly very close to this sister who so obviously craved her company. She felt guilty and flattered and determined to make it up to all the younger ones. Addie obviously now was doing well in her life and had managed to put the past behind her, as Verity had. She felt in a way they owed this to Mum, whose resilience and fortitude had somehow inspired them; a strong, yet somehow broken bough whose spirit, however, remained unbroken.

"Let's ask Frank to take us home as soon as we've finished," she murmured. "I'd very much like to spend some time with you."

After the lunch speeches in honour of the deceased man droned on for about an hour, there were prolonged goodbyes. Verity stood about for some time greeting those relatives she hadn't seen for years or whom she was meeting for the first time. There were promises, which would clearly never be fulfilled, to meet again before too long.

Gran, who had been very dignified throughout the long drawn out procedures, looked tired. She was, after all, seventy-seven. She told Verity that she wished she could have stayed with her mother to support her. However Aunt Maude said that she was staying, and Verity was needed by the younger ones. Gran agreed the younger ones needed someone with them. She responded warmly to Verity's embrace and told her to come and see her soon.

Another promise made.

There was a lot more kissing, toing and froing, a few tears, before people began to disperse. The funeral had been at the parish church not far from Swayles' farm and most people lived locally. Like all good funerals the wake turned into an occasion for partying and there was laughter and even sounds of merry-making. Some, who had drowned their sorrows too thoroughly, went off staggering down the main street supported by those not quite so inebriated.

At last Verity with Peg, Ed and Stella climbed into Lord Ryland's handsome car and, waving frantically from the back window to the crowd still gathered outside the pub, were driven off.

After supper the children were sent protesting to bed. Ed, at fifteen, considered himself a man and Stella, although two years younger, felt very grown up too. However, it had been a long day and it was school tomorrow. Peg was in her last term and, at eighteen, was given the privilege of staying up late with her eldest sister of whom they saw so little that it was almost like having a stranger in the house.

Besides, it was not often that she had the chance to be alone with Verity, and Peg wanted to talk to her.

The two older sisters washed up and then, with mugs of cocoa in their hands, regenerated the dull embers of the fire until they had a fresh blaze going. Each sat on either side looking into the flames.

"I hope Jenny is all right with Mrs Capstick," Verity said anxiously. "Does she often stay with her?"

"Not often because Mum is hardly ever away; but she is

very fond of Jenny, very good with her. Jenny will be absolutely all right," Peg said reassuringly, her words followed by a long pause. She finished her cocoa and put the empty mug down carefully on the hearth.

"I know Jenny is Addie's baby," she burst out as if the knowledge had been repressed inside her for some time as, indeed, it had. "She isn't just the baby of some relative, as Mum says. She's Addie's. I've known for ages."

Verity looked at her encouragingly, saying nothing because she knew there was more to come.

"How can you have a baby without being married?" Peg said at last and slowly her cheeks reddened.

Verity realised that despite her grown-up air, her flirtatious manner with the young men at the funeral, Peg was confused. Although she was a country girl used to seeing animals copulating it was difficult to separate the facts of animal procreation from the ideal of human love and babies.

"It is desirable but not necessary to be married for a man and a woman to sleep together."

Peg looked puzzled.

"But sleeping isn't enough," Verity went on realising that the task of explaining the facts of human sexuality to her younger sister was more difficult than she had imagined it would be. However, she persisted and at the end of a quarter of an hour or so all had been revealed. It was obvious that Peg knew part – although most of that was surmise – but not all.

At the end of it her cheeks were redder than ever.

"Is that what was going on with all that noise when Mum and Jack slept in the same room?"

Verity nodded. "Yes I suppose so. It isn't always a happy experience, especially if people don't love each other. It has to be wanted by both parties. Then I am told, it can be sublime."

She stopped abruptly as if aware of how much she was giving away about herself.

"Did you and Rex . . .?"

Verity firmly shook her head. "Rex and I didn't sleep together. Sometimes I wish we had, but don't let that give you ideas. I thought that Rex and I would be married, and he did want to."

"Then why didn't you?"

"Because I believe that despite what he might have said to get his own way a man doesn't really respect a woman if she gives herself too easily, and I knew it was not for the best."

"But later you did regret it . . . after Rex . . ." Peg left the sentence unfinished.

Verity finished it for her, a trace of bitterness in her voice.

"After Rex jilted me, you mean? Yes and no. I wondered if it would have made him love me more, given us a closer bond? But then if he had still called off the marriage I might have thought it was because I had cheapened myself in his eyes. He'd lost his respect for me. So I'm glad I didn't, but I shall never know for sure."

She lightly touched Peg's head. "You mustn't condemn your sister either. I'm sure Addie loved Lydney Ryland and he loved her. He was going away to the war and she did what she thought was best. Maybe it was, and Jenny is a lovely baby . . ." She stopped as she realised that Peg was looking at her aghast.

"Lydney Ryland was the father of Jenny?"

"Oh?" Now Verity looked surprised. "Who did you think it would be?"

"I didn't know. We never talked about it. Addie doesn't know that I know to this day. She went to stay with Aunt Maude for months. We didn't know why. I knew she was sweet on Lydney, but never that. I thought it was someone in Bristol who she met through the college."

"You must keep it to yourself then," Verity said gently. "This sort of knowledge must stay in the family. Now," She poked the fire to stir the embers which flickered into life, "we must go to bed soon. It's getting late and you have to go to school too."

"Do you *have* to go tomorrow?" Peg asked appealingly.

"Yes I do, after Mum comes back. I have to be on duty at seven the following morning."

Peg twisted her hands awkwardly in her lap.

"I thought I would like to be a nurse . . . but now I think perhaps I'd like to be a journalist."

"A journalist!" Verity looked astonished. "That's a funny thing to want to be."

"Why is it funny?" Peg asked defensively.

"Well, I don't know, really. It seems a funny thing for a woman to want to do. Are there many women journalists?"

"A few and I don't know why there shouldn't be more."

"But what gave you this idea in the first place?"

To her chagrin Verity realised more and more how little she knew of her younger sister, in effect how much she had failed her.

"I do write," Peg announced shyly. "I like writing stories."

"I'd love to read some. Have you got any you could show me?"

Peg looked doubtful. "You might laugh."

"I would never laugh, I promise you. I would probably be impressed."

"I thought, you see, you could talk to Mum about me being a journalist. She wants me to be a teacher. She wants us all to teach. She thinks it's the most respectable thing you can be, apart from being a nurse, or a doctor and that's beyond us. She hopes Ed will teach and Stella will teach. I'm next."

"Then give me your stories to read tonight," Verity said, "and if I like them I promise that when she comes home tomorrow I'll have a serious talk with Mum."

Verity lay awake until after two in the morning reading the closely written pages that had been reluctantly given to her by her sister. Their maturity and seeming breadth of adult experience amazed her, especially coming from a young woman who had protested she didn't know the facts of life. There was nothing salacious or explicit about them, but they were all about love and unrequited love, about desire and rejection, about loss and growing up in the country and a love of beasts and flowers.

They were astonishingly resourceful and imaginative, poignant and sad. As far as she could tell they were also very well written for such a young woman.

To have nourished such a gift and let no one know was also a source of wonder to Verity. She was heavy-eyed when she put the pages down by the side of her bed and wondered how many other hidden talents, secrets such as Addie's, had been suppressed by members of a family apparently so inhibited, despite the great love they had for one another? Could it perhaps be put down to the terrible secrets that Mum had tried to hide from them all about the undoubted torments of her married life with Jack?

Would it have been better to have unburdened herself, told everything and shared it with the family? And was not she, Verity, herself heir to that tradition of concealment caused by an overwhelming sense of embarrassment and shame?

"I'll come often, Mother," Cathy said kissing her mother warmly on both cheeks.

"Make sure that you do," her mother pressed her arm and gazed solemnly into her eyes. "And take care of yourself Cathy, I worry about you."

"There's no need to worry, Mother, I am perfectly well able to look after myself."

"I sometimes wonder," Sarah Swayles said sadly, "if you did right to keep Addie's child. She might have been better off and less of a burden for you if . . ."

Cathy sternly held up a hand. "Don't even *say* it, Mother. I would never have allowed her to be adopted. I love her as my own and she is well looked after."

"Yes, but is Addie a good mother too? How often does she see her?"

"She is as good as she can be in the circumstances," Cathy said cautiously. "She loves the child, no doubt about that, but she now sees what a burden she would have had to carry if she hadn't left her with me. She cares for Jenny very much and provides for her. Her daughter lacks for nothing. No, there is no need to worry about me, Mother. I shall survive. I always have."

"I wish I could let you have some money, but your father left very little. I know that. We sold up the farm and the stock and now all we have left is this house. That is pretty much all there is. When I go it will be yours. Maude is well enough provided for. But you'll have to wait for that."

"But you are not going to go for a long time, Mother. You are well and strong and I don't want you to go."

"I shall miss Joseph," her mother sighed sadly, putting a handkerchief to her eyes. "I still can't believe he's gone."

"I'll come next week, Mother. I'll come regularly."

Cathy turned as she heard a hoot from outside and hurried towards the door. Opening it she found Frank, his amiable face beaming, on the doorstep.

"Ready, Cathy?"

"I'm just saying 'goodbye' to my mother, Frank. I'll be with you in a second."

"Right you are." Frank lit a cigarette while Cathy went back indoors to emerge again in a few moments with her mother and carrying her overnight bag, which Frank took from her, to stow in the boot of the car.

Then he shook hands with Sarah Swayles, offering her once again condolences on her loss.

Mother and daughter embraced. Cathy got into the car and Frank drove slowly away while Cathy's hand fluttered from the window. Looking after her rather wistfully, Sarah waved back. "I do worry about my mum," she said to Frank. "I wish I lived nearer."

"I'll take you there any time you want, you know that, Cathy." Frank glanced sideways at her.

"It's very *kind* of you, Frank. And of Lord Ryland to let you use the car. I do appreciate it."

Once more she looked round the capacious interior of the automobile gleaming with brass and soft, polished leather. "It *is* lovely. I bet you wish it was yours, Frank."

Frank laughed. "Not this perhaps, but I aim one day to

have my own motor car. This is the transport of the future and very soon ordinary people like me will be able to afford one. Tell me how did you find your mother?"

"As well as can be expected, seeing that we only buried my father yesterday. Of course there's only me and my sister, which is the worry, but my father came from a large family and all his nephews and nieces will gather round to help Mum. Still," Cathy gave a wan smile, "there's no one quite like a daughter, is there Frank?"

"I suppose not," Frank said. "Though never having had children myself I wouldn't know."

Cathy looked at him curiously.

"Why did you never marry, Frank?"

"No one would have me," he said gruffly. "I didn't think I was the marrying sort. I've always been shy and awkward with women. Not what you'd call handsome, a ladies' man, Cathy."

"That's what's nice about you, Frank." Cathy settled more comfortably in her seat. "You're a restful man to be with."

Frank coughed and looking in his mirror to be sure there was no traffic behind him, he drew up by the side of the road and stopped the car.

"Cathy," his complexion began to go a dull red from the neck up, "do you really mean that?"

"Mean what, Frank?" Cathy looked taken aback.

"What you said about me being restful to be with."

"Of course, I mean it."

"Because," Frank's voice went a little hoarse, "I do like you very much. Very, very much. I don't know really how to ask you this, never having done it before, and I know it's not really the right time just after your father's funeral, but . . ." his voice finally dried up altogether and he stopped.

Cathy gazed at him wide-eyed and made no effort to help him.

Frank loudly cleared his throat and began again: "The thing I'm saying, Cathy, is . . . might you consider, in time of course, marrying me? I know I'm no catch and I'm certainly not worthy of you, and it's not a good time to ask with your

179

father just buried, but I am very, very fond of you. I know you will want time to make up your mind and think about it, ask your children, and I know . . ."

"Stop, stop, Frank," Cathy said, laughingly seizing his arm. "Stop and get your breath." She patted her own chest. "I'm quite out of breath myself. This has come as a surprise to me, Frank, a shock but I want to tell you I am very honoured that you should ask me. But you know I am still married to Jack."

"I know that Cathy, but it's something you might want to end."

"We both want to end it, and I certainly have grounds. Jack has another baby with Blanche, but it is so expensive to get a divorce that it's out of the question at the moment."

"I'd offer to pay if it would help."

"Oh, but you *couldn't*."

"I could. I am a bachelor and have saved most of what I earned over the years. I would gladly help and there would be no strings attached. I mean it would not be a condition that you then had to marry me, only if you wanted to."

"There would be no chance for you of children, you know." She looked at him closely.

"I know that," he nodded. "That's not what I want. I want you and I would be a father to little Jenny. She and I like each other very much."

Cathy leaned towards him and spontaneously kissed him on the cheek. "You are such a nice man, Frank, a *good* man, and I promise to give it very serious thought." She drew away and looked up at him. "I'm very fond of you too, you know, though it might surprise you to learn it."

Verity wondered that her mother coming straight from her father's funeral should seem almost to run into the house with a light step, a smile on her face. Always slightly envious of her mother's looks – and wishing they'd been passed on to her – she thought now that she appeared very much younger than her forty-seven years and, really, quite beautiful with her soft brown hair, deeply recessed brown eyes and soft, warm skin.

"Goodness me," Cathy said as she kissed Verity, "you will never *guess* what has happened to me."

"What's that Mother? You look very flustered."

"Put the kettle on first, there's a good girl. I'm dying for a cup of tea. I'll just run upstairs and take off my hat."

When Cathy came down Verity had the tea made and she looked enquiringly at her mother as she poured her a cup, noting that she seemed more composed.

"How was Gran when you left her?"

"Bearing up. I promised I'd go and see her every week."

"Won't that be a chore for you?"

"Well," Cathy touched her hair and Verity noticed that there was still an air of suppressed excitement about her, with pink cheeks and a sparkle in her eye. "This is the thing I wanted to tell you about. Guess what?"

"I can't, Mother. Don't be a tease." Verity smilingly pushed a plate of biscuits towards her.

"Frank Carpenter has asked me to marry him! He just stopped the car by the side of the road on the way home and popped the question. I can hardly believe it!"

The reality of this sudden announcement was hard for Verity to take in. She'd been amused by what Peg had told her, but that was all.

"Frank Carpenter! Peg said he liked you, but isn't he married already?"

Cathy shook her head. "He's never been married. He's got a thing about his looks and, besides, he is quite shy, at least with women. But I don't think he's *that* bad looking and his shyness is appealing after Jack and your father being so much the other way."

She paused and her expression grew almost girlish, almost fey. "It's true I have a weakness for handsome men, and both Jack and Billy were very good looking. Frank is a little plain I'll admit, and he is also a little younger than me, but he has other qualities that make up for his lack of good looks. It's true I don't love him, not yet anyway. I never for a moment considered him as a husband, so it's all quite new to me. But

181

he is steady, hard-working and kind. He is very, very kind."

Cathy grew more and more animated as she outlined Frank's attributes, and Verity reached for her hand.

"It looks as though you have already made up your mind, Mum."

"But would you mind? Would the others mind?" Cathy gazed at her anxiously.

"I wouldn't mind and I'm sure they wouldn't. We all want you to be happy. You deserve it."

"And there are other things, you see, Verity." Cathy's excitement at his unexpected proposal grew by the minute. "Frank has a nice house on the estate and we'd be able to live there. Lord Ryland has been very good to me, but I know he wants this cottage for a new groom now that Frank is driving the car and chauffering his lordship about the place. Also I did point out to Frank that, legally, I am still married and I could never afford a divorce. He says he will pay for it so, at last you see, I'll be rid of that terrible man, for good I hope. And that would make me really happy. Frank would give me security and that's something I've been without for years."

"Then in that case I'm very happy for you, Mum, and I give you my blessing. Now," Verity looked slyly at her mother, "in exchange for my support there is something you can do for me. I want to talk seriously to you about Peg."

"Peg? What about Peg?"

"Peg does not want to be a teacher." Verity took a biscuit out of the tin and bit into it thoughtfully.

"But she told *me*—" Cathy began, but Verity held up a hand.

"Let me finish, Mum. Did you know that she wrote stories?"

"Oh, I know she scribbled things into an exercise book. She would never show them to me." Cathy sounded impatient.

"No. They are not scribblings but very good stories. She wants to be a journalist, not a teacher or a nurse, and I think she should be encouraged."

"Well, I don't." Cathy's good humour evaporated and she

stubbornly folded her arms. "I think it is nonsense to entertain ideas of that kind. I don't want her running about loose in London, not following a decent profession."

"But journalism *is* a decent profession and there are women journalists and good ones. The war has changed a lot of things, you know, Mum. She can train as a stenographer and get a job in a newspaper office. That's the way to start, and if she doesn't succeed then, at least, she has a professional training and can always earn her living as a secretary.

"Frankly, as she's so pretty I don't think she'll be in any sort of employment for very long. And as for where she will live it will be with me. When I do my midwifery course I am going to leave the nurses' home and rent a flat. It will be fine for both of us. I feel I should start growing up and being independent too, and I am really looking forward to getting to know my little sister better."

Verity gazed at her mother whose expression, though less severe, remained doubtful.

"Go on, Mum, you support us and we'll support you. You know in many ways it's a chance for the three of us to make a fresh start in life."

Thirteen

Addie pulled her coat around her to try and keep out the cold from the blustery wind that blew through the playground during the mid-morning break. She had a free period immediately afterwards and she felt badly in need of the cup of hot coffee that would await her, maybe a chance to glance at the morning paper.

Addie had done her teaching practice at the mixed infants' school in Dorchester which had taken her on as junior mistress after she passed her exams. This was her first term.

She liked the school and she liked the people. She was also near enough to Sherborne to go and visit Jenny and her mother at least once a week, sometimes twice. She would go by bus or, occasionally, Frank would come down in Lord Ryland's car and take her home and bring her back to her lodgings in one of the old streets behind the prison.

The shock of the idea that Frank and Mother would marry had subsided and was now welcomed by her children, even Ed and Stella who were Jack's.

He had always been an inadequate father, almost a threatening presence in the house. His violence had been tangible and audible, the effect on a mother beloved by them all obvious, and his natural children as well as the stepchildren who had hated him were glad to see him go.

Frank had almost become part of the household while he waited for Cathy's divorce to come through. The result was that Cathy appeared to bloom like a young woman. Although the proprieties were strictly observed, Frank was always coming down with armfuls of flowers from the garden, fruit from the greenhouse, a plucked chicken or a piece of pork from the home farm and then one of Lord Ryland's cars was always there in case of need.

Occasionally he and Cathy would go on a day's outing, to see her mother or to have a picnic by themselves. It was a strange but rather touching romance that seemed to grow daily.

Because it so obviously made Cathy happy, her children shared in her joy, and little Jenny had already come to regard Frank as a father who doted on her and spoiled her, already calling her "my poppet".

Arms akimbo in the windswept playground, carefully watching her charges, Addie reflected on the changes brought about at home and the possible effect on her daughter.

The thought of Jenny always troubled Addie, however much she tried not to let it. There was no doubt about her intense love for her, but she never felt very close to her or motherly towards her. It was as though she was someone else's child rather than hers. She supposed that, if she was honest, she would admit to feeling slightly jealous of her mother's closeness to Jenny, who never showed Addie any obvious signs of affection other than what she gave the other children. She was, however, passionate about Cathy whom she called "Mummy" and to whom she clung whenever a stranger came or anyone she didn't know very well, and sometimes this included Addie, despite her frequent visits. At the sight of her she would run up to Cathy and cling to her skirt or climb up on her knee if she could.

Maybe in her childish, insecure little heart she was indeed afraid of being taken away.

Addie knew that one day, if she was to establish any kind of relationship with her daughter or claim her as her own, she would have to do just that. It was all right for Cathy to pretend that she was her mother, and probably better for the child who would have to withstand the taunts of other children when she grew older. But it would also lead to difficulties if and when Addie was able to acknowledge her openly as her daughter.

"Windy morning, Miss Barnes." A voice in her ear made her turn round to see Harold Smith, the deputy headmaster, standing by her side. "I didn't think you'd heard the bell."

"Oh, dear, has it gone already?" Addie looked down at the bell he carried in his hand. "I'm afraid I was miles away."

The children had already been assembled into their crocodile to go back into class, doubtless by Mr Smith who Addie thought was looking at her with some disapproval.

"I have a free period," Addie said hurriedly. "I'll see them into their class."

"No, that's all right, Miss Barnes." Mr Smith appeared to thaw a little. "I'll see to that. You go and get your coffee. It's a bitterly cold day."

And with a chilly smile he went up to the crocodile of children standing obediently and marshalled them inside. Addie, still deep in thought, followed them separating once she was inside and going to the staff room. She took off her coat and put it on a hook by the door. Then she felt the coffee pot standing on a table beside it. It was lukewarm, but it would do. Empty coffee cups stood around on the tables where the rest of the staff had had their break. Addie saw a copy of the morning paper and took it, together with her cup of coffee, to an easy chair facing the window. She slumped down, gulped down her coffee before it got even colder, and shook open the paper.

The overseas news was still depressing as economic conditions worsened. The German mark continued its dramatic fall that threatened further unrest in that unhappy country so penalised and humiliated by the victorious powers at Versailles. In Italy Benito Mussolini had declared himself the leader of a Fascist state. The terrible war, instead of settling things, had stirred up a hornet's nest.

But here in rural Dorset it was hard to feel in any way affected by what was happening overseas. There was enough unemployment and hardship at home, and Addie turned to the pages containing local news.

"Would you like fresh coffee, Miss Barnes?" Mr Smith

appeared by her side, holding out a jug. "I think what was left might be cold."

"That's very kind of you, Mr Smith." Addie held out her cup. "The news from overseas is so depressing, isn't it?"

"It is. Very." Mr Smith poured a cup for himself and sat next to Addie, thoughtfully stirring his coffee. "Sometimes you wonder what we went to war for."

"Just what I was thinking. Were you in the war, Mr Smith?"

He shook his head. "Alas, I was rejected for active service," he nervously pushed his spectacles up his nose, "on account of my poor eyesight. Also the country had to have teachers. We couldn't all go to war."

"So you were here all during the war?"

"No, I was at a school in Sussex. I've only been here two years. But I like Dorset. You are a Dorset woman, aren't you, Miss Barnes?"

"Yes, I was born in Bournemouth."

"And have you brothers and sisters?"

"Yes, I have three sisters and a brother."

"How lucky you are." Mr Smith gave a deep sigh. "I am an only child. Too long a mother's boy I'm afraid. That's really why I left Sussex." He paused and carefully examined the dregs in his coffee cup. "Do you like walking? I wondered if this Sunday you might like to go for a walk after church, say Weymouth if it's not too windy?"

"I always go to see my mother on a Sunday. She lives near Sherborne," Addie said.

"Perhaps Saturday, then?" Mr Smith once again pushed his spectacles up on his nose in a nervous gesture she was to grow familiar with.

"Why not?" Addie smiled at him. "Yes, I'd like to."

The following Saturday it rained. However, Addie met Mr Smith at the appointed time in the middle of Dorchester and they took a bus the few miles to Weymouth. By the time they got there the rain had lessened and the sun was trying hard to come out above the grey clouds.

They walked the whole length of the promenade saying little, rather an awkward silence between them in fact, because of course they scarcely knew each other. At lunchtime they explored the surrounding streets until they found a little café where they both ordered fish and chips, which were served with bread and butter and a cup of tea.

"This is really very agreeable," Mr Smith said expanding a little. "I'm enjoying my day. Are you . . .?" he paused and smiled at her. "Might I call you Adelaide?"

"If you like, but mostly people call me Addie."

"Addie, then," Mr Smith said happily. "And I'm Harold."

"Do they ever call you Harry?"

"Never." Mr Smith seemed to find the idea most unpleasant.

"Harold, then. Actually I prefer Harold."

"What are the names of your brothers and sisters?"

Addie told him and also a little about what they did. About Verity and the war (but not about Rex), and Peg who had gone to London to learn to be a stenographer. She left out that she wanted to be a journalist, surmising, somehow, that Harold might not quite approve of this. Both her half-brother and sister were clever, and Ed was even thinking of being a doctor if he could get a scholarship. Otherwise he would teach, as would Stella. But she didn't say anything about Jenny, and she didn't think she ever would.

It was not difficult to speculate on what effect that news might have on Harold who, she suspected, as a regular churchgoer, would be a stickler for morality.

She had known that Harold liked her. He had been a supervisor for her teaching practice and was on the board that appointed her to the school. He went out of his way to be helpful and to be nice to her.

Harold Smith was not a man whose immediate attractions were sufficient to turn a girl's head, especially a young girl's. For one thing he was over forty, a bachelor who had lived for most of his life, before taking up his post at Dorchester, with his mother. He was very tall and thin and, perhaps as a consequence of feeling awkward about his height, walked with a slight stoop. His face was pale and his cheeks sallow, as though despite his enthusiasm for walking he did not in fact take much fresh air. He had, however, rather friendly and attractive blue eyes that were not seen at their best behind spectacles, which always seemed too heavy for him so that he kept on pushing them up his nose, perhaps about eight or ten times an hour.

He had a good head of fairish, slightly wavy hair and was in many ways presentable; he was a solid, reliable-looking sort of man which had earned him his assistant headship. However, despite his undoubted good qualities he had nothing of the charm or fascination of Lydd.

What did Addie think about Lydd after the passage of three years? She still felt that Lydd had been honourable and they would have married, something her mother discounted on the grounds that he had never mentioned her to his family. Her mother, she knew, and Verity too thought Lydd had pretended to love her to lure her into bed; but she knew differently, and she treasured her love for Lydd in her heart and felt she always would.

But Lydd was dead and now there was Harold, unlike him in every possible way, but alive and interested in her. Above all he seemed eminently suitable, someone she wouldn't hesitate to introduce to her family.

After lunch they continued their exploration of Weymouth, looking at the shops and the old harbour, and walking back along the promenade where they had a cup of tea before taking the bus home.

Addie felt that friendship, rather than intimacy, had been established. In fact Harold was her first date since Lydd. She knew she looked bookish and schoolmarmish and didn't make the best of her appearance. She hadn't the natural beauty, allure or the feminine wiles of her sister Peg. She knew she had good features, fine bone structure, dark brown eyes and thick brown hair which she wore in a loose bun at the nape of her neck. But recently she had let herself go, perhaps from despair at losing the man she considered the love of her life. She was convinced that no man would ever be like Lydd, so there was no point in making an effort for something she wasn't really interested in: the attraction of the opposite sex. She had given herself to Lydd, she had paid a heavy price and she remained true to his memory.

Or that's what she told herself until Harold asked her out, and she realised that despite her lack of effort she still, after all, possessed the power to attract, though many would consider Harold, a confirmed bachelor and set in his ways, no great catch.

The day by the sea at Weymouth was followed by many other outings, usually on a Saturday, that continued throughout the winter of 1921 and into the following spring, by which time Addie had grown not only used to Harold but really quite fond of him, relishing his good qualities and glossing over the bad.

He was rather spinsterly, excessively tidy, meticulous and precise, extremely devout. He never missed church on Sundays and was rather shocked at her lack of interest in the divine.

They seldom went out at night. Harold didn't like dancing but he did take her to one or two lectures of an improving nature to do with the fauna and flora of Dorset. He was very correct in his behaviour, never made improper advances and, although by the spring they had only got as far as holding hands, she realised that he was very fond of her and she had to face the fact that if things continued as they were going now in all probability Harold would one day ask her to marry him.

This posed Addie with a dilemma. She liked Harold. She had grown comfortable with him, but he was no romantic, no Lydd and her one experience of lovemaking had shown her, under Lydd's guidance, just what sexual passion could be. She doubted if she would feel the same about Harold.

By late spring Cathy had grown rather curious about this man who was obviously courting her daughter and, as the date for her own marriage grew closer, she suggested that Addie might bring him home for a visit.

Frank went to the station to collect Addie and Harold, and Cathy stood nervously at the door waiting to welcome them with Jenny, dressed in her best, a bow in her golden curls, tightly holding her hand. Stella and Ed were also spruced up for the occasion. For reasons they didn't understand its importance could not be emphasised enough; the first meeting with Addie's young man. Well, not so young Cathy thought, but never mind. The main thing was to get this daughter, who many would consider damaged goods, safely married. From what she had heard from Addie, Harold was eminently suitable: a bachelor with a position, soon perhaps to be a headmaster and, hopefully, a little money behind him.

She was determined to do all she could to make a good impression.

Frank was in time and the car drew up at the door. Addie got out, followed by Harold.

Cathy immediately liked the look of him, upright and sensible, not handsome but that didn't matter. In fact, it was an advantage as far as she was concerned. Billy and Jack had both been very handsome, and they'd both had their faults, the one more than the other. The first impression made by Harold was one of wholesomeness, and that did matter. Tall, nice suit, white shirt, blue tie, spectacles and well-brushed hair. What more could a putative mother-in-law wish for?

She greeted the new arrivals with Jenny, and Addie made the introduction.

"Harold this is my mother. Mum, Harold."

"Very pleased to meet you," Cathy said with the little bob she usually reserved if she encountered guests of Lord Ryland.

"This is Jenny my adopted daughter," she said drawing her forward. Harold bent down and smiled kindly at Jenny, taking her hand.

"Hello, Jenny."

"Lo," Jenny said shyly trying to hide behind Cathy's skirt.

Addie endeavoured to kiss Jenny, who averted her face.

"She's very shy," Addie said nervously, "even with me."

"Not used to strangers," Cathy, a little flustered, explained.

She too had been rather dreading this meeting, as she knew that Addie had not told him about Jenny. At the back of Cathy's mind was always the worry about Jenny, not only about what would happen to her but also about losing her. To her she was not only the sixth child, but in many ways the most beloved. Of course she had loved all her other children, but Jenny was special. So special. Maybe this was because there was a little lost look about Jenny, as though somehow she was aware of things hidden in her past.

She had also spent more time with Jenny, they had not had the distraction of a man like Billy or Jack. It was true that now there was Frank, but he wasn't yet part of the household, he wasn't a threat, and there was no doubt that he loved Jenny almost as much as she did.

Tea was quite a jolly occasion. Cathy had been baking for two days and, as if there were not enough cakes, Mary Capstick had sent down another. They all wanted to make a good impression on Harold, and Harold was making an excellent impression on them. He was most attentive to Cathy, friendly to the children and kept on sending affectionate glances towards Addie who positively basked in the approbation she could sense her family was bestowing on Harold. Family approval meant so much to her, and Harold really was going down well.

Trying to look at him dispassionately in this environment she decided that Harold did after all fit in. She hadn't been sure, which was why she'd kept him under wraps for so long. Mum was clearly impressed by him, Frank treated him with respect and the children were at home with him. He was used to children and knew how to make them feel at ease. Although he was a deputy headmaster he didn't talk down to them, but entertained them with stories of various things he'd seen and done, that sometimes had them all in fits of laughter. Harold's humorous side was quite a surprise.

In fact Addie was seeing a completely new aspect of Harold and wished she had brought him home before.

"Another cake, Mr Smith?" Cathy passed him a plate, but he shook his head.

"I couldn't eat another thing, Mrs Hallam, and you must call me 'Harold'."

"Well that's very kind of you – er, Harold. Another slice of tart?" she suggested in a wheedling tone.

"Nothing, Mrs Hallam, but another cup of tea would be very welcome."

Cathy looked at the clock and turned to Stella and Ed who, though attentive, had scarcely said a thing, obviously a little in awe of the deputy headmaster.

"Time for choir practice, children. Don't keep the vicar waiting."

"Oh, the children sing in the choir, do they?" Harold looked pleased. "Addie didn't tell me. I am delighted to hear that. Do they go to church every week?"

"Every week," Ed said, "except when the vicar has his summer holidays and then we have a holiday too."

"My son is very interested in the church, aren't you Ed?"

Ed nodded, blushing.

"He's thinking of studying theology at university and then he'll see. Won't you, Ed? He may teach or he may apply for Holy Orders." Cathy looked very proud at the thought that her son might enter the church.

"I thought Ed wanted to be a doctor?" This news was a surprise to Addie who had no idea that Ed was so devout. It seemed to emphasise to her how cut off she'd become recently from the family, concentrating on her own affairs and not attending enough to theirs.

"I think he's gone off medicine. He doesn't really like the sight of blood, do you, Ed?"

193

Ed grimaced.

"He was impressed by what the chaplains did during the war. Were you in the war, Mr Smith?"

"I was deferred military service owing to poor eyesight, to my lasting regret I might add."

"It's nothing to be ashamed of. Sometimes I wonder if the war was worth fighting, don't we, Frank?"

"You do wonder," Frank said touching his leg under the table. "I have a gammy leg from a shooting accident when I was a lad. That kept me out."

"You don't have to make excuses," Stella said. "War is horrible. Mum, if we don't go now we're going to be late." She pulled her chair away from the table and looked at Ed, who also got down. "Will you be here when we come back, Mr Smith?"

"I, er . . ." Harold looked at Addie. "Will we, dear?"

"I thought you and Addie might like to go up and have a look at the castle," Cathy said, "and then perhaps stay for supper. We have some lovely home-cured ham. Frank will take you back to the station for the train."

"How can I resist?" Harold said with a disarming smile.

Cathy thought he was charming, the perfect gentleman, and her heart filled with hope for her daughter.

"Isn't he *nice*?" Cathy said to Frank, indicating the two going up the road towards the castle as he helped with the washing up after tea. "They'd make a lovely couple, don't you think, Frank?"

"He *is* a little old," Frank said. "Forty, did you say? And Addie only twenty-four. Sixteen years is a lot, my dear."

"Go on with you," Cathy dug him affectionately in the ribs. "You're younger than I am."

"But not by so much."

"I don't care. I think he's nice and he's good for Addie, and I'm sure she's very fond of him. Just look how she's changed. She was getting quite frumpish due, in my opinion, to pining for that Lydd."

It was true that Addie over the past few months had indeed made an attempt to smarten herself up, perhaps in an effort to impress Harold. If so, she had succeeded. She had had her long hair cut almost right off and it now curled about her jawline in a fashionable bob. For the important visit home she wore a pretty green jumper suit and had discarded her spectacles which, as her mother had suspected, she didn't really need.

"Now a whole new world has opened up for her again," Cathy continued. "She couldn't do any better, if you ask me. And he has such prospects. She says he is very well thought of and respected at the school. Imagine her being a headmaster's wife, if that should come about." Cathy put her hands to her cheeks, quite pink with excitement.

"What did she tell him about Jenny?" Frank asked, looking at the little girl who was playing contentedly on the lawn. A solitary child, she was quite happy amusing herself, inventing stories and playing them out.

"She's said nothing yet. No point." A frown crossed Cathy's brow and, the dishes being finished, she took her arms out of the hot soapy water and started to dry them on a towel.

"Will she tell him?"

"I don't know what she'll do. I only hope . . . well, as you know, I dread losing Jenny, to tell you the honest truth, Frank."

"Addie is her mother, and if she wants her . . ."

"But *does* she?" Cathy looked appealingly at Frank, who was carefully putting the plates away. "I don't think she knows in her own mind what she feels about Jenny. I honestly don't."

"Very hard for her, not seeing her much." Frank shook his head. "You can see she's torn. It's an artificial situation. Maybe if she and Mr Smith do marry it will settle the matter. It is a problem, Cathy. There's no hiding it, and what would Mr Smith have to say if she *did* tell him?"

"Don't ask me," Cathy shook her head. "I don't even like

to think about it. He's that nice. She'll be lucky if she finds another like him."

"It's a lovely place for you to have grown up in," Harold said appreciatively. "My first home was in a dreary London suburb."

"I didn't really grow up here. I was eight when Mother married Jack."

They were standing at the top of the hill; the castle was visible to one side and the lake below them. In the distance was the town of Sherborne with its beautiful abbey church rising above the roofs. It was a lovely spring day and the lakeside was ringed with daffodils, while little waves skimmed across the surface of the lake, hastened by the gentle breeze. It lifted Addie's hair above her head and she raised an arm to smooth it. Harold put an arm round her waist and drew her to him.

"You never talk much about your stepfather. You didn't like him, did you?"

Addie shook her head. "He wasn't very nice. He treated Mum badly."

"I can't understand how anyone could do that. I like your mother so much."

"And I could see she liked you." Addie was strongly aware of his arm around her waist and her heart began to beat a little faster.

"I can see where you get your looks from." The pressure of Harold's arm tightened. "You look very pretty today, Addie." Then he frowned. "But you never told me your mother had an adopted daughter. Who does she belong to?"

"A relation," Addie said and the happiness, almost the euphoria she'd felt, had been replaced by a sudden fear. Should she tell him? Should she confide in him now? Would it not be right, the honourable thing to do? And yet . . . she looked at his face smiling innocently down at her.

"Will you marry me, Addie? I think you must know how I feel about you, and I dare to hope you feel the same way about me."

"Oh, yes," she said with a heartfelt sigh. "Yes," and she sank into his arms and surrendered to his gentle kiss.

Now was certainly not the right time to tell him about Jenny.

"Let's tell your mother," Harold cried after breaking away. "I think she'll be pleased."

Hand in hand they ran all the way down the hill and burst into the kitchen where Cathy was laying the table while Frank, with his boots off and feet up, was reading the evening paper.

"We're engaged!" Addie burst out.

"I just asked Addie to marry me. She said 'yes'." Harold's face beamed with pride. "I can't believe how fortunate I am."

"Oh, I'm so happy." Cathy threw herself into Addie's arms. "What wonderful news, isn't it Frank?"

"Couldn't be better," Frank said, hastily putting on his boots. Then he rose and warmly shook Harold's hand.

"Congratulations. You couldn't have a nicer girl."

"Don't I know it." Harold's arm was once again around Addie's waist. "And aren't I lucky to think I'm going to have you all as a family?"

He kissed Cathy warmly on the cheek and then, looking at the little girl who stood shyly in the doorway, finger in her mouth, held out his hand. "And Jenny too."

Cathy went over to Jenny and, putting an arm protectively around her, gave her a little push.

"Jenny, Mr Smith is going to marry Aunt Addie. Go and give him a nice kiss. He'll be your new uncle."

But Jenny shook her head and, breaking away from Cathy, ran out of the room.

"Shy," Cathy said, as if trying to find an explanation. But she avoided Addie's eyes, and it seemed to her then that a sudden cloud had darkened the horizon.

And up to then it had been such a bright day.

Fourteen

As Addie came down the aisle of the church on Frank's arm, the sun from the west window caught the head of the man standing waiting for her at the altar and her heart missed a beat. It was Lydd! Lydd, standing there waiting for her. Lydd was not dead after all, but had returned safely from the war. All these years had been a bad dream.

The notes of the Bach toccata stopped, and as the man turned she saw the amiable, bespectacled face of Harold smiling at her encouragingly.

Frank felt her hesitate and the pressure of his hand on her arm increased. "Only a few steps more," he murmured and then there she was standing by Harold's side while the vicar in a white surplice smiled benignly upon them.

"Dearly beloved we are gathered here in the sight of God . . ."

Little Jenny fidgeted, standing first on one leg then another. She looked angelic in her long lemon-coloured bridesmaid's dress, a garland of fresh flowers on her golden hair which was parted in the middle, a thick lock falling each side of her pale oval face.

She almost eclipsed the bride, even though Addie lived up to the tradition of the bride looking her best on her wedding day. She wore a long lace veil that her mother had worn when she married her father, and her grandmother before that. A simple dress of white silk with three-quarter sleeves, because it was midsummer, was set off by a single-strand pearl necklace which had also been in the family for generations. Addie's short fashionable hairstyle was so arranged that it was combed across her brow, peeking from beneath her veil and curling softly under her ears towards her cheeks. She looked reposed, solemn rather than happy, especially after that momentary vision of Lydd.

It was warm in the church and Cathy waved her order paper in front of her face. Frank had now joined her and was perspiring heavily. Their own quiet wedding had taken place a few months before and she had changed her name for the third time in her life. Today she wore the outfit she had chosen for her own wedding, a pretty blue suit with a long skirt and a broad-brimmed blue straw hat. Frank kept on gazing at her proudly, thinking that his wife was as comely as any woman there that day.

From time to time as the service progressed Cathy looked anxiously at Jenny, but under the watchful eyes of Peg and Stella, the senior bridesmaids, the little girl settled down. Cathy's heart, though otherwise full of joy on Addie's wedding day, felt heavy as she looked at the little bridesmaid, because she knew she would soon lose her. Once they were married, and when the time was right, Addie was going to tell Harold the truth.

Reflections on the past as well as thoughts for the future jostled in her mind as she followed the course of the ceremony, singing the hymns, saying the prayers, but her mind was invariably elsewhere. Never very far away from her thoughts was Jenny and the question of what her future would be.

Harold had just applied for a headship at a school in Devon. When he got back from his honeymoon he should know the result. It was a large mixed infants' school with a house attached, a substantial dwelling with a view over the sea.

Ed read a lesson. He read it beautifully, sonorously. He had taken his scholarship exams and hoped to go to Durham University to study divinity.

Cathy could visualise her only son in a few years' time in the place of the vicar in a white surplice and stole. He was a fine-looking young man, physically like Jack, but so different, for which she thanked God. It was one thing to have Jack's looks but another to have his temperament. But there was no fear of Jack's restlessness, violence and liking for strong liquor as far as Ed was concerned. Just the opposite.

Verity sat on her mother's left and also found her eyes straying to her young niece fidgeting away behind the bridal pair as they began to make their vows.

"Harold Gordon Smith will you take . . ."

Verity gave a deep sigh. It was such a solemn moment.

"Rex Edward Harvey will you take Verity Annabel . . ."

A lump came into her throat. So nearly . . . They should have married before he went away. She should have gone to bed with him and then there would have been a bond that could never have been broken. Maybe he felt she had rejected him; she was too formal and correct, and maybe the woman he'd met in Kenya had been more accommodating, more fun. Perhaps if she had gone to bed with him, like Addie, she might have become pregnant and then . . . but no, mentally she corrected her train of thought. It would never have done. She knew that. This was all fantasy brought on by a sentimental occasion. There was no possible outcome between her and Rex but the one that had happened and she had to be realistic about it.

From the aisle Peg glanced at her as though she could read her thoughts. Verity and Peg now shared a flat together in north-west London, in a tree-lined road not too far from Hampstead Heath. They got on well. Despite Peg's youth they were close. Verity found that she was able to confide in her a lot. She'd even wept telling Peg how she'd really felt about Rex, how resentful and let down; and after that she had felt a lot better. To her surprise, her young sister had a breadth and maturity beyond her years. Now she was working as a stenographer in a newspaper office. She already had a young man. Of course she would, she was so pretty. Verity smiled at her and Peg winked as if she understood, as if she also was thinking "in other circumstances this could have been you".

"I now pronounce you man and wife."

An audible collective sigh seemed to rise from the large congregation. The vicar ascended the pulpit and began his sermon with the words "Whom God heath joined together let no man put asunder." The bride and groom, now man and wife, sat a little uneasily on their gilt chairs, looking steadfastly at the vicar and not at each other.

Verity smiled across at her but Addie either didn't notice, or pretended not to. Her sister, Verity decided, did indeed look pretty. She had let herself go after Lydd was killed. She'd been through a lot. Harold, who everyone agreed was a very nice man, a perfect match for Addie, had put the bloom back in her cheeks, the shine in her hair, the lilt in her steps. But now, nervously fingering her new wedding ring, she kept her eyes on the vicar as if her very life depended on listening to his words.

It was a long sermon for a hot day. People were mopping their brows, Frank looked as though he was about to burst out of his suit and Mum kept on glancing anxiously at him. It was wonderful to see Mum happy, as she and Frank undoubtedly were, and so well suited. The future looked good for them. Despite his single status Frank had long ago been given a house by Lord Ryland, big enough for a family man, out of respect for his senior position as a member of the castle staff.

The only thing was that Mum would so miss Jenny when she went to live with Harold and Addie, but Devon wasn't so far away. Ed and Stella would remain at home for a while and Mum would adjust. She always did. The only unease in Verity's mind was what Harold would say when he knew about Jenny. Addie would have been much wiser if she'd told him before.

The sermon ended, the couple walked to the altar and knelt for prayers, then went to sign the register in the presence of Cathy, Frank and Harold's mother who was making a first appearance. She seemed a little in awe of Addie's large family, but perhaps a few drinks at the reception would help calm her nerves.

The couple emerged from the sacristy, the organ blazed forth and Addie and Harold, to the acclaim of the congregation, walked down the aisle as man and wife: Mr and Mrs Smith.

The wedding had been at three and by early evening the reception, held by kind invitation of Lord and Lady Ryland at the castle, was well under way. Most of the staff from the castle had been invited, as well as numerous Swayle and other relations who had last been together at Joseph Swayle's funeral two years before. Mrs Capstick and Cathy had been cooking for days to provide the lavish buffet to which Lord Ryland had also made a contribution, providing lamb and beef, ham, eggs and various salads from the home farm and gardens.

Unfortunately, or perhaps fortunately as far as they were concerned, Lord and Lady Ryland had gone to Scotland for the shooting and were unable to put in an appearance.

There was also a plentiful supply of beer, wine, cider and spirits which kept on having to be replenished.

Harold came from one of those sad families who had few relations, or none at all. In his case he only had his mother, Rose Smith, who was clearly out of her depth amid all this jollity. Yet, nevertheless, now that the occasion was here, she seemed determined to enjoy it. It was not her fault that she was a rather reserved middle-class lady who had lost her husband to illness in the early years of her marriage and had brought up her son alone on very little money. She too had been an only child, and so had her husband. Her relief that her only son, so long a bachelor, was now married knew no bounds. She sat chatting with an unusual degree of animation, like a prisoner suddenly released from solitary confinement, and aided by a plentiful supply of whisky, to Grandma Swayle who was otherwise surrounded by cohorts of her husband's relations who had all come up from Bournemouth by charabanc.

There were speeches, toasts, the bride and groom cut the

triple wedding cake and then a small band, tucked in a corner of the large castle ballroom where the annual staff party was held, struck up and dancing began. The bride and groom reluctantly led with a few faltering steps before the throng joined in with more enthusiasm.

The din was quite deafening when a woman slipped in through the main door and stood watching the jollifications, looking as though she thought she had made a mistake and might make a quick exit.

Luckily Frank spotted Lord Ryland's daughter just in time and went across the room to welcome her.

"How very *nice* to see you, Miss Violet. How kind of you to come."

"My mother and father sent their apologies and best wishes for happiness to the bride and groom. As you know they're away shooting."

"Please come and say 'hello'." Frank politely steered Violet Ryland through the throng to where Addie and Harold had just begun making the rounds to say their goodbyes to friends and relatives so that they could get the last train to London.

"Miss Violet has come to wish you well," Frank announced proudly. "Miss Violet, may I present Harold, Addie's husband."

"How do you do?" Violet smiled graciously at him. "And may I congratulate you on your choice of a bride. You're really most fortunate."

"I think so, Miss Ryland," Harold said shaking her hand.

Violet turned her attention to Addie. "Addie, you really do look lovely today."

"Thank you, Miss Violet." Addie, already rather pink-faced because of the heat, noise and bustle, went crimson. "And thank his lordship and her ladyship *very* much for all they have done for me today."

Violet leaned forward and to Addie's embarrassment kissed her on the cheek. "They wanted me to wish you and your husband the very best and—" she stopped as Cathy came up to her, holding Jenny by the hand.

"How *very* kind of you to come, Miss Violet," Cathy said warmly. "Have you been offered something to eat and drink?"

"No, I'm going out to dine, thank you." Violet was indeed looking very svelte and elegant in a long dinner dress, an embroidered bag under her arm. "My escort should be here in a few minutes." She bent down and gazed at Jenny. "And who have we here?"

"Jenny, Miss Violet," Cathy said diffidently, "my adopted daughter. You remember . . ."

"Of course I remember Jenny! She's just grown so big, and so *pretty*." Violet took her by the hand, continuing to stare at her as if mesmerised. "She reminds me . . ." She stood up, a puzzled expression on her face as though she'd forgotten who she did remind her of, and left the statement unfinished. She consulted the exquisite marcasite watch on her wrist and exclaimed: "I must hurry or my date will think I've forgotten all about him, but I did want to say every happiness to you both." She blew a kiss in the direction of the by now bewildered-looking bride and groom and then, escorted by Frank once again, left the room.

"How very *nice* of Miss Violet to come," Cathy said looking at Addie. "When you think she lost her fiancé in the war . . . Well, it was kind of her, that's what I think." Her expression, however, was troubled as she gazed after the visitor, wondering who Jenny had reminded Miss Violet of and how long it would take for her or any of the Ryland family to put two and two together as the child grew more and more to resemble – as she already uncannily did – her dead father.

Just then Frank bustled back, also looking at his watch.

"The train goes in half an hour," he said urgently, "if you are to catch it . . ."

"Goodbye, goodbye." As many as could crammed on to the castle steps to watch the bridal pair take off in Lord Ryland's Rolls Royce, to whose back bumper a boot and a horseshoe had been attached.

Addie, wearing a navy silk dress with white trim and a broad brimmed navy hat with a large white bow flew down the steps avoiding the confetti, followed by Harold, tall and spruce in a grey double-breasted grey pin-striped suit, white shirt, red tie and grey spats over his well-polished brown brogues.

Frank held the car door open for them, and just before they got in, Addie turned and threw her bouquet high into the crowd. It was aimed for Verity, who dodged it in time and so it was caught by Peg who burst out laughing as everyone pointed to her and said that she would be next.

Peg ran after her sister and kissed her through the open window of the car. "*Please* take care. Have a wonderful time." Verity joined her and then Stella and Ed with Harold's mother, all wanting to say last-minute goodbyes.

Cathy, anxious to join them, urged Jenny forward but in the mêlée surrounding the car she let go of her hand and the tired little bridesmaid, breaking away, hurried up the steps and into the castle.

"She'll be all right," Frank whispered, "you know she's shy."

"Sometimes I think she *knows*," Cathy whispered back, "though I don't know how."

"This is Addie's day," Frank said urgently, "Addie's and Harold's. Go and give her a kiss now and stop worrying about the future."

Frank jumped into the driver's seat and Cathy, holding tightly on to her hat, just managed a hurried kiss with Addie and a wave to Harold as with a "toot toot" the heavy car went swiftly up the drive to the cheers and waves of those who were left behind, and for whom a night of jollity lay ahead.

Baedeker guide in hand, heads shaded from the hot Spanish sun by straw hats, the tourists gratefully entered the shade of Santiago de Compostela's glorious cathedral and stood for a while gazing around them. Harold, who was gently perspiring, took out a handkerchief and wiped his forehead. Addie

Nicola Thorne

fanned her face with her tourist guide, and then she seated herself on one of the chairs in the nave and gazed about her. The interior of this famous baroque-fronted basilica was indeed an awe-inspiring sight.

The honeymoon had been most instructional as the newly-weds travelled from one cultural spot to another, embracing Italy, France and now Spain. Addie's brain was so full of facts that she felt it would be hard to take in any more, and was glad that this was their last port of call before home.

She appreciated Harold's knowledge and erudition, which were far superior to hers. He knew everything about the great Gothic, Romanesque and baroque cathedrals and churches of the continent, the monasteries and art galleries. He was a mine of really useful information, no denying that, and at times as she listened making little contribution herself, she had felt inferior.

By this summer, August 1923, most of Europe had managed to cast off the obvious clouds of the aftermath of the war, though poverty and unemployment were universal problems. But Germany's financial situation had made the climate in that country desperate – there were 622,000 marks to the pound – so they had given it a wide berth. However, a cultural tour of such intensity, taken in August, especially in Italy and Spain, was exhausting. There was no let-up and as Harold lectured on she not infrequently felt herself nodding off and had to jerk herself sharply to attention.

". . . Begun in 1075 during the reign of Alfonso VI, but the church, originally Romanesque, was not completed until 1122. The great Azabacheria façade which we see today was not completed until 1750 and . . . Addie are you paying attention?"

"Oh yes, Harold." Up went the head, her eyes desperately trying to focus on her spouse who seemed to be lecturing her from a great height. She put a hand to her head.

"I am actually feeling a little faint, Harold. Do you think . . ."

"Oh, my dear." All consternation, he was immediately

beside her, Baedeker tossed on a nearby chair. "Why didn't you say?"

"I think I'm hungry."

"Of course you're hungry." He looked at his watch. "How selfish of me."

"No Harold, really I was most interested, but maybe we could come back when it's cooler?"

"You're right," Harold said, retrieving his guide book and shutting it, after carefully marking the page. "We'll have lunch and then we'll go back for a siesta. I must say I'm rather tired myself."

They went out into the square, still baking hot, and then, exploring the narrow streets surrounding the cathedral, found a restaurant with a shady courtyard at the back. They had paella and lovely dark Spanish bread with olives. Addie had a glass of cool white wine and Harold a beer or two and soon they felt restored. They sat well after they had finished their meal watching the lizards playing in the sun, and then they wandered back to their hotel not far away in the Rúa Nueva, another of the narrow cobbled streets which made up this most charming and fascinating of Spanish cities.

"We must see the *botafumeiro* before we go," Addie said, throwing herself on the bed once they reached their room.

"Of course, we'll do it tomorrow. I think it's only at High Mass but I'll find out." This was the occasion, unique to the cathedral, when an enormous smoking silver censer was swung from one side of the sanctuary to the other during Mass, to the applause of the congregation.

Harold stood in front of the mirror unfastening his tie. He looked just what he was: an earnest, knowledgeable school-master, the eternal Englishman abroad. He always dressed correctly, whatever the weather; today he was in grey flannels and a white jacket, a white shirt and blue tie, a tie, as ever, and, of course, there was always, and most sensibly, the white panama hat.

Watching him, Addie thought he was a curious contra-diction and she still found it difficult to realise he was her

207

husband. There was something very Victorian about Harold and she supposed it had a lot to do with his upbringing and his mother, his piety, because he was very religious, though strictly in the Protestant persuasion. Despite his veneration for continental cathedrals, monasteries and shrines, his profound knowledge of the various religious orders, friars, monks and mendicants, Harold had no time for the Roman Catholic religion which he thought was mere frumpery.

The intimate side of their marriage had not gone smoothly. It was hardly to be expected that it would with a couple who did not even kiss until they were engaged. It had been awkward, clumsy, almost furtive. She had never seen Harold naked, nor he her. They undressed, or dressed, in the bathroom along the corridor and one was always in bed before the other. Then the fumbling began.

Neither, of course, had had much experience. In fact it seemed that Harold hadn't had any. Addie had been surprised to discover that her forty-year-old bridegroom was a virgin, and had little understanding of the actual mechanics of lovemaking despite his extensive knowledge of biology. Addie felt similarly inadequate. Her brief experience with Lydd did not make her an expert. Anyway Lydd had told or shown her what to do and, what little knowledge she had, she tried to conceal out of respect for Harold's feelings.

She surmised that in time either you improved or it stopped altogether.

She respected Harold, especially his intellect, but he was not a passionate man and, she supposed, never would be.

Having taken off his tie and spent some time looking out of the window, Harold sat in a chair and opened the Baedeker again and Addie prepared for a lecture on the masterpiece that was the Basilica of St James the Apostle whose bones allegedly lay in the cathedral, having been discovered in the ninth century and given rise to Santiago di Compostela itself. She closed her eyes and then opened them as Harold abruptly abandoned his study of the guide and flopped down beside her.

"Hot," he said.

"Very. But a nice breeze from the window."

She thought Harold seemed agitated and was surprised when he suddenly rose and went across to the window and firmly closed the shutters.

Then in the near darkness he had created in the room she was aware that he was undressing. When he again lay down beside her he was completely naked and she felt rather shocked and wondered how many beers he'd had at lunch, or maybe it was the effect of the heat. Clumsily he kissed her and then he began to pluck at her blouse, the fastening on her skirt, and she wriggled uncomfortably about until the lower part of her body too was bare.

Harold drew back the sheet and covered them both with it as though to hide what they were doing from a chance onlooker. The lovemaking took longer than usual and she felt that Harold was more tender, understanding, even passionate. She experienced a degree of pleasure she hadn't felt before, and her responses seemed to make him happy.

They lay for a long time in the hot room, both sweating profusely, and then Harold went to sleep and she dozed or, maybe, slept too because when she opened her eyes it was almost dusk.

Harold reached for her hand and kissed it.

"I do love you," he said. "You know that don't you?"

"Yes."

"Do you love me?"

"Of course."

"And this . . . . this will come all right between us in time. It's because I was never with a woman before."

Addie sat on the side of the bed and removed the rest of her clothes, her brassière and blouse which had remained on during their lovemaking. She felt curiously happy and exhilarated. The atmosphere between them had changed. Harold had never been so tender, bold and open with her. Never so exploratory. Never completely nude. Never had he seemed to possess her so completely. She felt a surge of love and trust for this man she had married, who up to then had really been almost a stranger.

It was terrible that people should try and be so intimate, have to be so intimate, just because they were married, when they scarcely knew each other. The actual night of the wedding had been a shambles.

She felt that now was the time to be honest with the husband she loved and trusted. There should be no more concealment from him. She put on her robe and sat on the bed beside him. He reached again for her hand and she clasped his tightly, not quite sure how to begin. Then:

"Wasn't little Jenny sweet at the wedding?"

"Oh, adorable," Harold said, reaching out and lighting a cigarette. "I hope we have a daughter like that." He blew smoke over her head. "What made you mention her, dear?"

Addie took a deep breath. She felt very nervous now.

"Harold there *is* something I must tell you." Playing for time she rose and threw back the shutters, gazing for a moment at the splendid towers of the cathedral outlined against the azure evening sky.

"What is that, Addie?" he asked, smiling at her.

"Jenny is my daughter."

The silence lasted a few seconds. Then:

"I beg your pardon?"

"Jenny is my daughter. You knew she was adopted."

"You said that she was the daughter of a relation." Harold agitatedly stubbed out his cigarette in the ashtray by the side of the bed.

"Of Mum's. Well, I'm that relation."

"You really *are* serious?"

"Absolutely."

Harold sat up in bed hugging his knees.

"Why didn't you tell me before?"

"I couldn't. Now, just now I felt we were so . . . well, happy together, you know what I mean. I felt you'd understand."

"You mean you tricked me, you deceived me . . ."

"No, *no*, Harold," Addie cried, shocked. "I was afraid it might affect how you felt towards me."

Harold turned his back to her and reached for his robe. Then he got out of bed and came slowly towards her drawing the cord tight. "Well, I'm afraid it has. It has shocked me completely. The fact that you could give yourself to a man without being married really *astonishes* me. I'm sorry, but it does. It alters the whole basis of our relationship."

"Oh, no, Harold, please. No." She gestured imploringly towards him but he repulsed her.

"I wish I'd never told you," she said throwing herself into a chair.

"I wish you hadn't either." Harold lit a fresh cigarette. "I don't know how I'm going to get over this. I really don't."

Addie began to feel hysterical. "I thought you *liked* Jenny, that's why I told you. You always seem to get on well with her and I do so want her to come and live with us. You see I don't really know her and she *is* my daughter. Even though I'm her mother, she runs away from me. It's hurtful. Mum has brought her up almost entirely."

Harold looked at her coldly.

"I'm sorry, Addie, but I couldn't possibly have another man's child in my house. I couldn't entertain it."

"It was something that happened. Something to do with the war."

Harold held up a hand. "Please Addie. I don't want to hear about the sordid details."

"They are *not* sordid," Addie said hotly. "Jenny was a child of love. I loved her father. He was a soldier who was killed in the war. We were engaged to be married."

Harold lifted his hand in a threatening gesture and she fell silent.

"I don't want to hear about it, do you understand? Not another word. I'm not sure now how I feel about you and I have to have time to myself to think. I think if you'd told me before I would never have married you." He turned on his heels and left the room hurrying towards the bathroom along the corridor.

Addie leapt out of her chair and ran after him. "He was killed giving his life while you were *safe* at home," she screamed. "I loved him. What we did was lovely and noble—"

Harold slammed the bathroom door in her face and Addie fell to her knees in front of it, weeping. "I loved him," she whimpered. "I loved him, and I wished I'd married him, not you."

Cathy kept on looking out of the window for sight of the car, nervous and apprehensive at the prospect of the first meeting with her daughter since she had returned home from honeymoon. Frank had gone to meet her at the station and when she wasn't looking for the car from the kitchen window she was watching Jenny playing happily on the lawn with a puppy that Frank had bought for her from a new litter up at the home farm.

Happiness, Cathy thought, was a few short moments snatched occasionally from the relentless march of time which was otherwise full of apprehension and sadness, and the sight of Jenny so innocent, young and beautiful made her very happy indeed. The sadness would follow when Jenny was gone, and she imagined that life might seem unbearable, even though she would see her from time to time.

They were such a united happy family; she, Frank and Jenny. It was like starting all over again, as though she and Frank had their own child which she would so much have liked. What a good, natural father he would have made. He was the perfect husband, kind, thoughtful and tender. His expertise as a lover had come as a revelation to her. She had never expected excitement and passion in this marriage; but alone as Frank might have been for so many years in his bachelor-like existence, he had certainly not lacked female company.

At least they'd have each other, but the thought of losing Jenny was too painful. She'd dressed her up in a pretty blue dress with a white lace collar, long white socks and black patent leather shoes, a bow in her gleaming curls for this meeting, this crucial meeting with her mother. For Cathy was sure that Addie had come to tell her that she wanted to take Jenny away, and when.

Cathy's eyes filled with tears but at that instant she saw the car coming in through the massive wrought-iron gates, hastily dried her eyes on the kitchen towel and ran to the door just as Frank stopped the car and Addie got out.

She had changed, Cathy thought immediately. In a few weeks what a difference marriage had made. She looked now like a woman: mature, thoughtful, in control of herself. She, who had never cared very much about clothes, wore a short camel-haired coat buttoned up to the throat over an ankle-length skirt of the same material with a tight-fitting brown velour cloche hat over her shingled hair.

Addie's eyes lit up at the sight of her mother and, pausing to thank Frank who immediately drove on, she flew up the path and hugged her.

"Oh, Mum it's wonderful to see you," she cried breath-lessly.

"And you, dear." Cathy stood away and looked search-ingly into her eyes. "Did you have a wonderful time?"

"*Wonderful*," Addie linked her arm through her mother's as they approached the house, "but it was very hot." She waved a hand in front of her face. Then she paused as she saw Jenny and her new puppy playing away, as if oblivious of her presence. If Jenny noticed her she betrayed no sign of re-cognition. "How's Jenny?"

"Oh, she's fine. Frank bought her a puppy. He's always spoiling her. She's bound to want to show it to you later."

Cathy hurried Addie into the house dreading to hear those words, anxious to prolong the time she would have with her sixth child.

"Tell me what you did." Her mother sat on one side of the kitchen table while Addie took a seat opposite her and slowly peeled off her gloves, speaking quickly, animatedly.

"Oh, we went all over France and Italy, finished in Spain, where it was particularly hot. I thought I'd die in the Spanish heat, but it was wonderful, most instructive. Harold is so *very* knowledgeable about everything you could possibly imagine. I felt quite inadequate. He knows all about art and architecture, music and painting and I sort of trailed along behind him listening, wishing that I'd read more, studied more."

"But he's a lot older than you, dear."

Addie lowered her eyes. "Yes, I suppose so."

"Would you like a cup of tea?" Cathy rose and went over to the stove. Something about Addie's attitude worried her. She felt something was wrong. Unusually for Addie there was a lack of sincerity. Somehow she suspected that Addie was not being quite honest.

"Mother . . ."

Cathy turned abruptly, kettle in her hand. Addie only used the term "mother" if she was about to say something serious.

"Yes, Addie. What is it, dear?"

"Mother," Addie passed her hand wearily across her forehead, "everything was *not* quite all right on our honeymoon."

Cathy, kettle still in her hand, sat opposite her again, waiting for her to proceed, giving her time.

"The thing is," Addie nervously plucked at her skirt, "I told Harold about Jenny. He was shocked . . ."

"I suppose that was natural," Cathy said quietly.

"It was a *very* difficult time. Harold didn't understand at all."

Cathy pursed her lips grimly. "I see. In a way you surprise me. I thought Harold was a compassionate man and, although he was bound to be shocked at first, that he would understand."

"Some things he couldn't understand and that was one of them. In fact he said . . ." tears sprang to Addie's eyes, "he said that if I'd told him before our wedding he would not have married me. He thought I was a virgin, as he was."

"Oh, I see." Cathy looked away. She thought this explained

a lot about Addie's demeanour and behaviour. Though intellectually stimulating, the honeymoon might not have been such a success physically with a man who had spent forty years of his life without making love to a woman, something that was hard for Cathy to contemplate.

"We had a terrible scene after I told him. It was a particularly hot day and I blame the heat for much of it. I thought it was well timed, but it turned out not to be. Harold immediately left the hotel where we were staying and didn't come back until the following day. I have no idea what he did or where he went. I was beside myself with worry, as you can imagine, thinking he'd done himself some injury. I passed a sleepless night thinking my marriage was over and I should end up like Verity, but when he came back he was quite calm and said that he had thought about it, prayed about it – Harold, as you know, is very religious – and he'd decided to forgive me. However he said he didn't want to discuss this ever again or entertain the idea of Jenny living with us.

"He asked if she knew I was her mother and I told him she didn't. He said that was how he wanted it and that she should never know."

Addie bowed her head and Cathy could see tears welling up again. She thought rather bitterly that Harold had tamed her once spirited daughter, and she considerably revised her former high opinion of him.

"I am going to respect his wishes, Mum. He said that, despite everything, he wanted to stay married to me because he thought there was a lot of good in me despite what I'd done in the past. As you know, he has been offered the new headship to start after Christmas, and we want to make a fresh beginning. He could hardly arrive with a child of six years and a new bride."

Cathy bit her lip. "I suppose not. It would take a lot of explaining."

"Harold would want to avoid scandal at all costs."

"Did you tell him about Lydney? That it wasn't a casual thing, but you loved him?"

"I tried," Addie dabbed at her eyes with a hastily produced handkerchief, "but he wouldn't listen. It is a subject he says that must never be mentioned again. Harold does want to have a family, our own family. Not someone else's."

"That's that then." Cathy rose and went over to the window. Although she was sad for her daughter, she had difficulty suppressing the sense of joy she felt in her heart. Jenny was nowhere to be seen but she could hear the puppy barking somewhere out of sight. She crossed over to Addie and put a hand on her shoulder.

"My poor Addie. I am sorry but you know you have never really been *close* to Jenny. You couldn't help it and you love her, but I don't think you love her as I do. You thought you were doing the right thing by her and that does you justice, it really does.

"If you are happy with this arrangement I am happy too, and if ever things should change or Harold changes I'll do what you want. But you know Frank loves Jenny. He will be a good father to her. She will always be here for you to see and visit and I think that what has happened has happened for the best.

"You can start your marriage afresh and I can keep the little girl who is, after all, my own flesh and blood, whom I have come to love so much."

"Oh, Mum." Addie threw her arms around her and by this time Cathy's own cheeks were wet with tears. "You're the most perfect mother. I hope that if ever I do have more children they will all be just like you."

A short while later Jenny was called in for tea and brought the puppy to show Addie. Addie took Jenny on her knee and kissed her and she realised that, for the first time since her birth, she felt easy about her daughter and at ease with her. She had always felt guilty about Jenny, and that had prevented her from establishing a relationship with her.

But now she had made her decision, or Harold had made it for her, and the conflict had gone. If she could not be a mother

216

she would be a good aunt to her which, as she grew older, Jenny would imagine her to be.

Jenny also seemed more relaxed with her as though somehow in her childish wisdom she had divined all that was going on.

Finally it was time for Addie to go. Frank came back down the hill with the car and stood anxiously at the gate watching Jenny, Cathy and Addie come out. He seemed relieved to see that Jenny was not wearing a coat or Addie carrying a suitcase. Cathy beamed at him as though to say that all was well.

At the gate Addie stooped to hug Jenny, threw her arms round her mother and got quickly into the car. Then, as Frank drove off, she lowered the window and frantically waved.

Jenny, tightly clutching Cathy's hand, waved back, for once a broad smile on her face. It was almost as if she knew that a crisis had somehow been resolved, and that now she had the person she loved most in the world all to herself for ever.